THE KILLING CIRCLE

PAUL J. TEAGUE

Storm
PUBLISHING

Copyright © Paul J. Teague, 2024

The moral right of the author has been asserted.

To request permissions, contact the publisher at rights@stormpublishing.co

Ebook ISBN: 978-1-80508-495-2
Paperback ISBN: 978-1-80508-497-6

Cover design: Lisa Horton
Cover images: Shutterstock

Published by Storm Publishing.
For further information, visit:
www.stormpublishing.co

ALSO BY PAUL J. TEAGUE

The Fallen Girls
Her Last Cry
The Fifth Girl

11/29

0952

PROLOGUE
TUESDAY, 12:52

Kyle knew they'd be waiting for him, but there was nowhere to hide. If they didn't get him at school, they'd find him on the way home. He was more vulnerable walking through the estate. At least on the school grounds, a crowd might gather, the teachers alerted, and it would be broken up before things got too bad.

He hung back at the end of the lunchtime study session. Kyle deliberately packed his books, one at a time, pacing himself with the teacher, who was shutting down his laptop and organising some papers before heading back to the staff room.

'Is everything okay, Kyle?' Mr Bridges asked. He glanced over at Kyle, pausing from his packing up, a kind expression on his face.

It was not, and it was unlikely to be okay ever again after what Kyle had done. But there was nobody to talk to and he daren't even hint at what was going on. The supervised session over the lunch break had provided him with some temporary protection, but there were still ten minutes to kill before lessons resumed.

'Yes, sir. I'm just repacking my bag.'

Beyond the door, one of the students made a throat-cutting

motion with his fingers, pointing at Kyle in case he was in any doubt that he was the intended recipient of the threat.

Kyle's mouth was dry, he could barely swallow and was sweating profusely.

'Are you sure, Kyle?' Mr Bridges asked, his voice caring and a look of concern on his face. 'Only you don't seem to have been yourself recently. You know I'm always happy to talk if you've got something on your mind.'

Mr Bridges was one of the few adults that Kyle would have confided in. He'd reached out to him before, sensing perhaps that all was not well, whereas most other teachers seemed completely oblivious. For one moment, he really thought he might confess everything to this teacher. But he baulked and the words stuck in his throat.

Mr Bridges moved over to the door, his laptop bag in his hand, an expectant look on his face. Kyle thought his legs might give way. He hadn't grasped quite how scared he was.

'Well, if you change your mind, feel free to speak to me any time,' Mr Bridges encouraged him again, his voice gentle and reassuring. Kyle knew he meant it, too. Mr Bridges was one of the good guys, a teacher who remembered the little details about the students' lives. He'd set up the lunchtime homework sessions in his own time, offering a haven for those youngsters who struggled to make it through the social hell of the hour-long lunch breaks.

Kyle headed towards the classroom door. The corridor was dim, the movement sensitive lights having switched off. He knew the student was waiting for him, standing still out there, marking their prey. He stepped out, his body tense, his nerves on fire.

Mr Bridges had already disappeared round the corner to the staffroom.

'Don't kick up a fuss. You know you've got this coming. You should have just shut the fuck up.'

He knew that whispered voice behind him; they'd gone through school together, though never been friends.

Kyle began the walk along the half-lit corridor towards the staircase to the ground floor. He didn't resist. The corridor was now empty, the teachers grabbing last-minute coffees before the afternoon sessions began, all the students out on the field or in the playground areas. Lunch break would end in a matter of minutes.

Kyle let them guide him. The student holding his arm was trembling, but their grip was so firm, it felt numb.

Kyle had only done it to help his mum. But it had gone too far.

As they made their way down the stairs and exited onto the school field, there were others there, too, familiar faces every one of them. They all had a reason to despise him.

They were taking him to the old outbuilding, he could see that now. Away from prying eyes, a place where nobody would intervene. Long ago marked for demolition, the red-brick and heavily vandalised structure no longer fitted in with the image that the academy wished to present. It was abandoned now, the rotting doors torn off their hinges, fizzy drink cans and crisp packets strewn across the ground, and it had become a natural gathering place for pupils, despite the notices to keep out.

Kyle fell onto the filthy floor of the old storeroom, grazing his hands which began to bleed. He rubbed them on his trousers as if that would do any good.

He counted five of them, but there might have been more. The girls were there, too; he hadn't expected that.

He sensed the tension. As a group, they appeared uncertain, like a cautious predator, sure of victory but reluctant to commit to the first attack.

'We have to do it,' came the ringleader's voice, urging them on.

As Kyle began to push himself up from the floor, a violent

kick landed on his jaw and sent him crashing to the ground. There was a gasp from the group, as taken aback by the violence as Kyle was. Whoever delivered the blow was wearing a heavy boot. The force of it shocked him, a sharp pain lingering where he'd been hurt. His head struck the concrete floor. This was it now. He couldn't resist. He just hoped it would be fast.

A heavy punch was followed by a kick in his ribs. It was one of the girls; it didn't hurt so much, but the speed of it made him gasp.

Then they all piled in, emboldened by the first blows. He heard sobbing as punch after punch, kick after kick rained down on him. He could barely feel it after a while, the pain was so intense.

At last, it stopped, and he wondered if he might get away with a warning. That was better than he might have expected; was there a chance he might walk away from this?

There was a pause at last; they were going. But then, footsteps. Someone had returned.

As Kyle drifted in and out of consciousness, dazed, bloody, and sore, a final kick from the heavy boot struck him – delivered with such power and hate. He slumped to the floor. It was over, and now their secret was safe.

ONE

TUESDAY, 13:58

Hollie's mind raced as her eyes darted between her sat nav and the road. She didn't know the Crestwell Academy, but she could picture what it would be like from its name; a modern building sited on the Kingswood estate, which had just started being built while she was a student in the city.

Kingswood was a safe, quiet neighbourhood, the sort of place where people got on with their own business and very little drama occurred. A shit storm was about to descend on their calm, cosy lives.

Seeing that it was almost two o'clock, she pressed the dial on her car radio to catch the local news headlines.

'We're receiving news of a serious incident at Crestwell Academy on the Kingswood estate in Hull,' the breathless newsreader announced.

Damn, they'd got the story already. A small part of her had hoped they might miss it until the next bulletin and at least give her a moment to catch her breath. Not a chance, this had all the prerequisites to become explosive. There were kids, parents, and a fatal assault; she'd have the world's press at her door before she knew it.

'Police officers are in attendance and members of the public are asked to stay away from the area, pending an official update once the emergency services have the situation fully under control.'

Yeah, that'll do the job keeping the area clear, Hollie thought to herself as she ran through the series of actions she was going to have to take the minute she stepped out of her car. Before long they'd have every concerned parent or carer in the neighbourhood there, wanting to know if their kids were safe.

The sat nav dutifully directed her to the main academy gates, and she had her ID ready for the uniformed officers who were posted there. It was only when she saw the number of police vehicles on the scene that she truly grasped what she was walking into.

Uniform had got there first, and they'd done a good job, but it was the turn of the Scenes of Crime team now, and her own Murder Investigation Team.

'Good afternoon, sergeant,' she said, straight down to business as she made for the senior on-site person. His hair was flecked with grey streaks; his face showed the stress of being first on the scene. He looked like he might be due for retirement soon.

'What am I walking into here, Sergeant—?'

'Sergeant Reynolds. We're barely forty minutes on the scene ourselves, ma'am.'

Hollie noticed the relief on the sergeant's face, he seemed over the moon to be handing this one over. It was like the worst game of pass-the-parcel ever.

'Is this an ongoing situation?' she began.

'No, ma'am, we've swept the grounds and premises and spoken to the staff. There is no assailant loose on the premises; from early accounts it appears to be a targeted and self-contained attack.'

'So we're certain the children are safe and secure on the premises?'

'Yes, ma'am, the school is in lockdown and all classes are now contained in the classrooms.'

'Good, this is great work, officer. Give me an overview, please.'

Reynolds consulted his notes.

'The body was found at quarter past one in an old outbuilding at the back of the premises by two of the younger students. School lunch break finished at one o'clock, so we're assuming it's only been there for a short time.'

'Do we have the school sealed off, officer?'

'We've found three exits, ma'am; this one, a rear gate which the staff use for vehicular access and a gap in the fence on the school field which is pending repair.'

'And they're all blocked?' Hollie checked.

'We have officers stationed at both exits, ma'am—'

'I want an officer posted at that gap in the fence, too. Nobody comes in or out of this site until we've had a chance to work out if the killer – or killers – are still on the premises. That means deliveries, parents, teachers – I don't care what the reason is, this building is sealed until we get a grip on this thing.'

'Yes, ma'am.'

'Do we have a name yet?' she continued.

The sergeant looked flustered, but this was no time to beat about the bush.

'Yes, ma'am, but no formal ID. It's believed to be'—he consulted his notes again—'Kyle Wilson, a sixth former. That's been worked out via the registers, but we've not yet got a formal identification. Some kids alerted the teacher on duty, who checked for signs of life, but was unable to identify the person in the panic. The victim was in a bad way. The principal made sure nobody entered the area until the first officers and ambulance arrived.'

'Well, that's a good start at least. Where are the kids and the teacher?'

'The kids are being comforted by a teacher and have been moved to a separate room in the admin block. The same with the teacher, he has a PC with him.'

'How was he killed?'

'As yet uncertain, ma'am, we've got confused information.'

'Right, so we have a disturbed crime scene, I'm assuming. Make sure SOCO has the name of that teacher and the two kids, so they know to eliminate them from the crime scene. I want them spoken to by my team ASAP and I'll want to see them, too. Have the ambulance crew confirmed the victim as dead?'

'Yes, ma'am.'

The officer followed Hollie's gaze over towards the main gate.

'Here's the first parent arriving. I thought that nobody's supposed to be listening to local radio these days.'

Hollie had wondered how many milliseconds it might be until word got around. Social media was like a wildfire; the public often knew more than the police did at the beginning of an incident.

'This gate needs to be secured, because you're going to have a crowd of anxious parents out here in no time at all.'

Hollie thought of Noah and Lily; she'd be out of her mind if this had kicked off at their schools. She considered what she'd need from the police. Was it my kid? That's all she'd want to know. And was there any ongoing danger to the students? They couldn't announce the name of the child, not until they'd got a formal ID and the family had been informed. As for the safety of the children, at least they could offer that reassurance.

She estimated that the building had to hold at least a thousand students. Each one of those youngsters could have seen something important, or perhaps been a witness. They might not even know it yet. It was a nightmare of evidence gathering and a powder keg of hormones that was about to explode, if it hadn't done so already.

'Okay, is the headmaster inside? I take it they're my main point of contact?'

'Just a heads-up, ma'am, it's a he and he prefers to be called principal.'

The sergeant's face told her all she needed to know about that painful exchange.

'And we're dealing with a management team, rather than just one person.'

'Thank you, officer, I appreciate you letting me know.'

DS Anderson had just arrived, with DC Harry Gordon and DS Amber Patel. Amber was a logistics genius in the office; Hollie hadn't had a chance to observe her working a crime scene yet.

She thanked the sergeant and was pleased to see him straight onto the radio to get the exit at the fence covered. Hollie gave Anderson a wave and made her way up the steps into the main building. The moment she walked into the foyer, she drew out her ID and headed over to the man she assumed was the school principal.

'Sorry to interrupt, I'm DS Hollie Turner. I'll be the officer in charge here.'

'At last, DS Turner,' the man replied, studying her identification. 'You've taken your time getting here. I'm Bernard Canfield, the principal.'

Hollie knew his type: full of himself and the status of his position. She hoped he wouldn't be a problem. Canfield didn't hang around to get things off his chest.

'I've got over one thousand students shut in their classrooms and the school day ends in less than two hours. I hope you've got a good plan up your sleeve, DS Turner, because this has all the makings of a disaster.'

TWO
TUESDAY, 14:13

Hollie and Anderson made themselves known to the Crime Scene Manager and got themselves suited up.

'My son is the age of this kid,' Anderson said, solemn and thoughtful, as he made sure his shoes were protected with plastic overshoes.

'It's just horrible,' Hollie replied, bracing herself for what was coming next, a dull sensation of nausea sitting in the pit of her stomach.

Doctor Ruane was just finishing off when they walked through the forensics team's tent and into the outbuilding. It was everything she'd expected a disused structure like that to be. There was a larger area, with a couple of broken doors leading off it to what looked like cupboards. She could only think that it might have been used for storage, as it didn't appear suited to anything else.

There were discarded confectionery wrappers and vaping liquid bottles strewn across the floor. Once upon a time that would have been cigarette stubs, and they might have secured some useful DNA. Spray-painted ball-and-cock pictures filled the plastered walls. In the middle of it all was a slight, skinny body in the foetal position, black and blue from bruising, the face bloodied and swollen, lying in a small pool of blood.

Hollie pushed back the tears gathering in her eyes. This might have been one of her kids.

'Doctor Ruane,' Hollie began, steadying herself. 'What do you think?'

'I'll need to examine the body properly, but it's a very sad state of affairs. I see no reason to dispute the reported time of death; he's been dead for just under an hour now, I'd guess. It's not an exact science, of course. He's taken a terrible beating; you don't need me to explain what your own eyes can see.'

Hollie couldn't recall the time she'd seen a body like that. Older people tended to bruise badly if they'd been attacked, but it was unusual to see that level of damage on a younger body.

'Why the blood?' Anderson asked. 'A beating wouldn't be responsible for all that, would it?'

The blood had pooled around the upper half of the boy's body.

'If you step round the body carefully and view him from the front, you'll see the source of the wound.'

Doctor Ruane stepped around the various markers which had been put in place by the crime scene officers who were meticulously working around them.

It was all the more shocking to see such a young face, red raw, heavily bruised and battered, but looking like he was fast asleep and might wake at any moment. It was just a regular teenage kid, tall and gangly, with a lame effort at facial growth on his chin, and Doc Marten boots on his feet.

Ruane sighed. 'I'll need to examine the body more thoroughly to ascertain the actual cause of death. It's possible he might have had a heart attack during the beating, for instance. I can't rule that out at this stage.'

Hollie was waiting for the but – Ruane was clearly building up to something.

'I'm sorry to inform you that you're looking for multiple perpetrators, detectives. In simple terms, it looks like several attackers set about the victim. This assault was made by at least three assailants, and most likely more, perhaps as many as five or six. You can tell that from the angle of the bruising and the position of the body. He's been given a good kicking.'

'What about the blood?' Anderson asked once again.

'That's coming from a wound to his neck,' Ruane answered.

'Is this a knife stabbing?' Hollie asked aloud. 'I was told this wasn't a knife incident.'

It was becoming more and more common in secondary schools if the press were to be believed. It was a scourge of modern life which terrified Hollie when it came to her own children.

'Once again, I can't be sure until I can examine the body properly. But if you asked me to hazard a guess, that looks to me like somebody pushed a chisel into his throat. It leaves a distinctive wound. And if you pushed me even further, I'd speculate that this youngster wasn't killed as a result of the beating; it was likely the chisel wound that finished him off. Which means that the two attacks might have happened separately.'

THREE

TUESDAY, 14:26

'Damn, this is grim,' Hollie said, surveying the interior of the outbuilding and looking everywhere for signs which might give them some early momentum in the case.

'What kind of a murder weapon is a chisel though?' Anderson asked. 'The sort of murder weapon a teenager could easily lay their hands on from the woodworking rooms?'

Hollie nodded.

'You're right, DS Anderson, good thinking. If I remember my time at secondary school correctly, the woodworking tools were all identical and probably bought in bulk.'

'You did woodworking at school?' Doctor Ruane asked. 'It was just the boys who did that in my days.'

'I did one term,' Hollie replied. 'The wooden box I made was such an abomination of craftsmanship, they moved me swiftly back to cookery classes.'

'How did that work out for you?' Anderson wondered.

'I seem to recall the word *abomination* being used again in that year's school report.' She shrugged.

All three turned back to the body as if there had been some

temporary collusion between them to indulge in a brief moment of respite.

'We're going to need to get a formal identification. If we don't release a name fast there's going to be a riot outside those school gates. Was there any ID on him, Doctor Ruane?'

'Sorry, nothing at all to work with,' he replied.

'Not even a name tag at the back of his clothes? Those things were the bane of my life back home – back in Lancaster, I mean.'

There it was again, a minor clarification about her domestic situation. She was still getting used to being away from the kids.

'Maybe not so unusual for the older kids,' Anderson observed. 'And what about his lanyard? I've already seen enough kids in passing to see that they all seem to have them here.'

Anderson fiddled with his own lanyard as if illustrating his point.

'They have lockers to store their bits and pieces a lot of the time,' Hollie suggested. 'Though I think they still carry bags around. That's how it works at Lily's school.'

'Any sign of a school bag or books?' Anderson called over to one of the SOCOs. Whoever was under the white suit and face mask shook their head.

'He's clear of personal belongings. No phone, no bag, no ID,' the officer confirmed.

Hollie took out her phone and dialled urgently.

'DS Patel, I need you to get the word out to the teams. There's likely a school bag, a lanyard and a phone missing, possibly a coat or a jacket, too, I'd guess. I can't believe the victim didn't have a phone; they all have phones these days. Check if the kids use lockers here. If they do, nobody gets in them at home time. And I want a master key, we're raking through the lot of them. There'll be a list of which locker belongs to who. We'll prioritise this by year group and the victim's social circle, when we confirm who he is. If we get the victim's phone, I'll put money on us finding out what's gone on here. I'm guessing there might be a laptop or tablet, too, so let's keep an open mind.'

She ended the call.

'There has to be something that can help us to narrow this down. So far, we've got a school full of teenagers as our list of suspects. There are a lot of footprints here, I see they're taking some casts, hopefully that will give us a head start.'

'I can tell you more when I have the body back at the morgue,' Doctor Ruane offered, 'but I can only offer a limited opinion at the moment.'

'I'll take anything at this stage,' Hollie replied. 'I don't care if it's complete conjecture, I just need to pick up a trail.'

'I'll get a better idea of the bruising patterns when I can remove the clothing from the body. That should give me a good impression of how many people were involved. At the moment, I just have the face and the hands to work with.'

'Explain why you think the murder weapon may be a chisel?' Anderson said to Ruane.

'You can tell by the entry wound,' he began, pointing to the broken skin with a large pair of metal tweezers. 'I've seen that before, I'm afraid. It's very different from a knife wound.'

'If it is a chisel from the woodwork rooms, it might suggest this was premeditated,' Hollie conjectured aloud. 'If you needed to silence someone and you weren't a violent person, what would you use for a weapon? A kitchen knife? A craft knife? There aren't that many options.'

'It would be easy enough to sneak out a chisel,' Anderson added. 'I once nicked a biology book from my school.'

Hollie and Doctor Ruane looked at him.

'It's a sad tale of teenage hormones in overdrive, I'm afraid. There was no internet back then, so the only source of nude pictures was biology textbooks. I'm not proud of my criminal past. I even tore out all the good pages and kept them under my mattress.'

Hollie was thankful for the levity. Every time she looked at the curled-up body she wanted to scream. It was oppressive in there, but she knew the importance of walking and talking the murder scene as soon as possible. The meticulous photographic record created by the SOCOs would be invaluable for memory jogging and evidence, but there was nothing quite like taking in the smells, the size of the space, and the environment, first-hand.

'When we're finished here, pop over to the woodworking rooms and find Doctor Ruane one of the chisels that the kids use. Until we find the murder weapon, that'll help us match it to the entry wound at least.'

Anderson nodded.

Hollie scanned the small outbuilding. It was just the sort of place she'd expect kids to gather when they were up to no good.

'Why is this building still here?' she asked, not expecting an answer. How would her colleagues know?

'Might be asbestos,' Anderson suggested.

Hollie turned to him, encouraging him to continue.

'You have to get specialist contractors in to get it removed, I know that much.'

'They'd have to make it like Fort Knox to keep the kids out though, wouldn't they?' she asked.

'I'm no expert, but I think the issue is with disturbing asbestos. It's fine until you move it. We'd have to check that out.'

'Okay, let's raise that with the head teacher – the principal. Did you notice any CCTV when you entered the site?' she added.

'Yes, in the foyer,' Anderson replied.

Hollie spent her life scanning for CCTV, it was often their best and most reliable witness if it happened to be pointing in the right direction. As a younger cop, more times than not, the

CCTV operators had recorded over the videotapes. These days, though, the cameras recorded on hard drives and the available archives often went back several weeks.

'Anywhere else?' she asked, looking at the doctor.

'I do human bodies only.' Doctor Ruane shrugged.

'What's your impression of DC Gordon?' Hollie changed the subject, turning to Anderson. 'Is he up to handling a bit more pressure?'

'He's keen and ambitious, that's for sure,' he answered. 'Why?'

'I'm going to push him a bit harder on this case and see what he's capable of. If you think he'll respond well?'

'Go for it,' Anderson confirmed. 'I reckon he'll rise to the occasion.'

Hollie took out her phone.

'DS Patel, it's me again. I need to know about CCTV in and around the school premises. Find out who's responsible for it and let's get scouring the footage for clues. Oh, and tell DC Gordon that I want him to lead a sweep of the school field and all interior and exterior bins. There has to be a phone out there somewhere.'

She paused momentarily, then continued.

'Send the principal and his deputy over here ASAP, will you? I hope they've got strong stomachs, it's high time we confirmed this kid's name.'

FOUR
TUESDAY, 14:39

'Is Canfield suited and booted yet? I want to get this done.'

Hollie was anxious to get her formal ID. The sergeant had given her a name, but it was little use to her until she got her confirmation and could follow-up with family and social contacts.

Hollie turned to leave the outbuilding, taking care to use the route designated by the SOCOs. They reminded her of ants, crawling all over the area and leaving no stone unturned. Their job was so much different to hers; it was a process of observing, cataloguing, and recording. Most of Hollie's breakthroughs came from hunches and conversations. But she knew the painstaking groundwork was essential for securing a conviction, and it was that thought that got them all out of bed every morning.

Bernard Canfield and a colleague were being checked over by a member of the crime scene team to make sure they would not leave any traces of their presence when they walked into the dilapidated building.

'Thank you for agreeing to do this,' Hollie started. 'I know this will be difficult for you, but you'll be sparing a family member from this pain if you can give us a positive ID. I'm sorry, I don't think we've been introduced—'

'I'm Olivia Dreyfuss,' she replied. 'Mr Canfield's deputy.'

'So that makes you vice-principal?' Hollie checked. Modern education seemed laden with jargon.

'Yes, that's right. I used to be a police officer before entering education,' she continued. 'I'd rather hoped I'd never have to see a scene like this again.'

'What made you leave?' Hollie asked.

'I got fed up with picking up the tab after people were broken. I decided to try and make a difference before the damage was done.'

Hollie couldn't be certain, but she thought she heard Anderson muttering under his breath.

How's that working out for you?

When she turned to look at him, he was gathering information from one of the SOCOs. She'd have to watch herself; she was putting words in his mouth now.

'It was Mrs Dreyfuss who advised us what to do immediately after the death was reported,' Canfield interjected. 'I fear you'd have had half the staff in this area if she hadn't advised against contaminating the crime scene.'

'That was a solid call, Mrs Dreyfuss, thank you.'

Hopefully it would make life easier for SOCO, but there appeared to be so many footprints mixed up in the dirt-covered floor already, she didn't fancy their chances.

'I'm afraid there's no way to sugarcoat what you're about to witness. I know I don't have to say it to two people of your seniority, but you must not discuss anything you see today with anybody who's not in this area right now.'

'Understood,' Canfield confirmed. He seemed eager to get it over with.

'I believe the registers suggest this is a sixth-form student – Kyle Wilson?'

'Yes.' Canfield nodded, solemn and subdued. 'I can't believe this has happened to one of our students—'

'Why is this building still here?' Hollie asked, remembering their previous conversation about asbestos. She could see she'd hit a nerve.

'Because some local history group wants to get it excavated,' Canfield answered. 'This whole area used to be marshland, but they started draining it in the sixteen hundreds. Would you believe there were windmills here once upon a time, which were used as part of a drainage project? Some bright spark seems to think this building was constructed on top of one of those windmills, so we've been locked in a dispute since the academy site opened. Any excavation could open up a huge can of worms.'

Hollie didn't need to know more, but she'd got her explanation and was happy with it.

'Okay, let's go in. Follow my lead, please, and don't disturb anything. Keep to the designated pathway that the crime scene team have set out for us.'

Canfield gasped when he saw the body lying curled up on the ground. Dreyfuss acted like she'd seen it all before. Perhaps she had, but nobody with any sense of humanity could not be affected by the sight of that dead child.

'Yes, it's Kyle Wilson,' Dreyfuss said, her voice calm and certain.

'You're sure?' Hollie asked.

'Oh God, yes, poor Kyle,' Canfield picked up. 'It's definitely Kyle Wilson. How could this have happened?'

'That's what we're here to find out.'

'Oh no—' Canfield's face was white. 'His mother is one of the parents waiting at the school gates.'

'One moment,' Hollie said, taking out her phone.

DC Jenni Langdon picked up in the office immediately. Hollie knew she was bored doing desk work and in that moment broke her promise to herself that she'd give her colleague plenty of time to recover. After her recent injuries from their previous investigation, Hollie was treating her colleague with kid gloves.

'I want you over here at the school,' she said, hoping it wouldn't be too soon. This case was going to require Jenni's empathy. She detected the lift in Jenni's spirit over the phone.

'I'm going to need your people skills around the school. Bring your laptop though, you're still to take things easy—'

'I promise,' Jenni replied. She sounded like she'd just won the lottery.

Jenni confirmed that she'd get it sorted and they ended the call. It would be good to see Jenni Langdon back on a case. At least the academy environment was an easy entry back into field work.

'What can you tell me about Kyle?' Hollie asked Mr Canfield.

'He's a quiet boy, and a bit of a loner. He's what you might call a sensitive child,' he began, his voice shaky.

'What's his family background?'

'Single mother, father off the scene soon after he was born. I don't think Kyle has a relationship with his father,' he continued.

'Any siblings? Is there a new partner on the scene?'

Dreyfuss answered this time.

'No new partner as far as I'm aware. Kyle doesn't have siblings either, he's an only child. I heard once that his twin died at birth.'

'That's probably why she's...' Canfield interjected.

'She's what?' Hollie pushed.

Canfield and Dreyfuss exchanged glances.

'This is all confidential?' Canfield checked.

'Of course,' Hollie reassured him. 'Anything you can tell me will help with our investigation. Please don't hold anything back.'

'She's quite overprotective,' Dreyfuss answered on his behalf. 'We see a lot of her in school.'

'Why's that?'

Another exchange of glances. She'd have to watch these two.

Canfield sighed.

'She's been in school a lot over the past few weeks, saying that she's worried about Kyle's behaviour.'

'Was there any reason for her to be worried?'

'He's been on report several times in the past month.' Dreyfuss sighed. 'It's not like Kyle. He's usually one of those kids who never causes any trouble. But he's been unsettled recently.'

'Do you know why?' Hollie pressed.

'No, no idea.' Canfield paused. 'I guess he was in trouble of some sort.'

'Did Kyle have any friends? Was there any hint that he might have been bullied?'

Hollie caught Canfield and Dreyfuss lock eyes again as she asked the questions.

'He was always quite aloof. Kyle was the sort of child who didn't like sports or physical rough-and-tumble, and that excluded him from a lot of social activities—'

'You said you thought he might be in some sort of trouble,' Anderson picked up. 'What kind of trouble would a student like Kyle get involved in?'

Canfield's voice faltered as he began to answer.

'I'm sorry, officer, I just need a moment. It's all very overwhelming.'

He stepped back into the tented-off area outside the building.

Hollie took the opportunity to quiz Dreyfuss without having to defer to her boss.

'If you're a former police officer, I take it you'll have seen things like this before?'

'Never a child,' Dreyfuss replied quietly. 'I never saw anything like this.'

'Look, I know how it works these days. Nobody working in education admits that there's any bullying, life at school is just one happy family and all that. But I'm not one of the governors, neither am I an Ofsted inspector, so I can't put you in special measures. Be honest with me; is there much bullying at this academy?'

Dreyfuss glanced over to where Canfield had exited as if checking he was out of earshot.

'Unofficially and off the record, it gets worse and worse. I don't know how the kids can bear it.'

She was speaking like a human being at last, rather than as a suited official.

'These damn smartphones, they're to blame.'

'Have you had a particular problem here?'

'We tried to ban them from the school premises once.'

'That's quite dramatic. Why did you go for a ban?'

Hollie's eye was caught by one of the forensics officers who had just moved Kyle's body very slightly to take a sample from his clothing.

'It was an incident involving some of the older children,' Olivia Dreyfuss continued.

Hollie looked away from the body and picked up her conversation.

'How old? Sixth formers? Any of the kids who knew Kyle?'

'There was an outcry about it, and we had to cave in.'

'You still haven't told me about the incident, Mrs Dreyfuss.'

She paused as if recollecting. While she was thinking about it, Hollie glanced back at the officer taking samples.

'When I started teaching,' Olivia Dreyfuss continued, 'it was as simple as breaking up fights in the playground or suspending kids from school. Nowadays, all the bullying takes place where the teachers and the parents can't see it. We don't even know it's going on most of the time. And the poor kids can't escape it at home. It's twenty-four seven. It's relentless.'

'Okay, I get the point. So, what was it that caused the principal to take such dramatic action?'

Olivia Dreyfuss checked that nobody had come into earshot, and she drew closer to Hollie.

'It was Kyle. He'd been filming the sixth formers without their permission. Nothing dodgy, but they didn't want him to do it.'

Hollie's ears pricked up immediately, but as the forensics officer gently moved Kyle's leg, she spotted something concealed on the ground.

'There, over there!' She pointed, shaking the officer out of her deep concentration. 'Get a photo of that and somebody pick it out with tweezers.'

Hollie moved up close to study the retrieved item. It was a blood-stained business card and written clearly across it was the name and address of a local sex shop.

FIVE

TUESDAY, 14:54

Hollie ended her call with the press officer and steeled herself for what was coming next.

'Let's get this business address checked out, and then I'll do my piece to the press outside the school gates. Radio and TV are there, and DCI Osmond is being briefed in the principal's office.'

Hollie wondered if Kyle had just fallen on the business card, rather than it being something he owned. She read the wording from a photograph she'd taken on her phone.

Dirty Little Secrets

Adult Store

Fetish wear, Lingerie, Sex Toys, DVDs, Magazines and Erotica

Over-18s ONLY

DC Jenni Langdon was getting the shop checked out back at the office before driving over to the academy. DS Patel had joined them.

'Ha, I bet DCI Osmond loves that,' Anderson chuckled. 'The cuckoo in the nest, throwing the principal out of his own office, that's Osmond down to a tee.'

He was at it again.

'Well, remember he is our superior officer, and he can make things happen for us if we need him to. I prefer allies over enemies. But he is a bit of an enigma, I will admit.'

'An enema more like,' Anderson mumbled.

Hollie still didn't know Osmond well enough to form a solid judgement just yet, but he'd already been more of a help than a hindrance to her, even if his manner was a little unusual, and occasionally abrasive.

'Okay, we need to get straight to it. We're on the clock. DS Patel, I want you to coordinate a classroom-based response with the school, interviewing the children in small groups. We'll be dealing with minors here, and there'll be vulnerable children, too, so we've got safeguarding issues as well as the usual pressures. You'll be leading on this, Amber, once I've briefed the school's senior team. Oh, and the two kids who found the body and the teacher are in holding rooms. I'll also want to speak to them personally as they're so pivotal to the case.'

'Yes, boss.' Amber nodded. 'We've got a psychologist coming in to speak to them, too. They'll need it after what they just witnessed.'

'Good call, Amber. Where are the kids and the teacher?'

Amber pointed across the foyer.

'The kids are being questioned at the moment, but the teacher is in there waiting for his interview. He's a guy called Nick Yerbury—'

'I'll nip in and introduce myself. I'd like to hear what he has to say.'

Hollie scanned her brain, thinking it through. Cases got messed up because the senior officers failed to think ahead.

Ask the team.

She'd learned it early in her career. These detectives had as much, if not more, local experience than her. She had to use that, not ignore it.

'What can you tell me about this place? What am I missing?' she asked.

Anderson took the lead.

'The school is four years old, it's got a decent catchment area, and none of the troubles that you tend to get in some of the other city schools.'

'Great, good, any more?' Hollie encouraged.

'Excuse my language but this is a freaking logistical nightmare, ma'am,' Amber said, her voice lowered. 'We need more feet on the ground, surely?'

'Point taken,' Hollie acknowledged, a little annoyed by the remark. 'But DCI Osmond has already reminded me on my drive over that we have to make do with limited resources. You know the drill – budget cuts, Police and Crime Commissioner's pet projects and the Delivering More For Less initiative—'

'Squeezing blood out of a stone, more like,' Anderson added.

'Exactly, but we're a great team and we'll do what we've been asked to do,' Hollie reminded them. 'Remember, a child died at this school today, and within the past hour or so, too. The kids are going to be frightened, so are the staff. Rumours will spread like a rash, and emotions are going to flare up. Put your best game face on and let's get this school scoured before it all bubbles over.'

The two senior detectives were off faster than a teenager at a fast-food restaurant. Anderson was about to interview Nick Yerbury, so she got ahead of him and headed for the room where he was awaiting questioning. She tapped on the door and opened it, to see the teacher chatting to a female police officer. It seemed informal and relaxed; the officer straightened up as soon as Hollie stepped inside. She studied the teacher; he didn't look like a man who'd just come across a dead student. Perhaps it was the shock; she and her team often used humour to deflect from a dark situation.

'Nick Yerbury?' she asked, knowing the answer already.

'That's me,' he replied.

'I'm DI Hollie Turner, I'm leading the case. I hear you were first on the scene.'

'Sort of,' he began. 'Two of the younger students got there before me.'

'DS Anderson will go through this in detail shortly, but is there anything immediate you can tell me which might help? Did you spot anybody in the area, for instance? Was there any indication who might have done a thing like this?'

DS Anderson came up behind her, accompanied by another detective. He was ready to get on with the formal interview.

'Nothing that comes to mind,' Yerbury said. 'It was all a bit of a blur, I'm afraid. I'm still shaking now at the thought of it.'

He didn't seem to Hollie like a man who'd been rattled by recent events, and she hadn't particularly warmed to this teacher from her first impressions of him.

She studied his face; he wasn't telling her everything. She'd leave him to Anderson: if there was anything to discover, he'd draw it out.

'I'll leave you to get on with it,' she said to DS Anderson, exiting the room.

Hollie sought out the principal once again. If they were going to keep her lean on officers, she'd use the academy staff. They'd all be cleared for safeguarding purposes, and it was the most effective way to get a grip on the situation.

'Mr Canfield, might I speak to you and the senior team in your office or somewhere private?'

'Mrs Dreyfuss has them assembled in the conference room,' the principal confirmed.

Bernard Canfield escorted her to the small room to one side of the foyer.

Hollie took a beat before addressing the assembled group of

five senior staff. The phones could be heard ringing off the hook at the reception desk through in the foyer; Hollie didn't have to ask to know that was concerned parents inundating the academy with frantic calls.

'Firstly, and I'm sorry to have to do this, but the students are going to have to stay in their classrooms for now, and for as long as it takes—'

Bernard Canfield was about to speak, but he stopped himself.

'Has anybody left the academy site since the body was discovered?'

'The lunch staff will be about to leave shortly—' Canfield began.

'I need them to stay on the premises until we've had time to speak to them,' Hollie interrupted.

Canfield nodded, and Mrs Dreyfuss moved over to the phone in the middle of the conference room table and placed the call to the kitchens.

'Why is that fence broken on the school field?' Hollie asked, more accusatory than she'd intended.

Canfield was suitably rattled. 'Oh, er, yes, it's less than ideal, I know. We've been trying to fix it, but we have such a level of financial accountability required as an academy that it's proven more troublesome than it should have.'

'Here's the situation,' Hollie began, taking a deep breath. 'We need to ascertain, as quickly as possible, who was in the area and who may have seen something. The sooner we can assemble and sift that information, the better. The children will also need to be told, in a sensitive way, that a student has lost their life.'

'We can ask class teachers to speak to the children and mark those who think they saw something on photocopies of the class registers,' Olivia Dreyfuss suggested.

'Yes, that's a great idea and we'll have to follow up swiftly with those children. I'll also need my officers to come into the classrooms to speak to the kids. Are the sixth formers in classrooms at the moment?'

'Yes, those who weren't in lessons made for the nearest classroom when the lockdown alert sounded,' Canfield replied.

'Okay, we're going to be placing a particular focus on the older sixth-form students who will have mixed with the victim. How much freedom do they have here? Can they come and go?'

'If they're not in lessons and don't have study periods, they're allowed off the site,' Dreyfuss said. 'They have a designated sixth form area. I'll find out who used their lanyard after lunch.'

'So you use the lanyards to swipe in and out of the academy?'

'Sixth formers are supposed to use their lanyards to check themselves off the premises if they leave during lunch break or go off for a driving lesson. It's not perfect because often one student will use a lanyard to let in a group of students. We can supply you with a printout if you want. It's not perfect, but it'll give you a start though,' Mrs Dreyfuss explained.

'Excellent, can you also make sure my team gets copies of the visitor's book, too? I want to know about deliveries, contractors on site, everything.'

There wasn't much warmth in Olivia Dreyfuss, but Hollie had no doubt at all she was going to get the job done.

Bernard Canfield seemed irritated that his deputy had got herself assigned a series of key tasks, so Hollie thought she'd better get him deployed quickly, before his nose was put out of joint too much.

'Mr Canfield, as the senior member of the management team, I'm going to need to rely on your skill and experience in this delicate matter.'

Ego stroked, he looked eager to be assigned a task of his own.

Hollie glanced out of the conference room window and towards the school gate.

'The children are going to be the least of our problems today, Mr Canfield.'

A group of distressed and angry parents was gathering out there already. Word had spread fast.

'It's time for you and me to speak to the parents, and we will be calling in Kyle's mother to give her the terrible news.'

SIX

Okay, so here goes, my first recorded diary.

I do enough writing at school, and there's no way I'm leaving a regular diary around the house for Mum to find.

Besides, it looks silly when you write it down.

I can password protect these audio files, so only a geek will be able to break in.

I'll encrypt them, too – you can never be too careful.

Thanks for the security tips, Mr Yerbury!

I prefer this stream of consciousness thing.

I don't feel like I've got anyone I can talk to about this stuff, so I may as well talk to myself.

Let's see how it works out.

So, anyway, my name is Kyle Wilson, I'm seventeen years old and my life has just turned to shit.

Mum told me she's got Motor Neurone Disease this evening.

She's had it for ages apparently and she never told me.

She was all serious, like she was when she told me about the birds and the bees.

She'd been working up to it all evening, and I could tell something was coming.

I didn't expect that.

She'd kept it from me as long as possible so it wouldn't worry me.

She was hoping I'd get away to university before she had to break the news, but it's too bad now and she can't conceal it.

She cried. I hate it when Mum cries.

She doesn't do it often, which is why I know it's serious when she does.

I didn't even really know what Motor Neurone Disease is, so I looked it up on my laptop.

Fuck, it's horrible. She's basically going to deteriorate in front of my eyes.

This is when I wish I had a sibling, or Mum had a partner.

It feels like too much shit for me to handle on my own.

I wish I had someone to talk to.

I might mention it to Miss Drake.

She's super cool, all the lads fancy her.

Anyway, I thought if I keep a diary, it will help me to talk things through.

I'm keeping it on an SD card where nobody can find it.

Right now, I just want to cry.

I don't want Mum to know, but I need to be strong for her.

Sometimes, I hate my life.

SEVEN

TUESDAY, 15:03

There was no easy way to handle what was coming next. The Family Liaison Officer, DC Fran Hayes, had arrived already. Alongside Hollie and Canfield, they were going to try and discreetly bring Kyle's mother into the school to break the news to her. Hollie and Canfield would then manage the press briefing between them and announce Kyle's name at the same time as the teachers were informing the students. That way they could control the sharing of Kyle's name via social media. After that they had to get the children off the premises without allowing any vital pieces of evidence to slip out under their noses. Hollie had enjoyed nightmares more.

She wondered how she'd be right now if it was her children locked up in the school, and she was out there, terrified at what might have happened, fearing for the worst. What they were about to do would bring one parent's life crashing down around them.

The three of them stepped out of the foyer, onto the steps at the front of the building. The sound of camera shutters going off was instant. Hollie thought it was all digital now, but someone in there was still old-school. The press knew they couldn't take pictures of the children, but the principal and case lead were fair game. She sensed Canfield's hesitation.

'You can do this,' she reassured him. It was her own capabilities she wasn't so sure of.

'You can't keep them locked up in there!' one of the parents shouted.

'Bloody police, keeping us waiting like this. It's barbaric, that's what it is. We have a right to know if our children are safe.'

'Will you be making a statement to the press?' a reporter called over.

'Can you confirm there's been a death?' came a shout from the back of the press pack.

Hollie kept her face straight and didn't meet any eyes. Canfield stood in front of the barriers. He'd have spoken to these parents on so many different occasions. She doubted he'd ever had such a difficult task in his entire career.

DC Hayes left her side and unobtrusively mingled with the crowd of parents who'd gathered there. She'd been given a description of what Kyle's mother was wearing by the principal.

Canfield spoke directly to the parents.

'I'm so sorry we've been unable to update you any further on the incident that occurred in our academy this afternoon—'

'When can our kids come home?'

'Why won't someone tell us what's going on? It's outrageous!'

'We've heard someone died,' a woman shouted out, anxious and on edge.

Canfield ignored it all, as they'd agreed, and pressed on.

Hollie scanned for DC Hayes. She'd located Kyle's mother now and had got her attention.

'Detective Inspector Turner and I will be giving a full briefing to parents and the press shortly. I would beg for your understanding at this time; we're doing our very best to assist the police and take care of your children—'

'Then let them come home!'

It was one of the male parents this time. It was a demand rather than a request.

'Just tell us what the fuck's going on,' a woman's voice followed, dripping in anger and frustration.

Canfield paused and looked into the sea of distressed faces.

'I would ask you to think of our small academy community at this time and refrain from conjecture until all the facts are known.'

Chance would be a fine thing. Several parents had their phones out filming and livestreaming his announcement to the rest of the world.

Then a woman's faltering, desperate voice silenced the crowd.

Hollie hoped she'd never have to hear a sound like it again. The wall of parents fell instantly silent.

'Oh no, Kyle—'

There was no hope in the woman's voice; it was instantaneously desolate and empty. Hollie immediately noticed that she used a stick to help her walk; she couldn't have been older than forty.

There was no concealing this, they all knew what it was. The mood changed to one of sympathy.

'Isla, I'm so sorry.'

'My God.'

Gentle hands reached out to guide Kyle's mother to the front of the barriers, as DC Hayes slowly led her towards Hollie. Each touch was an insufficient attempt to offer comfort and sympathy.

A uniformed officer pulled open the barrier, and as Isla Wilson stepped down onto the asphalt, her legs gave way. Canfield moved in swiftly to support her. She released a pained, anguished cry and seemed unable to form any words. Even the members of the press were silenced, though Hollie could hear the cameras recording every move.

The walk up the steps to the school entrance seemed endless. Hollie and Canfield gently supported Isla's arms. DC Hayes carried her stick. DS Anderson had made sure the foyer was as clear as possible, so it was possible to get her into the principal's office without a crowd.

DCI Osmond was lurking in the background; he gave Hollie a gentle nod. She'd never seen so many tears in police officers' eyes. None of them would have wished this task on her.

They escorted Isla into the private space, where three chairs had been hastily arranged in front of Canfield's desk, along with a box of tissues and a glass of water on a nearby set of drawers.

Isla took a seat and closed her eyes as if steeling herself to hear the words. Hollie knew there was no point delaying it any longer.

'Mrs Wilson – Isla – I'm sorry to have to tell you that your son, Kyle, was found dead on the school premises just after the lunch break today.'

It looked as if Isla was trying to cry, but she couldn't. She made a gagging sound, as if her body was attempting to scream and eject her pain but it couldn't find a place to begin. Eventually, her eyes reddened, and her tears began to flow. She took a sip of the water which Canfield offered her.

'Oh no... no... not Kyle. Not my precious Kyle. No, it can't be him. I only just waved him off to school. I want to see him. You must be mistaken.' Isla attempted to get her frail body out of the seat, her eyes filled with distress.

Hollie reached out and placed her hand on Isla's arm.

'I'm so sorry, Mrs Wilson,' Canfield continued, all signs of pomposity now gone. 'Kyle was such a special student.'

'How? Why? Who would want to hurt my little boy? Is this because of the terrible things those children said?' she sobbed.

Bernard Canfield seemed suddenly anxious, the defensive principal eager to keep the academy's skeletons firmly locked in the closet.

'It was a storm in a teacup, Mrs Wilson,' he said softly. 'It was just Kyle being Kyle. He was filming the students chatting and playing games in the common room and he didn't ask their permission first. He learned his lesson and it was quickly resolved, after we spoke to him about the importance of seeking consent beforehand.'

His answer seemed more for Hollie's benefit than Mrs Wilson's. Hollie clocked that exchange but filed it for later. Isla Wilson had just lost her son. She couldn't begin to imagine the anguish she was experiencing having already lost a child. Hollie desperately wanted to talk to her own children, and she wished she could pull all three in close right at that moment and keep them safe forever.

'How could you have let this happen?' Isla lashed out in her grief, desperate to find some meaning in this bleakness.

Hollie let her speak, mindful of what still had to be done. She felt like this day might never end, there was so much to do, and it was so difficult to manage with all the children on the premises.

'Isla, this is DC Fran Hayes, she is what we call a Family Liaison Officer. DC Hayes will stay with you now and answer any questions that you have. She'll take care of you while we try to work out what happened to Kyle.'

Hollie could see she wasn't taking much in, but she leaned into Isla, giving her a hug.

'I'm so sorry,' she whispered.

Hollie knew this wasn't in any police handbook, but she was desperate to reach out to Isla, to connect with her as a mother and reassure her in any way that this wasn't just another police case to her.

Canfield followed her lead, and they stepped out into the foyer, leaving DC Hayes to do what she did best.

'What's the stick for?' she asked him.

'Mrs Wilson has MND,' he replied. Seeing that she required further explanation, he filled in the details. 'Motor Neurone Disease. It's fairly well advanced, but Kyle is, in effect, her carer. She's had to reduce her hours at work, and I think they're under some financial pressure at the moment. It's all very sad.'

'Is that why he might have been getting into more trouble at school recently?' Hollie suggested.

'Perhaps,' Mr Canfield replied, non-committal.

Hollie walked over to the main doors and paused for a moment to gather her thoughts.

DCI Osmond joined her.

'How was it?'

'As bleak as you'd expect.'

He gave her a respectful nod. She'd just drawn the shortest straw in policing.

'Ready?' he checked.

Hollie could see the press gathered outside, cameras poised.

Hollie swallowed and steeled herself.

'Let's do this,' she said.

EIGHT

TUESDAY, 15:11

It wouldn't have been Hollie's preference to do things that way, but there wasn't much choice in the matter. She'd invited the gathered parents and press members into the foyer. It didn't seem appropriate to make the announcement out on the street. BBC, ITV were there, independent radio, the lot. Canfield had asked that they stand in front of the large welcome sign so that the academy's branding would be seen in the press coverage. It seemed that even in crisis his mind was on maintaining healthy admission numbers.

DCI Osmond was speaking first. He opened his mouth as if he was about to say something, paused, and waited for everybody to fall silent in expectation.

'I'm very sad to have to inform you that at 13:14 today, the body of a male, age seventeen, was found dead on the school premises.'

There was a rumble of chatter. DCI Osmond waited until it had completely subsided before continuing.

'For obvious reasons, I would urge the press and the local community to remember that a young life has been lost here today and that conjecture, gossip or speculation are not helpful. The name of the victim is Kyle Wilson, a sixth-form student here at Crestwell Academy. I can confirm that the family has been informed and the children are being told by their teachers as I speak. Our deepest sympathies go out to Mrs Wilson and all of Kyle's family and friends.'

Hollie looked over to the parents, a sea of concerned faces. If that information wasn't racing its way across social media at that very moment, she'd get up and tap dance right there in front of the press.

'I would also remind you that we are dealing with young people and there is a legal obligation not to identify or harass them at this time. There will be a lot of frightened youngsters in this academy, and I would encourage you all to remember that.'

Good luck with that.

'I will now hand you over to the principal here at Crestwell Academy, Bernard Canfield.'

Canfield shuffled his feet. He was more accustomed than any of them to addressing groups of parents, but Hollie could sense his unease in this situation.

'I'm devastated that our close community has lost one of its own today. Before we send the children home, we will gather every year group in the main school hall for a special assembly to offer them support and prayer at this difficult time.'

That was news to Hollie, but she could make good use of the opportunity; it would be the only time they had the entire school gathered before they had to let them out.

'School will close a little later today, possibly as late as five o'clock, and any students using school buses will have their transport delayed until our special assembly is over. We are sending out an email immediately after this briefing to update all parents and carers on the situation.'

'We want to see our children now!' came a shout from one

of the parents. There was a general mumble of approval. Canfield ignored it and ploughed on.

'As a mark of respect to Kyle, we will be closing the school tomorrow, though the police may request the presence of some pupils on the premises if they're needed for further questioning—'

'Bloody police harassment, these are our children!'

'Detective Inspector Turner will give you full details of the police investigation momentarily. In the meantime, the days ahead are going to be very difficult to navigate. We are all going to want to see justice for this young man. I would urge you to think of the children first in the days ahead.'

DCI Osmond made sure Canfield had finished, then picked up again.

'Thank you, Mr Canfield, and you have my personal assurance that Humberside Police will be doing everything possible to bring to justice the person – or persons – responsible for this tragic incident at your academy. I'll now hand you over to DI Hollie Turner who will bring you up to date with how we'll be managing this investigation.'

'Thank you—'

Hollie paused and tried the DCI Osmond technique. It worked. The old dog had some new tricks to teach her.

'Clearly what has happened at this school today is shocking and distressing, and I'd like to extend my heartfelt thanks to Mr Canfield and his management team for assisting us with our investigation so far.'

It never hurt to keep the key players onside. She could almost feel Canfield preening.

'I would like to apologise to parents and carers for having to place the school on lockdown this afternoon. The welfare of your children is paramount, and we have taken great care to work our way through the school so that we might assemble an early picture of the tragic incident which took place here. I'm sure you will appreciate that, whatever the circumstances, the police must do things in a specific order. Nevertheless, I apologise for the delay in being able to bring you details of what happened here today.'

She paused for a moment. She seemed to have their full attention.

'We will likely need to call in some of the children tomorrow to ask them some follow-up questions.'

There was a murmur from the parents; it was difficult to tell if it was friendly or hostile.

'I must stress that nobody has been arrested or charged in this investigation, but the children might be able to share vital information that will help us find who is responsible quickly. You have my word that all safeguarding matters will be attended to.'

Hollie was trying to sound reassuring but knew this was going to be a nightmare. They'd need to coordinate counselling services with the school and make sure none of the detectives waded in there with their size elevens.

'In the days ahead, we will be setting up a small police hub in the conference room in the academy. If you have any information to share, you can do so, in confidence, at any time. You should also call the Crimestoppers number if you prefer to remain anonymous. Thank you, we'll now take some questions.'

'You say no arrests have been made so far—'

It was the BBC, a TV reporter as far as she could tell.

'—yet there are over a thousand potential witnesses in this academy. So how come you're not able to give us more details about what went on here?'

DCI Osmond picked it up. He handled it better than she was going to.

'I'd remind you that we're in the first hours of this investiga-

tion and that the fatal incident occurred in a remote area of the
school. Rest assured, once we are able to safely release your
youngsters from the school premises, we will be reviewing the
vast amount of information at our disposal and seek a swift reso-
lution to this tragic case.'

'How safe are the rest of the children?' came a shout from
the parents. 'How do we know there's not some nutter going
around the school killing children?'

The press loved that. An angry parent with the inevitable
How safe are our children? question. It was a clickbait headline
forged in heaven.

Hollie took the question.

'As part of our initial investigation, all bags are being
searched in a sensitive manner in classrooms—'

'Fucking police state!'

She couldn't win. They wanted swift justice with zero
inconvenience.

'Students will not be permitted to access lockers when they
leave school today, pending a full and comprehensive search of
the premises—'

'Are you still looking for the murder weapon?' somebody
from the press asked. 'Is this a stabbing incident?'

'We have a right to know if our children are in danger!'

'Okay, let's call time on this,' Osmond said quietly.

'Thank you, everybody,' he said, addressing the parents and
the press. 'That's all the questions we're taking for now.'

With that, he got up and Hollie and Canfield followed
directly behind.

'Well, that's that done,' DCI Osmond announced as the
uniformed officers stepped in to escort the parents and press
from the building. 'I think it remained quite calm, given the
circumstances.'

Hollie was relieved it was over, too. They could buckle in
and get on with the investigation now.

'DI Turner, would you give me a quick tour of the building?' Osmond changed the subject. 'I'm keen to get a sense of the layout.'

Hollie was eager to catch up with her team members, but knew it was best to indulge Osmond in his request. She led him off down the main corridor, observing the CCTV camera as they passed it.

'As you can see, sir, the lower school have this single point of access and egress, so that simplifies matters.'

They'd come to a stop by a stark concrete staircase at the furthest end of the corridor, which led to the upstairs classrooms. The afternoon sun was shining directly through the windows to the extent that Hollie had to squint in order to face DCI Osmond.

'From here you can access the sixth-form common room in that direction.' She pointed. Something caught her eye under the staircase, a glint from something.

'One moment, sir—'

She cut herself off, mid-sentence, and headed over to the staircase, under which was a dark recess where a couple of sweet wrappers had collected.

She lowered herself onto the cold tiled floor that covered this area. It was unforgiving on her knees, but she wanted to see where that glint had come from.

It was almost like entering the beginnings of a dark tunnel getting in under the concrete steps, and she turned back to glance at Osmond who had a look on his face that suggested he was doubting her sanity.

Hollie fumbled for her mobile phone and shone the torch to see what it was that was catching the light. She gasped when she saw what it was.

'Over here, boss,' she called, her voice sounding hollow in that concrete recess. Osmond came closer so he could see what it was that she'd found.

Hollie moved to the side so that he could get a clear view of the object that had been kicked in there.

It was Kyle Wilson's lanyard, its Crestwell Academy ribbon drenched in blood.

NINE

DS Gordon

Harry Gordon looked across the academy's sports field and tried to calm his nerves. The thought of instructing the small group of police constables at his disposal had filled him with terror when DI Turner asked for him to take the lead, but he didn't want her to think he wasn't up to it. He could see how she was trying to encourage him and build his confidence, but he constantly worried that he'd screw something up again.

As a new detective, he'd walked onto a crime scene, completely forgetting the protocols and making life difficult for the SOCOs. It was an early dressing down and Anderson wouldn't let him forget it. Where DI Turner was all for pushing him, DS Anderson was sometimes reluctant to remove the trainer wheels lest he crash into a wall.

Harry turned away from the team of uniformed officers so he wouldn't be observed and took a sertraline. He'd given up with the Cognitive Behaviour Therapy; it was all too light-weight as far as he was concerned. Anxiety ran deep in his bones, and it wasn't something he could just think away or switch off with some positive thinking.

He watched as the team of police officers made their way slowly along the length of the academy's field, painstakingly examining each square foot, following his instructions. He was younger than all of them, yet they'd accepted his seniority without question. They'd searched, labelled, recorded and stored the contents of all bins throughout the academy site and found nothing.

Harry stood in the middle of the field, observing, waiting in readiness for a shout. None came. The officers returned to the academy end of the field, and they assembled along the next section of grass and began to make their movements to the other end.

Harry noticed the stud imprints from multiple football boots in the mud; it almost seemed like the ground was perforated. He had little expectation that they'd find anything, but he knew Anderson would want his assurance that no square metre of it had been left unchecked.

Width by width they crossed the field, until at last they came to the far side, where the outbuilding was located. Boundary fencing ran directly behind it, but there was a very narrow gap at the rear, along which a ditch ran.

Harry recalled how there had been a small, shallow stream running at the back of his school and, although it was forbidden, they would often race Coke cans or plastic bottles along its length during the lunchtime, with one of the group on perpetual watch for any patrolling teachers. If Kyle's killer wanted to get rid of something quickly, that would be an excellent place to do it.

He could see that the team of constables had become dispirited by their search, having yielded nothing in the way of clues. Eager not to report to DI Turner empty-handed, Harry spilt the group into two teams, one to search the lower ditch area, the other to work over the upper ditch. He detoured over to the scenes of crime officers who were working around the gap in the fence, taking casts of any footprints which were clear enough to record.

'You might want to check in with the rest of the team and scope out the rear of the outbuilding,' he suggested. 'There's plenty of room to hide behind there. It's just possible you might pull a footprint or two if we get lucky.'

The officers gave him a look as if to suggest that they knew better than a kid like him, but they agreed to follow it up anyway.

'If I'd been a student here, that's where I'd have hidden or gone for a fag,' he joked, hoping it would encourage them in their conviction.

'We were sharing joints when I was in secondary school,' one of the officers laughed, 'so we could have done with a hidey hole like that.'

Harry walked back over to his allocated section of ditch, and he saw that it was deep enough to contain slow-running water, which appeared to be discharged from a wide concrete pipe running under the farthest boundary fence. There was nothing in the ditch, other than crisp packets and discarded cans, but he was interested in the drain.

Fearing for his shoes, he hung on to the root of new-growing plants to lower himself down for closer investigation. The mouth of the pipe was littered with more debris, and the light was poor inside. Carefully keeping his feet clear of the water, he took out his phone and switched on the torch.

He shone it up the concrete pipe. Halfway along, bundled up and hastily discarded, was what looked like a coat. Remembering how things worked when he was at school, he knew this item of clothing might belong to any bullied pupil at that academy, tormented by a group of youngsters who'd thrown it somewhere that was out of reach.

Harry activated the flash camera on his phone, taking several pictures to capture the item in situ. He then reached into his pockets and pulled out a pair of latex gloves, quickly working them onto his cold hands.

With his left hand, he clasped the side of the wide concrete pipe, stretching his right arm as far as he could reach into its mouth. He almost sprained his arm stretching, but at last he succeeded in catching it with his middle finger. Slowly he hooked it out, calling over to one of the SOCOs who'd just exited the outbuilding further along the field.

It was a Primark jacket. He moved his hand from side to side, anxious not to contaminate this vital piece of evidence in any way. As he twisted it to the right, he caught sight of a sewn-in name tag, attached just below a small nylon tab.

It read *Kyle Wilson*.

TEN

TUESDAY, 15:23

Hollie was delighted to find that Jenni was waiting for her in the foyer. It was good to see her back on a case.

'How are you doing?' She smiled.

'I'm desperate to get started,' Jenni replied.

Several weeks of desk work was enough to drive any copper insane, but Hollie was there when Jenni's head slammed the paving slabs after being struck by a motorcycle. There was no way she was pushing her too hard, too soon.

'You're restricted to light duties for now,' Hollie explained. 'I'm sorry, but I'm not overruling the medical profession. My expertise only extends as far as sticking on plasters and giving magic kisses—'

'Well, if there are any going—'

'Ha! Good to see your sense of humour is still intact. I already think you're back too soon so, sorry, I'm going to limit your movements to the academy campus, or you can accompany me for home visits if any come up.'

Hollie could sense Jenni's frustration at not being given a free rein. Her hair still hadn't grown back properly from the operation; it was remarkable that she was even back at her desk.

Getting struck by a motorcycle down a dark alley in pursuit of a nun-killing murderer had almost ended her colleague's life. Every now and then Hollie would catch a glimpse of the scars left by the staples in her head and it would make her shudder.

'So, what did you find out about this Dirty Little Secrets place on that calling card?'

Jenni pulled a printout of one of the photos that had been taken of the business card before it had been sent off for forensics testing. She'd scribbled some notes on the page.

'It's an adult shop on Chanterlands Avenue – you know, one of those places with the windows blacked out.'

Chanterlands Avenue wasn't so far from Hollie's flat, but she'd never noticed it there.

'The owner seemed fine. He confirmed they have business cards on the counter and that they're strict about kids coming in and always challenge for ID if they seem too young.'

'Okay, thanks. We still don't know that the card belonged to Kyle, of course. I'm still going to want to pay a visit there to check the place out.'

She was suddenly hit with a wave of dread knowing where they had to go next.

'Right, we need to get over to Isla Wilson's. Let's see what we can find that will help us paint more of a picture of Kyle.'

'How is she?' Hollie whispered as DC Fran Hayes opened the door.

'Out of her mind with grief,' Fran replied. 'But also very angry. We've got a couple of detectives in here working their way through the house and going through Kyle's things.'

Isla Wilson was sitting in an armchair, looking like a woman who had no more tears left to cry. Her face was gaunt and expressionless, a parent bereft from the death of her child. A woman Hollie assumed was the sister sat beside Isla quietly, waiting to do whatever small thing she could whenever her sibling needed it.

Hollie walked slowly up to Isla, took her hand and cupped it in hers. It was cold and lifeless, much as this poor woman must be feeling inside. Her stick was perched at her side, ready to use if she needed it.

As Hollie glanced around the room she observed a pile of opened post on a table. It appeared from that distance to be bills, the majority of them red.

'I am so sorry about Kyle, Mrs Wilson. I can't imagine what this must be like for you. I want to assure you that we will do everything possible to find out what happened to your son and to make sure that they're held accountable.'

She turned to Jenni. 'This is my colleague, DC Jenni Gordon, who's assisting me today.'

'Hello, Mrs Wilson, I'm so sorry for your loss.'

Jenni walked up to Isla and gave her a hug. Hollie would never have done that, but there was something about her young colleague which made it the most natural thing on earth.

Fran Hayes had already settled into the home environment now and was comfortable telling them to take a seat and heading into the kitchen to boil the kettle.

'I know you've spoken to my colleague since I last saw you,' Hollie picked up softly, 'but it would really help me to get a first-hand picture of Kyle and to gain a sense of the kind of boy he was.'

Isla began to cry, but they were dry tears; it was the tortured sounds of a body trying to expel a deep grief.

Jenni started the recording app on her phone.

'He was a beautiful boy,' Isla sobbed. 'I just don't know why this would happen to him.'

Fran came through with the drinks. There was a packet of biscuits on the tray. They were own-brand and plain, the cheapest that were available in the supermarket. It seemed to Hollie that things were tight for the Wilsons.

'Was there something going on between him and the kids at school?' Jenni asked gently.

Isla shook her head.

'You think you know your child. He was worried about my Motor Neurone Disease, I know that much. But he kept himself to himself,' she sobbed before going on. 'I used to hear him up there talking to somebody. I don't know what he was doing, but I assumed he was FaceTiming or whatever it is they do these days. You know what teenagers are like. He's entitled to a bit of privacy.'

'What was he like?' Jenni spoke softly. 'I'd like to know more about Kyle.'

Isla sobbed a little, then wiped her eyes.

'He lived for his little films. He filmed everything. I used to have to tell him to switch his phone off in the house. He was obsessed with it. He wanted to be a film maker. He had a good eye for it, too. I'm sure he'd have made it—'

Jenni shuffled up to Isla on the sofa and put her arm around her.

'He got into trouble at school, too. His mates didn't like him filming them without permission. It got a bit tense, I think—'

'You don't think that's why Kyle got hurt, do you, Isla?' Hollie suggested.

Isla looked up and thought about it.

'No,' she replied. 'Not really. It all blew over. Kyle stopped filming in the common room, and everything returned to normal. I just don't know why anybody would want to hurt him.'

She started to cry again, and Fran Hayes made a face at Hollie.

'I'm going to suggest that DI Turner takes a look around Kyle's bedroom, Isla, while you have a cup of tea. Is that okay?'

Isla nodded.

'It's on the right up the stairs.' Fran motioned.

The Wilsons' house was a recently built modern semi. It was homely enough and tidy, but the furnishings were basic and selected from budget ranges, and it was no more than functional. The décor was magnolia, a sure sign that the property was most likely a rental.

Hollie figured that, as a single mother, Isla Wilson might not have as much money around, but she didn't want to jump to stereotypes, she'd ask DC Hayes away from the property. The pile of unpaid bills was not a good sign, though.

Hollie got up slowly and Jenni followed her lead. Hollie noticed the computer tucked underneath the staircase. It was sun-faded and well-used, and the screen was of the old-fashioned variety, rather than being flat and lightweight; it looked like an antique already. She'd ask about it later.

Kyle's bedroom was much like she'd expected. The wall was covered with posters, music and film stars. His bookshelves were packed with Penguin Classics – presumably for his studies – and Young Adult fiction, a couple of titles which she recognised from Lily's reading choices. There were various cartoon and TV-related ornaments around the room, with a small desk in the corner.

'You'll have to tell me who the people in these posters are,' Hollie said to Jenni. 'I know that's Harry Styles, a mother's nemesis as far as young daughters are concerned.'

'I know most of them,' Jenni replied. 'That's Adam Lambert, Billie Eilish and somebody I don't recognise—' She pulled out her phone, flicked through her apps and held it up at the poster.

'That's Brandon Flynn, apparently. He starred in a Netflix series for teenagers.'

'How did you know?' Hollie asked.

'Google Lens on my phone. It's great for detective work.'

'I'll need to remember that. I'll make room for it by uninstalling Myspace.'

She caught a snigger from her colleague. It was good to have Jenni back, she'd missed her.

'This is not a sports jock's bedroom, is it?' Hollie remarked. 'It's not a million miles away from my daughter's bedroom.'

'It's not a million miles away from my bedroom.' Jenni smiled. She knew well enough to keep her voice down.

Hollie was suddenly drawn to a book that was sticking out slightly on one of Kyle's bookshelves. It wouldn't have caught her attention if the other books weren't quite so tidily ordered. Its spine was broken halfway across. She asked one of the Scene of Crimes officers for a pair of latex gloves, and she walked over to it, pulling it out and opening it up. The inside had been cut away to create a hidden chamber in which to conceal things. A small plastic holder fell out.

Jenni moved to examine it, and Hollie showed her the book.

'This is a plastic case used to store an SD card.'

'Let's get it bagged up,' Hollie said, addressing the detective nearest to her, who was looking a little sheepish at having missed the clue.

Hollie was finished in the bedroom; she'd see what had been checked in as evidence when she returned to base. Their best hope was of finding a diary, but she knew that in the digital age that the chances of coming across a conventional, handwritten journal were as likely as DS Anderson leading a staff training day on nuance and subtlety in workplace interactions.

Isla Wilson seemed a little more settled when they returned to the lounge. The second detective was just about to start dismantling the old-looking computer set-up which was tucked in the nook under the staircase.

'Do you mind if I take a look before you take it to HQ?' Hollie asked.

'Be my guest,' they replied, knowing better than to obstruct the lead officer on the case.

'Kyle didn't use it, apparently,' DC Hayes said.

'Well, he only used it for gaming,' Isla corrected her. 'I got a bit confused about that when I was speaking to you. His whole life was on his laptop and his phone, but he would play online games when he was in the house by himself. He liked the bigger screen on the computer. He used it to play *vintage games* as he used to describe them—' Isla became choked up at the recollection.

'May I take a look?' Hollie asked.

'Of course, but I don't think you'll find anything,' she sobbed.

It was switched on already. Hollie moved the mouse to activate the screen.

'Here, I'm going to let you lead the way, DC Langdon, you're probably more adept at this than me.'

Jenni sat in the wheeled chair next to the computer and clicked around the screen.

'He has a separate login,' Jenni said as she brought up the welcome screen. 'Oh good, he's on Microsoft, and he uses a PIN for access instead of a password.'

'Is that good?' Hollie asked.

'It's better than a password, there are fewer characters to guess.'

'Okay, let's work through the obvious,' Hollie began.

With Isla's help, they ran through the regular numbers: Kyle's date of birth, Isla's date of birth, the house number, Kyle's lucky number, and Kyle's mobile phone number. Hollie made a note of the mobile number, as she'd just had an idea about how she could use that. At last, they exhausted everything obvious.

The distraction appeared to have been good for Isla Wilson; she'd become intent on helping them crack the code.

'I think we'll have to send it to the tech team,' Jenni said, a little crestfallen.

'I wonder if he used the birth date of his twin?' Isla suggested.

It was worth a try.

'I assumed they were born on the same day,' Hollie replied.

'It was the seventh of May 2007,' Isla continued. 'The day before Kyle. Alex arrived just before midnight and Kyle arrived just after.'

Jenni input the numbers 0705, 070507. Nothing.

'Try them the wrong way around, the American way,' Hollie suggested. She didn't expect it to work, but if they could bypass the tech team, this would speed things up considerably.

Jenni entered 0507 and tapped the return button.

They were in.

ELEVEN

Fuck!

Mum has had to reduce her hours at work with immediate effect.

That means we can't afford to pay the bills.

Fuck!

She told me over breakfast.

She's bought me Coco Pops for a treat, too, I should have known something was up.

Mum showed me the spreadsheet she uses to work out the money.

I'm shit at maths, but even I could see the problem.

There's not enough money coming in to meet our expenses.

It was tight enough as it is. I'd have tried to raid the fridge less if I'd known.

She asked me if I had any ideas how we can tighten our belts.

I'm so busy with my studies, I can't really afford the time for a part-time job.

I must get this place at uni, I can't stay in Hull forever.

We need an extra three hundred pounds a month to make ends meet.

Where the fuck is that coming from?

I considered for the first time today that I might have to give up my place in Manchester.

I can't even think about it yet.

It's all I ever wanted – to study on the film and media studies course.

When they offered me a place, I thought I was set for life.

But I can't leave Mum, not now.

They do a similar course at Hull Uni.

It's not what I want, but I may have to see if they'd consider me.

I talked to Yasmine Drake about it today, she's so nice.

I cried a bit, and she made me feel like it didn't matter at all.

Thank fuck we have a school counsellor, I'd be lost without her.

TWELVE

TUESDAY, 15:38

DS Patel

There was nothing Amber Patel liked more than a puzzle. As a child her father had struggled to keep up with her appetite for jigsaws. She'd started with six-piece ones as a toddler, then swiftly moved on to fifty, one hundred and, her crowning glory as a student, a 5,000-piece puzzle of an antique world map, completed over her final year at university to relieve stress.

Where most police officers started with the corners and assembled the edges, it was the tricky inner pieces that challenged Amber most. And she was trying to place one of those in the complex patchwork of clues at that moment.

She was concerned about Hollie, too. She'd taken to her new boss swiftly. Not only was she a good laugh, but she also had shit-hot policing skills. She kept the pressure up on the old-timers, too. As a young, female Asian police officer Amber had had her fair share of jibes and digs, all under the guise of office banter. DS Turner stood for none of it and she'd already, in a short time, succeeded in turning around the mood in the office.

Amber had thought it was just how things were with DI

MacKenzie at the helm, and she'd been as shocked as the others at his violent demise – Hollie's predecessor met a gruesome end in the line of duty. She wouldn't have wished it upon any of her colleagues, but the change in the office atmosphere since Hollie arrived had been a breath of fresh air. It meant more time for solving puzzles and fewer distractions handling people nonsense in the office.

Olivia Dreyfuss had supplied her with a printed-out list of lanyard assignations and a map of where the scanning points were. She'd also explained how security worked at the academy. The CCTV was being scoured by one of her junior colleagues, but Amber wanted to make sure they hadn't missed any crucial movements which the lanyards might reveal. Kyle's lanyard had been sent over for testing, but that didn't mean the victim's last movements couldn't be tracked still.

She'd been given an access-all-areas pass card so she could see how the system worked. She touched it against a plastic panel at the side of one of the building's side entrances. It beeped and the door unlocked so she could push it open. She stepped outside, let the door close, then tried it in reverse. She got the same beeping confirmation and re-entered the building. This was a tennis court side door; she checked it on her map of the school.

There were four CCTV cameras in the academy, excluding one which had been disabled in the sixth-form common room area. Apparently, a group of English Literature students had been studying 1984 as one of their texts and they'd got a bee in their bonnet about being under surveillance. Canfield had agreed to unplug that camera. Amber bet he was regretting that decision right now.

The foyer had CCTV, the rear exit to the staff car park had CCTV, as did the main arterial corridor, and there was one in the dining hall. The younger students only entered and exited via the foyer; after that, they were on academy premises and monitored by registers, so that meant they were accounted for at all times.

Side doors were opened by teachers on duty at morning, lunch and afternoon breaks and, with the exception of the damaged fencing at the far end of the school field, they were, for all intents and purposes, penned in during school hours. Only a parental note, medical emergency or pre-arranged pick up would mean a lower school pupil could leave for more than the duration of one lesson without anybody knowing.

The gap in the fence was a major point of failure in their ability to be absolutely certain who was on the school premises and who was not. Also, the sixth formers were the only year group who had freedom of movement, apart from the staff. Their lanyards were supposed to keep a record of who was in and who was out, but as Olivia Dreyfuss had explained, the students sometimes swiped themselves in and out in groups.

Amber found Kyle's lanyard ID on the list and checked his movements. The first evidence of movement was during the morning break. He'd scanned out by the tennis courts and, ten minutes later, scanned back in again. All that was around that area were benches which ran alongside the adjacent sports hall. Why was Kyle out there, when normally he should have been with his mates in the sixth form area? Perhaps he was keeping out of the way? Maybe he'd nipped out to vape or smoke a cigarette?

After that, there were three more records. Kyle had scanned himself into the corridor where the lunchtime study room was based. Mr Canfield had already explained to her that the lunchtime sessions were supervised and that students either stayed there for the duration or spent their lunch break on the school field or playground, if they were lower school. Sixth formers could do what they wanted, including leaving the premises, but they had to scan out so that fire safety records were always complete.

Kyle was recorded as entering the corridor at 12:13, so it seemed like he'd skipped lunch to attend the study class. The next scan was at 12:51. She knew from the staff already that study group finished at 12:50, so Kyle must have been dawdling or distracted as he made his way along the corridors.

He'd scanned out at a different door – at the exit which led out onto the school field.

Amber checked the information on the page, making certain there wasn't an error.

According to the timing of Kyle's death, his exit via this door should have recorded the final use of his lanyard, as he was known to be dead by 13.20 at the latest, and most likely by 13:10 or thereabouts.

So why was there a further scan with Kyle's lanyard at 13:27, when Kyle was already dead, and the emergency services were heading over to the academy?

THIRTEEN
TUESDAY, 15:54

Hollie was thankful for a couple of minutes to herself on the walk through the academy. She thought back to Isla Wilson's anguished cry when she learned of Kyle's death; she never wanted to hear a sound like that ever again. There was also the SD card holder, too; where was that SD card and why was it so important that it needed to be hidden? And there was the computer at the Wilsons' house. They'd cracked Kyle's pass code but found nothing obvious on the PC. It had been packed up and sent back to the digital forensics team. Hollie was frustrated that they'd not been able to find anything useful to help with the case. But now, she wanted to take a closer look at that gap in the fence and the place where Harry had found the coat.

She couldn't get too close, the area was still being combed by the team, but she pulled out her phone and found her location on Google Maps. Moving her fingers on the screen, she enlarged the view and tried to get a better idea of how this exit fitted into the geography of the place.

According to the map, which only showed limited detail, the gap in the fence appeared to lead to a narrow area of unused land, and then to a confined pathway which ran between a parade of shops. It was the perfect place to come and go without detection. The front and rear of the building were a bit like a fortress, in that there was no wandering in and out without having to pass the scrutiny of the CCTV, but this side entrance was going to be a problem, she could see that.

Hollie scanned the field, thinking through what they knew of the timeline. It would have been possible for somebody to hide, undetected, in that outbuilding, and make their escape via this broken fence. It was also possible that they might have hidden behind the outbuilding, as Harry Gordon had observantly suggested.

There was sufficient distance across the length of the field not to be identified should a student happen to glance out of a classroom window and see somebody making their escape. They might get a coat colour from that distance, but nothing much by way of a detailed description.

She looked over to the main block of the academy; most of the blinds were down in the classrooms, presumably to keep the glare off the interactive screens, or to stop the children drifting off and staring outside during lessons.

'How's it been broken?' she shouted over to a suited-up crime scene investigator who looked like she was still recording information about the footprints on either side of the break in the fence.

'A couple of bolts have worked loose,' she shouted back. 'Either that or one of the little buggers has had a go at them, you know what kids are like.'

'Anything else?'

'Sorry, it's a mess of footprints either side of this fence. I'll do my best, but it's going to be a tough job. Some of these footprints are obfuscated in some way. I've not encountered this before.'

'What do you mean by that?' she asked.

'It's like the shoes don't have a tread. It's unusual, that's all.'

Hollie's phone vibrated in her pocket. It was a text from Léon. Her husband had a habit of picking all the best times to get in touch.

> FFS! Noah needs to dress up as some book character tomorrow. How the hell am I supposed to sort that out at such short notice?

Hollie felt a glow of spiteful satisfaction. *That sounds like a you problem, Léon.* She'd let him stew with that little dilemma; it would give him the true 24/7 parenting experience. She would never moan that her estranged husband didn't pull his weight with the children, but the thankless jobs like coming up with *Bake-Off* standard creations for school fêtes and somehow creating fancy-dress costumes out of household items, often with less than twenty-four hours' notice, had usually fallen on her plate.

When it reached frenetic levels of panic, he'd no doubt phone her.

Hollie made her way back to the main building, mulling over what might account for the unusual footprints. She knew kids wore all sorts of weird trainers, and she resolved to keep her eyes peeled and see what the students were wearing around school; it might yield a clue.

The entire area was a hive of police activity. She pitied the teachers with the children cooped up in those classrooms. It would be like a pressure cooker in there before long.

'Have you got a moment, boss?'

DS Patel had caught Hollie on her way through a side entrance into the main academy building.

'How's it going, Amber?'

'We need to examine our life choices, boss. This is grim, isn't it? I had a date set up tonight, too. I've called it off.'

'With Duncan?' Hollie asked.

'Yes, he's got it bad. It's going well, dare I say. He appears to be completely and utterly normal. I don't even get a hard time when I should get one. I texted him to apologise for cancelling tonight and he just said we'd reorganise. I mean, some men I've dated in the past would have had me under twenty-four seven surveillance for daring to do such a thing.'

'Ah, a boyfriend who rejects stalking. He sounds like a keeper to me.'

The two detectives laughed, knowing it was only a momentary relief before they set their minds back to business.

'So, what brings you to these parts, Amber? I assume you didn't pop out for a crafty fag?'

Patel smiled again, then held up the papers that she was clutching in her hand.

'CCTV and classrooms, boss. I'm retracing Kyle's steps and marking everything that's key on this map of the school building.'

'I can always rely on you to do the detailed work, Amber.'

They walked through the corridors of the school. They could hear the voices of the teachers behind the classroom doors. The children sounded on edge, the teachers exhausted. Some of the classroom doors were open and uniformed officers, accompanied by teachers, were searching bags and speaking to students.

'So, don't tell me,' Hollie continued, 'the killer used their lanyard, and we can identify them from that list of yours. I'll get my coat, shall I, it sounds like the case is closed?'

'Ha, chance would be a fine thing, boss. What I can tell you is that whoever was with Kyle on the field, used Kyle's lanyard to exit and re-enter the building, so they were sensible enough to cover their tracks—'

'They then disposed of the lanyard at the stairs near the sixth-form common room, which is where I found it with DCI Osmond,' Hollie added. 'Doctor Ruane reckoned we might be looking at multiple assailants,' she continued, thinking aloud.

'He was assaulted and stabbed. And Harry is pretty adamant that someone might have exited the field via that hole in the fence.'

Amber Patel had just figured out where she was heading with this.

'So someone came into the school, after assaulting Kyle, because the use of Kyle's lanyard after his death confirms that. Which means we're potentially looking at someone who's a pupil here and someone who is not.'

'Exactly!' Hollie exclaimed, excited that the puzzle pieces were starting to show some shape.

They'd reached an open area midway along the corridor, where clusters of metal lockers were located. Anderson was standing with Harry Gordon, and they were clearly pleased to see Hollie.

'Go ahead and make sure the teacher and the two kids who found Kyle are ready for me to speak to, would you, Amber? Apologise for the delay. Oh, and see where we're up to with the CCTV. I ought to have heard something by now?'

Amber headed in the direction of the foyer.

'I was just about to call you,' Anderson began, as he walked up to join her. 'We've located Kyle's locker now, and Harry has the master key.'

Hollie scanned the rows of small metal doors. She was certain that one of these storage units would reveal some of Kyle's secrets.

'You've got the number, I take it?' she asked Harry.

'Number twenty-two, row five. I saved it until you joined us.'

Harry pointed to the far side of the row of lockers. It seemed like every child in the academy was allocated a space. Their doors were decorated with stickers and labels, and slogans and graffiti had been scrawled across several of them, and many of the doors were battered or distorted where they'd been kicked or manhandled. There were posters all around warning *Nothing to be attached to locker doors*.

Hollie gloved up and waited for Anderson to do the same. She took the key and opened up the locker door.

'Oh, Jesus!' she said, when she saw what was inside.

FOURTEEN
TUESDAY, 15:59

At the very edge of Kyle's locker was a pile of computer-printed notes on torn-off scraps of paper which appeared to have been pushed underneath the locker door. Many of them were scrunched up where they'd been pushed up against the pile of textbooks that Kyle had placed there. Hollie had been able to read three of them without disturbing anything, before calling for the crime scene photographer who was still on site.

Keep your fucking mouth shut Kyle.

You blab, you die!

Shut the fuck up Spielberg.

It was enough to make Hollie cry. These were kids, for Christ's sake – what were they doing making threats like this? Her daughter Lily was in secondary school now, too; was this the kind of language she was exposed to?

Stuck on the inner door of Kyle's locker was a poster of a young, attractive male.

'Who's that?' Hollie asked, certain she'd never seen this celebrity before.

'That's Olly Alexander,' Harry answered swiftly.

'Oh, right,' she replied, vaguely recognising the name. 'Still no school bag and still no phone,' she remarked, peering inside like that might somehow give her a better view. 'Okay, we need to get the contents bagged, recorded, and sent over to evidence. I'd like a record of all these messages for the briefing tomorrow. And handle it with great care; we may be able to pull DNA or prints off some of this stuff. Go and grab some more evidence bags, will you, Harry?'

Harry headed off along the corridor.

Hollie thought back to DCI Osmond's remarks about the forensics testing backlog.

'It's a good job old-fashioned police work is free. If we relied on the forensics lab, our killers would all be in retirement homes by the time we caught up with them.'

She instantly regretted the remark. Despite the overwhelming difficulties in which they were forced to work, she wanted her team to retain a positive outlook. She'd seen how the poison of negativity could mire investigation work in the muck and result in carelessness. She didn't want that; intuition, observation and instinct came for free, and the government hadn't yet found a way to cut them to the bone.

There were several other items in the locker and Hollie decided that she would carefully rake through the items now, rather than later, as it might be some time before the lab finished with everything. She adjusted the latex gloves, as if reassuring herself it was okay to proceed.

There were a couple of exercise books and textbooks in the locker. She pulled out a manual for video editing software and noted how many of the pages had been marked with the coloured sticky tabs.

'That's interesting,' she remarked to DS Anderson, reading

the scrawled handwriting inside the front cover. 'This is on personal loan from a Nick Yerbury. That's the teacher who found Kyle, isn't it?'

'Yes. He never mentioned this textbook when I spoke to him.'

'Did he suggest they had a close relationship?' Hollie wondered. Sharing personal textbooks seemed an unusual thing to do.

'Nothing more than a regular teacher and student relationship. He wasn't very forthcoming, so I've recommended a follow-up with him.'

'Great. I'm speaking to him and the two kids as soon as we're done here,' Hollie said. 'I'll ask him about it then.'

Harry returned with a collection of evidence bags and a storage box. Hollie selected a couple of the marked pages at random, taking great care as she opened them.

'He's been looking at file compression, metadata removal and the TOR browser and encryption. Does that mean anything to either of you?'

From DS Anderson's blank look, she could see there would be no help forthcoming from that direction.

'It's connected with uploading, security and privacy, boss,' Harry offered. 'I'm no expert, but it's something you'd use if you didn't want somebody to know you'd uploaded a video. You'd best ask the tech guys for a proper explanation.'

Hollie made a mental note to do just that and then placed the manual in one of the bags, sealed it and handed it over to Anderson, who labelled it and placed it in the box. Hollie lifted the exercise books one by one, checking the topics: Media Studies, English Literature, Psychology, General Studies. There didn't appear to be any clues in the books, but they'd need to comb through them one page at a time to be certain. They might just as well have been Hollie's from when she was at school, they'd changed so little in the intervening years, what with the doodles on the covers and plethora of teacher comments written in red ink.

At last, almost everything was bagged up and recorded, with the exception of one exercise book which Hollie was holding in her hand. She was most interested in the manual to see if it gave any clues as to what Kyle might have been up to, but they'd need to check it over carefully first before an officer could be assigned to work through its numerous pages.

'I guess we'll need to focus on the threats in those notes and figure out what they were about,' Harry remarked. 'At least we know this didn't come out of the blue. Like the teachers said, something's been going on between these kids. We just need to figure out what.'

Hollie considered this and nodded. She couldn't wait to see what came up from the interviews with the pupils which her colleagues were conducting around the school. As she turned to face Harry, something slipped out of the back pages of the exercise book and onto the floor.

'I'll get it,' Hollie said immediately. 'I'm gloved up already.'

Still holding Kyle's textbook, she stooped down to pick up whatever it was that had dropped onto the floor.

It was a piece of paper, folded, on which was scrawled a handwritten note.

It's not too late Kyle. Please text me at home. Tilly x

FIFTEEN

TUESDAY, 16:09

'Thank God, we've got a lead at last,' Hollie said, holding out the scrap of paper while Harry photographed it. She placed it inside an evidence bag which Anderson had to hand already.

'Find an officer to take over these locker searches, Harry. I want you to locate this Tilly and find out what she can tell us about Kyle. We're still looking for a school bag and a phone as far as I'm concerned. There may be a tablet or laptop, too. Have we found anything yet in the student bag searches?'

'No, boss,' Anderson replied. 'The biggest surprise from the bag searches was how many of these kids are vaping.'

'Seriously?'

'Yes, boss. It's like an epidemic. Even the teachers seem embarrassed. I've a feeling the principal may learn a few home truths after this incident.'

He could say that again. For all the positive slogans painted along the walls, the dark underbelly of academy life still seemed to be there. These were no halcyon days as far as Hollie was concerned; it had been tough enough when she was a teenager. But no amount of inspirational quotes painted along the corridors could conceal the fact that children could be a spiteful bunch at that age.

'Can we get to the woodwork rooms from here?' Hollie asked, thinking she could squeeze in one more location visit before carrying out some interviews. She was keen to see where the murder weapon had come from.

'Sure,' Anderson replied, 'it's not so far from here. I took one of the chisels for Doctor Ruane's reference, as you requested, and noted that, including that one, two chisels are missing. The murder weapon and the one I took.'

'Thank you, Ben. Good work. So we were right, it did come from the craft rooms.'

She much preferred praising DS Anderson; it was much easier than ticking him off for saying something inappropriate.

Hollie peeled off her gloves and walked up to Amber Patel, who'd just rejoined them in the locker area.

'Tell me you've cracked the case already,' Hollie said.

'Not yet, boss. I came to check in with you. My eyes are hanging out on stalks raking through all the information from this afternoon's interviews.'

They left Harry Gordon to the lockers, and Anderson offered to guide his two colleagues to the craft block.

As they walked through the corridors, it struck Hollie how little things had changed since she was at school. They were completely obsessed with those inspirational quotes, that was for sure, and more of the children's work was on display than she recalled. The corridors were bare when she was at secondary school; her memories were of a bleak building with bare-brick interior walls and noisy, uncarpeted corridors.

The craft block was clearly marked, but just before it was a set of double doors which looked like it belonged to some community arts group. It had been painted with Manga figures and would not have been out of keeping in a subway tunnel.

'That's where the sixth formers hang out,' Anderson explained. 'It's like a chill area—'

'Take care how you use that nowadays.' Amber smiled. 'You've heard of Netflix and chill? It has rude connotations.'

'Damn, you'll be telling me I can't use my favourite aubergine emoji in work emails next,' Anderson continued, his face completely straight.

'You haven't, have you?'

Amber looked genuinely shocked.

'I'm kidding.' He laughed. 'But it's where the sixth formers go to hang out when they're not in lessons.'

Hollie put her head through the doors. There were numerous old sofas about the place, a table tennis table, a table football game, and a couple of tables on which there were chessboards, Connect 4 and other board games. The board games made her think of the kids, but she pushed it to the back of her mind. They still loved playing snakes and ladders.

Exiting the common room, she noticed the CCTV camera above the double doors. The wires were clearly detached from its rear, presumably as agreed by Mr Canfield after the sixth formers' complaints about privacy.

They continued through into the craft block, which turned out to be a large, open-plan area. There were ten large workbenches placed equidistantly around the centre of the space, with heavy machinery – lathes, drills and the like – around the edges. The teacher's desk was located at a vantage point at the front, giving a clear view of the room.

'Which bench was the chisel removed from?' Hollie asked.

'That one.'

DS Anderson pointed to the first row of benches, furthest away from the teacher's desk.

Hollie walked up to the closest bench and took out one of the chisels from the tool set that was fastened to the side. She put her finger against the end.

'That's blunt, isn't it?' she asked. 'I mean, I'm more Bob the Builder than Isambard Kingdom Brunel when it comes to construction matters, but that wouldn't savage a piece of balsa wood, would it?'

Anderson ran his finger along the top.

'Blunt as f— ...yes, it's blunt.'

'Just check the others, would you?' Hollie asked.

Amber and Ben Anderson checked the tools while Hollie walked up to the teacher's desk. She hadn't been able to see it from the back of the room, but the teacher had the same type of toolkit as the youngsters. She drew out the chisel and ran her finger over the top.

'That's interesting – the teacher's chisel is blunt, too. You'd need a sharp chisel to pierce someone's neck like that, wouldn't you?'

'I'd guess so, boss,' Amber replied.

'Definitely, boss,' Anderson added.

'Are all the others blunt?' she checked.

'Yes, boss.'

'Interesting,' Hollie said, thinking aloud.

'There's one missing over here, boss,' Amber called.

Hollie thought it over. 'So, one of those missing chisels will be the one used to kill Kyle. The other will be the one I asked you to make available to Doctor Ruane for reference during the post-mortem—'

'Yet one of them must have been sharpened in order to be any use in killing Kyle,' Amber finished off her line of thought.

Hollie opened the drawer in the teacher's desk. She raked around, not entirely sure what she was looking for. Her hand found a wooden item pushed to the back and she pulled it out to take a closer look. At first glance it looked like a wooden pencil holder, but when she lifted the lid, there was an oiled stone inside. She recalled her father having something similar in the garage when she was a child.

'Any idea what this is?' she asked. 'It's for sharpening, isn't it?'

Anderson and Amber came up to the desk and took a closer look.

'Pass me your chisel,' Amber said.

Hollie took the tool out of the holder at the side of the teacher's desk and handed it over.

Amber began to move the chisel's blade expertly across the oiled stone.

'It's used for sharpening tools,' she explained.

'Bloody hell, it's like watching a master craftsman at work,' Anderson teased.

'Thank *The Repair Shop* on TV.' Amber smiled up at her colleagues. 'Need a sofa stuffing or a bicycle fixing? I'm your girl.'

Anderson started to speak; he had a look of excitement on his face, like he couldn't wait to get it out.

'Nick Yerbury told me he was supervising a class here just before lunchtime. The sharpening block is in the teacher's desk, and by his own admission, he returned here immediately after Kyle's body was found to retrieve his mobile phone. We have to speak to Yerbury again. We need to know if he used that sharpening block.'

SIXTEEN
TUESDAY, 16:21

Hollie took three slow, deep breaths in the few moments she was on her own in the foyer. If life had seemed dull over her lunchtime Pot Noodle, now it was racing at her all at once and she was in danger of becoming overwhelmed.

Isla Wilson had just lost her only child. Lives were about to come crashing down; hopes, dreams, and aspirations dashed on the rocks of a bleak reality. Sometimes life was shit; she hated it when youngsters were involved – the emotional bandwidth required went off the scale.

As she scoured the area, her eye caught something splashed on the inside of a large bin which was sitting just under the staircase that led up to the school library on the second floor. Harry Gordon and his assigned team of uniformed officers had worked through the bins before searching the field, and each one had been given a reference sticker for easy identification.

She'd be receiving a list of those bins at some point, along with their reference numbers and any contents of interest which had been retained as possible evidence, but she knew already from earlier discussions that nothing had been found in them.

New and empty bags had been placed in each bin, and the contents of the old bags had been retained in a safe place offered by the caretaker in case further examination was required.

So how, if everybody was still cooped up in classrooms and all officers deployed to the investigation, had something splashed up the side of this new bin bag?

Hollie suspected it was probably a discarded drink, but something made her check that supposition. She peered inside, spotting what appeared to be a splash of blood on the interior of the bin bag.

'Officer, have you got a latex glove I can use?' she shouted over to a uniformed officer who'd just walked into the foyer. He pulled one out of his pocket and handed it to her.

'Fetch me an evidence bag, will you?'

He headed off to do as requested. Before putting on the glove, Hollie drew out her phone and took numerous images of the bin and its contents. The sides of the bin bag had stuck together so it was difficult to make out what was sitting at the bottom of it.

The officer returned with an evidence bag, and Hollie handed her phone over to him. She placed the latex glove on her right hand.

'I'm going to push the sides of the bin bag apart, then you take lots of photos of whatever is in there so we can see it in situ.'

The officer seemed nervous, like he was being asked to hand over medical tools in an operating theatre. Hollie just hoped she wasn't cataloguing the retrieval of a discarded Starbucks cup.

The moment she pushed aside the edges of the bin bag, she knew her instincts had been right. The officer repeatedly touched the screen on her phone, recording everything should it be required later in the investigation.

'I'm going to pick it up now,' Hollie advised him. 'I'll do it slowly, keep snapping away.'

Anderson had joined her now, having made his way back to the foyer.

'We've located the student who wrote the note—' he began.

'One moment, Ben.' Hollie stopped him.

Carefully, she gripped the object that had been discarded in the bin. She could see now that whatever it was had been wrapped in paper towels, through which blood was leaking. The moment she felt the item that was wrapped inside, Hollie knew what she'd got.

'It's the chisel, Ben. We've found the murder weapon.'

SEVENTEEN

It's taken me three goes to record this.

Fourth time lucky.

I gave up my place at Manchester Metropolitan University today.

There, I got it out without crying at last.

Yasmine advised me not to, but I can see the writing on the wall.

Hull Uni said I can apply through clearing, but they don't see a problem, especially as I'm a special case what with Mum and all that.

I can see how difficult Mum's finding things.

It crushes my heart watching her.

I've started cooking the evening meals and doing much more around the house.

I feel like a right tosser for leaving her to do so much in the past.

These past few months, I've had to do some growing up.

I also have to face the fact that Mum is going to die.

Not now, not next week, but soon.

I'm going to be really young still when she does die.

I always thought I'd be forty or fifty or something like that when she went.

If I'm lucky – and I do use the word lucky with sarcasm – I'll be in my early twenties by the time she goes.

I can't even think about it right now.

Yasmine asked me today if I want referring for some psychological counselling.

I said no, they'll only tease me more at school if they see me getting hauled out of classes for that.

The whole sixth form already think I'm gay, just because I kept banging on about that TV show with Olly Alexander.

It's like fucking medieval times with Zach; he's all testosterone and bravado.

And he spurs on the others, too; they all follow his lead.

The bastard.

I wish someone would teach him a lesson.

EIGHTEEN
TUESDAY, 16:26

Once the chisel was bagged and recorded properly, Hollie caught up with Ben Anderson.

'Excuse my language,' she whispered, looking around for teachers and children, 'but how the fuck did that get in there after we searched all the bins?'

Anderson shrugged, then seemed like he'd been struck by an idea.

'The only members of the public who've been in here are the parents and reporters who you briefed earlier, plus whichever staff were around at the time.'

Hollie looked at him, realising what that meant.

'You think one of them put the chisel in there? How? We were all there. It would take some damn nerve.'

Anderson led her over to the bin which had now been cordoned off.

'Just think about it,' he began. 'They were all standing in front of this bin when you addressed them. Anybody might have dropped it in there in the hustle and bustle—'

'But who? Do we know who came into the foyer... where's the CCTV camera?'

She looked around.

'Damn, it's trained on the entrance. We must have caught them coming in. Ask Canfield, too, he'll know the names of the parents who came in.'

Hollie thought back to her inspection of the gap in the fence. Google Maps had shown her how it was possible to have sneaked through that gap in the fence, then doubled back to the academy. She shared her thoughts with Anderson.

'Again, you'd need some damn nerve to do that,' he remarked. 'But it's certainly one theory. We can't rule out the possibility that one of the kids managed to drop it in there after the school was locked down, but they've all been restricted to classrooms for the past couple of hours.'

'Yes, but they're being given supervised access to one of the toilet blocks which has been swept for evidence. I guess there's a small possibility one of them might have managed it.'

Hollie wasn't sure, but they had their murder weapon and their first named lead.

'Langdon is with Tilly now,' Anderson explained. 'She's in an empty classroom, Room 12G – we're running out of places to put everybody. She's a sixth former. The vice-principal said she'd sit in on the interview. Poor kid is shitting bricks, she looked terrified.'

'Okay, I'll be along shortly. If Jenni and Olivia Dreyfuss are with her, she's in good hands. I want to speak to these two kids now before we have to let them all go home.'

The two teenagers were playing with their phones when Hollie and Amber Patel walked in. The school counsellor stood up when they entered the room.

'No need to stand up,' Hollie said.

They made the introductions and Amber pulled up a couple of chairs.

Hollie couldn't believe how young the counsellor looked. She had to be around the same age as Jenni Langdon.

'Hello, I'm Yasmine Drake,' she introduced herself. 'I'm the counsellor here and I have part-time teaching responsibilities, too. I work part time.'

'What subject?' Amber wondered.

'I teach drama at A level. I also support the sixth formers with their university applications.'

'You're a busy woman,' Hollie observed.

Yasmine had a nose piercing, through which was threaded a gold nose ring. Her skirt was vivid and much shorter than Hollie might have expected in school, her T-shirt bore a logo and slogan which seemed like it might belong in popular culture, but which Hollie was unable to identify off hand. She wore yellow Doc Martens and dark, patterned stockings.

'So, what school year are you in?' Patel led the way.

'Year ten, miss,' the boy called Mickey replied.

'So that's, what, fourteen years old?'

'I'm fourteen, miss, Finlay is fifteen,' Mickey continued.

Far too young to be discovering dead bodies on school grounds.

'I know it's been a difficult afternoon for you, boys, but we just need to run through what happened this afternoon,' Patel said softly.

They looked at each other, and then at the school counsellor.

'It's okay, boys, you're not in trouble. It's a good job for everybody you were getting up to mischief.'

'We were skipping lessons, miss,' Finlay explained, 'so we were going to sneak out the gap in the fence. There are no cameras over there—'

'What made you make the detour to the outbuilding?' Hollie asked.

'Mickey reckoned it would be a laugh, miss. Besides, we saw Mr Yerbury checking the school field.'

Hollie was looking forward to her second chat with Nick Yerbury. She wanted to know why he'd loaned Kyle that textbook for starters.

'What time was this?'

Patel had her pen poised, even though her phone app was recording everything. Old habits die hard; Hollie often wrote things down even though it wasn't necessary these days. It helped to fix things in her head.

Mickey and Finlay had blank looks on their faces.

'Roughly,' Hollie encouraged them.

'It must have been about ten past one,' Finlay ventured after some delay. 'The warning bell had gone for lessons; it usually takes the field and playground a few minutes to clear, and we were halfway across the field when we changed course and decided to hide in the old building.'

Hollie wanted to move this on, so tried a bit of rapid fire.

'Had you played in the building before?'

'No, it was supposed to be out of bounds.'

'Was anybody there when you went inside?'

'We didn't go inside at first. We hid in the doorway until Mr Yerbury started making his way over—'

'So, Mr Yerbury was heading for the outbuilding. Had he spotted you?' Patel asked.

'Maybe. That's when we hid inside, miss.'

'Was anybody else in there?'

'There are a couple of small cupboard spaces in there, so somebody could hide, I suppose.'

'When did you see the body?'

'Officer!' the counsellor chided Hollie.

Yasmine was present in a safeguarding role after all, and the speed of this investigation was going to rely on maintaining the goodwill of the school staff.

Hollie tried again, gentler this time.

'What did you see when you entered the building?'

Mickey looked at Finlay. For the first time, she detected some tension between them. Amber clocked it, too; Hollie saw her eyebrows raise slightly.

'Finlay?'

'I thought it was just a pile of clothes at first, miss. I gave it a kick, then realised it was a body—'

He began to sob. Yasmine Drake looked agitated like she was unsure if she should call time on the interview.

Hollie gave Patel a quick glance to make sure she'd noted that the body had been kicked again. Doctor Ruane would need to know that, as would the SOCOs.

'A kick seems an unusual thing to do?' Amber commented.

'Not a hard kick, miss, just a tap with my foot. I was scared to touch it.'

'What about you, Mickey?' Amber asked.

'I didn't really see it until Finlay shouted. I was looking out for Mr Yerbury, in case he spotted us.'

'I know this is difficult to think about, but was the person alive when you saw him there?'

'He groaned when I kicked him, miss,' Finlay sniffed.

Hollie felt her heart pounding. She'd caught a scent.

'Think really carefully about this, boys. Are you certain the person who was on the floor was still alive?'

'It scared me,' Finlay continued. 'It was like a zombie movie.'

'I'm sorry to have to ask this question.' Hollie softened her tone. 'Was there blood on the floor when you saw the body?'

She got her answer from the blank look that the boys exchanged.

'No, miss, there was no blood on the ground,' Mickey confirmed. 'We were scared when we heard the groan, so we ran to Mr Yerbury because we didn't know what to do—'

'I thought it was a tramp or something,' Finlay added.

'You're certain there was no blood?' Hollie pushed again. This was crucial.

'No, miss,' they both answered at once. 'Only on the face,' Finlay added.

'Was there a coat anywhere in the area?' Hollie asked, recalling her catch-up with Harry Gordon.

'Yes, miss,' Finlay answered. 'It was on top of him, that's why it looked like a pile of clothes.'

The coat was removed after Kyle's death. The killer must have still been there. Harry was right.

'What happened after that?' Amber picked up.

'We shouted for Mr Yerbury to help. He told us to wait outside the building while he checked what was going on.'

Mickey was the more confident of the two boys. Finlay seemed shaken by having to recall the events.

'And then?' Hollie prompted.

'His face was white when he came out. He told us to come with him back to the school while he fetched help—'

'Did he call 999?' Amber interrupted.

Finlay shook his head. 'I can't remember, miss.'

'Maybe,' Mickey offered. 'We went back to reception, and he found somewhere for us to sit and told us not to move. Then he got some other teachers to help. Soon after that, the panic alarm went off—'

'The panic alarm?'

This was an education for Hollie. Her kids had never mentioned anything about panic alarms.

'We do regular drills in case there's an emergency in school,' the counsellor explained. 'Perhaps a knife crime, or somebody on school grounds who shouldn't be there.'

Jeez, this sounds more like a US penitentiary than a UK school.

'The panic alarm has a different sound to the fire alarm.

The students know that they have to stay in their classrooms. Doors are locked, blinds pulled down and the police are called.'

'How long until the alarm was switched off?'

'Well, I heard the sirens when the police and ambulance arrived. It was soon after that. About twenty past one, maybe as late as twenty-five minutes past.'

This was a detail about school life that Hollie wasn't aware of. Is this what it was like for her own kids? And why didn't they mention it to her when she was teasing out details of their school day? It appeared to be so mundane to them that it barely warranted a mention over the dinner table. The thought of it horrified her.

Hollie ran through what they'd said. She could see both boys had had enough now, and she was reluctant to push them too hard. They were slightly older than her own daughter, and she wondered how Lily would have coped in a similar situation.

'You've done a great job, boys, I just want to check one more time, because this is really important. You're certain the person on the floor was still alive when you entered the outbuilding? And you're positive there was no blood?'

They looked at each other again and nodded.

'Well, you've been very helpful. I'm so sorry you had to deal with that. We may have to speak to you both again, but we're finished for now, thank you.'

The moment Hollie and DS Patel stood up, the boys were back on their phones.

'I need to ask you not to post anything about this on social media, boys,' Hollie added. 'It's really important that this all stays private, is that okay?'

They looked up momentarily and nodded.

'Yes, miss.'

They exited the room after thanking the counsellor and the police officer for their help. Hollie sighed.

'What do you think?' she asked Amber when they were out of earshot.

'I think that I'm pleased I went to school in the nineties,' she replied. 'All I had to worry about back then was if my Tamagotchi was still alive and how many Pokémon I'd still got to catch.'

NINETEEN
TUESDAY, 16:45

'Hello, Mr Yerbury, thank you for your patience. Today must have been a shock for you.'

Hollie had gone directly from Yasmine's office to see Nick Yerbury. She wanted to be certain that the stories matched up. His feet were on one of the conference room tables; that wasn't the best start.

'Lovely to see you again, Hollie.'

He stood up and walked over to her with his hand outstretched. 'But, of course, it's terrible under the circumstances,' he added, recovering himself.

Hollie hesitated; shaking hands with witnesses in a murder case was not specifically mentioned in the etiquette book. Awkwardly, she fumbled, uncertain whether to reciprocate or not. She felt ridiculous.

She reciprocated anyway; it was soft and uncalloused, the hand of a man who didn't have to do manual work.

Yerbury returned to the chair he'd been sitting in. Hollie was relieved he didn't put his feet back on the table – it was one of her pet hates. In her mind, it displayed a presumptive arrogance, and it was guaranteed to wind her up every time.

She pulled up another chair and sat in front of him with the table separating them.

'I know you've already spoken to my colleague, DS Anderson—'

'Yes, he was very thorough—'

'I'll be catching up on your statement shortly, but I just wanted to have another chat with you before you leave the building.'

'By all means, fire away with your questions.'

Hollie activated the app on her phone to ensure it was all formally recorded for the police system.

He seemed confident and assured; it was not what she'd usually see in somebody who was one of the first to discover a dead child. There was no standard reaction, of course, and the bravado he was now displaying might well have been his coping mechanism.

She looked at his hands again, which were steady. She'd noticed a persistent tremble in many people in his situation, but Nick Yerbury was sure of himself.

Hollie examined his face. He was in his mid-thirties, she reckoned, well-groomed and tidily presented. There were fleeting flecks of grey in his hair, yet his overall demeanour was youthful and positive. He had great teeth, too, though she wouldn't be sharing that information in the next team briefing.

'So, how can I help you, Hollie? Or I guess I should call you detective while things are so formal?'

Hollie snapped her mind back into gear.

'Just walk me through the timeline of what happened this afternoon.'

'I have gone through this with your colleague already—'

'I know, but I'd like you to do so again. It's important we don't miss anything.'

'Sure, I won't tell you how to do your job. I was on lunchtime duty—'

'What does that involve?'

'At five minutes to one o'clock, I walk out into the playground and wait for the warning bell to sound. I supervise the children into the building and then, once the playground is clear, I do a circuit of the school to encourage any stragglers on their way.'

'Are you also looking for truants?'

'Always. So, when I saw Mickey and Finlay by the old building, I walked over to see what they were up to.'

'What can you tell me about the old storage building? I know you'll have explained this to DS Anderson, but this is for my benefit. I'm trying to get a sense of this academy.'

'Well, you know that building has been a bit of a thorn in the side of Mr Canfield, I assume?'

Hollie nodded.

'It's been a constant problem. The kids keep working the barriers loose and they sneak in there to vape, skip lessons and who knows what else? It was used for storage until fairly recently. I think it caught Canfield on the hop because he thought he could just demolish it, and the moment the planning application was announced in the local paper, all hell broke loose. The local archaeological enthusiasts spotted it and now it's on a perpetual hold while everybody figures out if the area should be excavated first.'

'What about that hole in the fence?'

'What about it?' Yerbury replied.

'Why was it left and not repaired? How did it get there?'

He smiled at her. Hollie reckoned his teeth may have been whitened.

'I can't tell you how it got there, it's probably loosened bolts or something like that. The security of school grounds is of paramount importance, so it's been at the top of the maintenance list for some time. I think we're just waiting for the contractors to come out, you know how long things take these days.'

She did. Simple requests for IT or office items took forever. When she was a police constable, there seemed to be a store cupboard which contained everything anybody could ever need. And, if what you wanted wasn't available, you'd go to the petty cash box and buy it yourself. These days you had to wrestle with a purchase order number and approved contractor before anything got done, and that was assuming you could prove it was value for money in the first place. As for petty cash, there was an entire generation of new workers who didn't even know what it was.

'Okay, thank you, that's very useful. Tell me what happened when you found Kyle's body.'

'Will I be able to leave soon? Only, I have explained all of this to DS Anderson already. He's got it all recorded in my statement.'

Here was the first resistance. Just for a moment, the charm was dropped and replaced by annoyance and impatience.

'I won't keep you long. It's just it's often handy for me to hear it straight from the horse's mouth. Sometimes things are missed or forgotten. This is a huge help to me, seeing as you're so integral to the case.'

He sighed, and then the charm was back.

'I thought I saw movement by the disused outbuilding so, being the diligent educationalist that I am, I walked over there to flush them out. Only, they called to me first.'

Hollie bristled at his turn of phrase. This man wasn't giving her many reasons to warm to him.

'Which of the children called you?'

'Mickey, I think. No, maybe Finlay. To be honest, I'm not sure. It may have been both of them—'

'And you ran over?'

'Yes, of course. At first, I was annoyed because they'd ducked into the building when they saw me on duty. But I could tell from the urgency of their shouts that something was up. So I ran over.'

'What did they say when you got there?'

'They were in a panic. I got the gist of it. I told them to wait outside, and I went in to investigate.'

'What did you see?'

For the first time since they'd spoken, Nick Yerbury looked like a man who'd witnessed something disturbing that day. He swallowed before answering.

'There was a body on the ground. It was in a foetal position. I didn't know it was Kyle then, his face was bruised and sore and bloodied—'

'Was he moving? Were there any signs of life?'

'No, nothing.'

Hollie made a mental note; the boys had been certain Kyle was alive.

'Was Kyle's coat there?'

Yerbury considered that.

'Yeah, I think it was. I'm not sure, but it was next to him, I think. Maybe even partially covering him.'

'What did you do then?'

'I rushed up to the body, gave it a gentle shake, and then panicked. It was completely unresponsive.'

'Was there blood on the ground?'

'Yes. No. No, there wasn't.'

'Yes or no, you don't seem sure?'

'There was blood on his face, but not on the ground. I didn't see any, at least. I'm sorry, I had to think about that.'

'Didn't you recognise who it was?'

'Have you seen the body?' Yerbury asked, with more than a hint of annoyance in his voice.

Hollie recalled Kyle's bloody, bruised and swollen face.

'Then you'll know he was a bit of a mess.'

That was a fair point. She decided to move on.

'Did you call 999?'

'No, I'd left my phone in my classroom.'

Hollie recalled Ben mentioning that.

'Do you usually do that?'

'No, but I'd forgotten I was on duty, and Mr Canfield can be a bit of a stickler about things like that.'

'What's he a stickler about?'

'He doesn't like us using our phones when we're around the children. They're completely banned in classrooms. I'd accidentally taken mine into the lesson I was covering before lunchtime and, to remove all temptation, I'd placed it in the desk drawer to stop me fiddling with it. I forgot to take it with me when I went to the staffroom for lunch. In fact, I only realised what I'd done when I needed to call 999.'

Yerbury had his phone with him now and he activated the screen to check the time.

'We're almost done, Mr Yerbury. This is so useful to me, I can't tell you how much I appreciate it.'

He sighed.

'So, what did you do next?'

'I told Mickey and Finlay to follow me over to the main building, and I rushed to reception, where I asked Mrs Robinson to call for an ambulance.'

'Did you alert the police?'

'Not straight away. To be honest, I didn't cope very well. I panicked, and I just thought whoever it was had passed out or something like that. I didn't know whether to stay with him or leave him.'

'Didn't Mickey or Finlay have phones you could have used to call for help?'

He paused and considered that.

'They're supposed to be in their lockers during the day, but that doesn't mean that they are. I'm sorry, I told you I panicked. I just didn't think to check.'

She studied his face; he seemed sincere and even a little sheepish about what he'd just admitted.

'What do you teach, Mr Yerbury?'

'Well, I'm a media studies teacher by profession, but with budgets being what they are, we're often moved around a bit. I might find myself supervising all kinds of lessons: Maths, PE, Resistant Materials—'

'Resistant materials?'

'Woodwork, metalwork, design and construction – that's what it used to be called.'

'Have you supervised woodwork lessons this week?'

She knew the answer; Anderson had mentioned it in the woodworking room. She was leading him.

'Yes, I stood in today. It was one of my free lessons. I was pretty annoyed about it, truth be told. That's where I left my phone, in the desk drawer there.'

Hollie nodded. She assumed Anderson had got all this on the statement, but past experience had taught her that the nuggets of an investigation were often found in the cracks. The same applied to job interviews. The gaps in employment histories were usually where the real stories were hidden: mental breakdowns, caring responsibilities, marital break-ups, dismissals and redundancies.

'Is that the same desk drawer that the tool-sharpening block was stored in?'

Nick seemed genuinely bemused by that question.

'Yes... that seems an odd question to ask.'

'Did you use that sharpening block while you were in the classroom?'

He seemed embarrassed by his answer, but not in a guilty way.

'Yes, I got bored, so messed around with the chisel that was in the teacher's toolkit. As soon as I'd sharpened it, I placed it in one of the far desks and picked up another one to sharpen. I didn't get any further, though, because one of the students asked for some help with some work they were doing.'

Only Mr Canfield and Mrs Dreyfuss knew about the wound to Kyle's neck, but that a chisel had made that wound was only known to the police. If Yerbury was guilty, Hollie reckoned he'd have been much more guarded about that answer.

'I'm almost done now. I just want to be absolutely clear in my own mind. You were alone with the body when Mickey and Finlay were there. You asked them to wait outside?'

'No. I'm not sure I like where this is heading.'

'Mr Yerbury, I'm just clarifying the timeline in my head.'

'Okay, but do I need legal representation?'

'As I said, we have your statement, and this is just an informal follow-up. It's a witness statement, one of many we'll be taking over the course of today and tomorrow. So, the body was also left alone when you walked over to the school building with Finlay and Mickey?'

'Yes. It was perhaps left for ten minutes, while the ambulance was alerted.'

'Who phoned it in?'

'Mrs Robinson from the reception desk. She has a first aid qualification, but Canfield told her to wait until the medics arrived. I think he was panicking about having a dead body on the premises, and Mrs Dreyfuss had told him not to mess up the crime scene.'

Nick Yerbury seemed confident about the order of events. They'd need to check the statements, match them against the CCTV if it had recorded the movements, see which children needed to be interviewed the next day and then piece together the jigsaw puzzle of events leading to Kyle's death.

But one thing was for certain, there were now three

windows where Kyle might have been stabbed with the chisel, apart from the main assault. There was the time when Mickey and Finlay found Kyle, the ten-minute gap while help was being summoned, and then there were the few moments when Nick Yerbury had been alone with the body.

'When did you return to the craft rooms to collect your phone, Mr Yerbury? I'd have expected you to stay in the admin area to await the arrival of the police.'

For the first time, Nick Yerbury looked rattled.

'Well – um – you're right, of course, I was terribly concerned about Kyle. Though I didn't know it was Kyle at the time.'

'Still, it was most likely one of the students from the academy. And your phone was more important?'

'I needed it to stay in touch, you know how it is with phones.'

'I do, Mr Yerbury, but on a hierarchy of importance, surely the welfare of children comes above a phone.'

'Yes, well, I agree, but...'

His face was now beetroot red, and he wouldn't meet her eyes.

'I noticed earlier that you loaned a personal textbook to Kyle, one that was all about video editing and security. We found it in Kyle's locker. Was there something about Kyle that meant you were closer to him than other students?'

Hollie noted how Nick Yerbury's eyes flashed with indignation. All hint of his former charm evaporated in an instant.

'I don't know what you're trying to suggest by that remark, detective, but there was nothing inappropriate about my relationship with Kyle and I take offence that you might think there was.'

Hollie had seen hollow protests before, but this did not appear to be one of them.

There was a tap at the door, which she ignored, as he was about to say more.

'I loaned that book to Kyle because I wanted to help him. And yes, he did get some special treatment, because I felt sorry for him about his mum. Kyle used to come around to my place to do his homework. But there was nothing more to it – nothing.'

TWENTY

TUESDAY, 16:57

Hollie was annoyed to have to break off her interview with Nick Yerbury. Amber Patel had knocked at the door to let her know that they were going to have to release the students to go home. Every bag had been searched, any child who'd seen something interesting had been spoken to by a police officer and the entire school grounds had been searched.

They couldn't put it off any longer. Parental shouting outside the school gates had reached a fever pitch. She could hear it all the time she was interviewing Nick Yerbury, but she had no reason to hold him yet, even though he'd just got himself added to a list of interesting persons. She'd told him they would speak further with him the next day.

Tensions were running high throughout the academy – some children were scared and tearful, others were getting restless and misbehaving. Hollie couldn't recall a policing situation that had required so much people management.

'The moment we let them out of those classrooms, they're going to go trampling all over any evidence which might be here,' she confided to DS Patel.

'It's not quite so bad, boss. The outbuilding is properly

cordoned off, the principal has agreed that everybody will leave via the front exit, and nobody will be able to touch their lockers. Jenni's waiting for you down there.' Amber pointed. 'You'll see the room, she's left the door open.'

Hollie was anxious to speak to Tilly before the students were allowed home; she'd have kept them there all night if she could.

Tilly Mann's body language told her everything she needed to know when she walked into the classroom. Jenni had set things up so they were completely non-confrontational, with some of the desks pushed aside and four plastic chairs pulled into a small circle.

Tilly's arms were tightly pulled into her stomach and there were streaks down her face where she'd been crying. Olivia Dreyfuss stood up as soon as she saw Hollie at the door and encouraged her back out into the corridor.

'She's in a right state,' Olivia whispered to Hollie. 'Can't this wait until tomorrow?'

'I'm sorry, Mrs Dreyfuss, so far Tilly is the only student we can directly connect to Kyle's death. She's not a suspect, but I think she can help us.'

'Well, go gently with her. She's a quiet girl at the best of times, she'll need handling with kid gloves.'

Hollie nodded.

Imagine this is Lily you're talking to. Treat her like you'd like your own daughter to be treated.

Jenni was holding Tilly's hand when they walked back into the room. She was speaking softly to her, reassuring her that everything would be fine.

'Hello, Tilly,' Hollie began, holding out her hand. Tilly snatched her hand out of Jenni's and clasped herself tight once again. Olivia Dreyfuss sat down to her right.

Hollie withdrew her hand. That was a bad start; she knew

from past experience that many youngsters chose not to shake hands.

'I'm Detective Inspector Hollie Turner,' she tried again. 'I'm the police officer responsible for finding out who hurt Kyle.'

Tilly screwed up her face and began to cry. She looked like she was on the verge of a complete breakdown.

Hollie let her be for a few moments, then took her phone out of her pocket. She held it close to her as she scrolled past some of the more gruesome images which she'd captured that day. She gently held out her phone and showed Tilly the photograph of her note.

'We need to ask you about this note, Tilly.'

Jenni leaned over and squeezed Tilly's arm.

'It's okay, Tilly, DI Turner only wants to help. You can tell her.'

'Were you friends with Kyle?'

Tilly gave a small nod.

'Would you say you were mates?'

'Yes,' she whispered. 'I loved Kyle.'

'Were you boyfriend and girlfriend?' Jenni asked, so casually that you might as well have been Tilly's mate.

'No, it was nothing like that.'

Tilly began to sob again.

'What was that note about, Tilly?' Hollie pushed.

She looked at the image of the note on her phone:

It's not too late, Kyle. Please text me at home. Tilly x

Tilly pulled her arms in tighter, gently rocking in her chair. The tears were streaming down her face.

'It sounds to me like you were trying to help your friend, Tilly,' Jenni said. 'Was he in trouble?'

Tilly closed her eyes and shook her head.

'It was just homework,' she said at last, her voice broken and weak. 'I was trying to help with a homework assignment.'

'Only it looks like you might have been trying to warn him about something, Tilly,' Hollie added.

'No, no, Kyle was my friend, I loved Kyle. I've known him since primary school. I was just trying to help him.'

Tilly was becoming distraught. Olivia Dreyfuss seemed on the point of intervening.

'Did you text Kyle again?' Jenni asked. 'If we asked to see your phone, would you let us take a look at it?'

'Kyle never answered,' Tilly replied. 'I slipped that note to him across the table yesterday, but he never texted me back... I wish he...'

'What do you wish, Tilly?' Hollie urged her. It felt like Tilly was on the verge of telling them something, but she was holding back. Was she scared of something? Or someone?

'I wish he was still alive. I just wish Kyle was still alive and none of this had happened.'

She began to sob again, and Olivia Dreyfuss leaned over to whisper in Hollie's ear.

'Can we leave this now? The poor girl is obviously upset, and she's not on your list of suspects, is she? I'd prefer for you to try again tomorrow, she looks traumatised—'

The school bell sounded.

'That's Mr Canfield for the special assembly,' Olivia said loudly. 'We'd best be on our way.'

'Can I check your phone before we go to the main hall for the special assembly?' Hollie asked. 'Just to be sure.'

'It's okay,' Jenni encouraged. 'It'll just help us find out what happened to Kyle.'

Tilly's eyes flashed with fear, and she looked at Olivia Dreyfuss for support.

'It's okay, Tilly,' Olivia reiterated.

Slowly Tilly reached into her bag and drew out her mobile phone.

'I'll just find the texts for you,' she sniffed.

Her fingers worked deftly across the screen, but after a couple of seconds Jenni stood up and moved towards her.

'No!' she cried, reaching out to take the phone.

'What?' Hollie asked, taken aback by her colleague's sudden movements.

'She's deleting them,' Jenni said, placing her hand on Tilly's phone. Tilly held on tight for a moment, then seeing she was outnumbered, let it go.

'There's just one left, it's in the recycle bin,' Jenni muttered, moving her fingers across the phone screen with similar dexterity to Tilly.

'Look at this,' she mumbled, turning the screen so that Hollie could see it.

I'm sorry, Tilly. I'm so sorry. I hope you'll forgive me one day. Kyle x

'If you want to avoid a nervous breakdown, don't check social media,' Amber groaned, looking at her phone.

'How bad is it?'

Patel screwed up her face. 'It's nasty,' she replied. 'And lots of it's come from the kids in the classrooms.'

'Oh, for fu—'

'Careful, boss.' Amber Patel placed her hand on Hollie's arm, signalling that the principal was nearby.

It might become her greatest professional challenge yet, not swearing inappropriately in front of the school staff or the students.

Anderson joined them. She was grateful to have her team working at her side; she didn't feel quite so exposed knowing they were on the case.

'Okay,' Hollie continued, 'Mr Canfield said I could say a few words during this special assembly he wants to hold. I'll explain to the kids what's going on then. Is everybody in place?'

'All sorted, boss,' Anderson replied. 'We're clearing the top floor first, then the ground floor. Everybody is restricted to the corridors and the cloakrooms are out of bounds. We've had lots of kids with overactive bladders, so we made one cloakroom area available after giving it a thorough check. God knows what forensics would find, probably several new strains of bacteria.'

'What about keeping everywhere else safe from contamination?' Hollie asked.

'I have uniformed officers making sure none of the lockers are touched, and all exits are blocked. They're walking from their classrooms to the hall, then once they're dismissed, they'll be released in year groups, through the foyer and out the front. School buses will pick up from the front only. It'll be a bit of a jam, but we've got a couple of uniforms out there playing referee. It's the best we can do.'

'Good work, Ben, thank you.'

He and Amber certainly knew how to do their jobs; she felt well flanked having the two of them in school.

'We'll release the staff soon afterwards. They can all exit via the rear car park. We should probably check vehicles, too.'

'It's a bit dystopian, isn't it, boss?'

Hollie considered Amber's point.

'We still need to find Kyle's phone and laptop, if he had one; it could be concealed in any locker, any school bag or any vehicle. It might have left the academy already. Every vehicle needs a search before it leaves the premises.'

Amber nodded.

'Have you heard from the digital forensics team, Amber? We cracked open the password on Kyle's PC for them, so I'd have expected an update by now?'

Patel's blank face gave her the answer. Hollie signalled to Mr Canfield, and the school bell was sounded. Within minutes, lines of children began to filter through the foyer and enter the double doors into the school hall. They walked in complete silence as if they'd grasped the gravity of the situation despite their young years.

There was an atmosphere of grim anticipation. Hollie gave

Twitter a quick glance to get a feel of what was happening on social media. Somebody had made an animated GIF from a short extract of her press briefing. The words *Blah! Blah! Blah!* were animated coming out of her mouth. The person posting the tweet was using the hashtag *#policebunglewhilekidssuffer*.

Hollie clicked off the app. Social media trolling was not going to help keep her mind on the job. She'd got the gist, there was no need to torture herself over it.

It took just over ten minutes to filter the entire school into the hall. Hollie followed one of the last groups through, watching the students and looking for any clues or giveaway signs as they filed past her.

Rows and rows of children sat on the wooden floor of the hall, school bags placed in front of them. Despite their uniforms, they still seemed like a rag-tag bunch. The boys' partly shaved heads appeared to be part of the uniform, they were so prevalent. *Peaky Blinders* had a lot to answer for.

Behind the lower school years, the sixth formers displayed their increased status by getting to sit on chairs. As the counsellor had mentioned to her earlier, they wore whatever clothes they chose, and from where Hollie was standing, there were a wide variety of different styles on display.

She thought back to her own sixth-form years; they seemed so bland by comparison. She'd worn culottes and Doc Martens back then, that was as edgy as it got. She envied them their flare and self-expression, wishing she'd had more self-confidence to do the same thing at their age.

Bernard Canfield walked up on the stage. The children had been sitting in silence, but as he prepared to speak, the fidgeting ceased and there was not a sound to be heard, with the exception of the last teacher to find a chair. It was packed in there, the teachers lining the hall at either side so they could watch over the kids.

'We'll start with the Lord's Prayer—'

Immediately, thoughts of her own school assemblies came roaring back into Hollie's mind. They always started with the Lord's Prayer, yet she'd never heard anybody saying it since she left for university. As Canfield ran through the words, she was surprised to find that she could still recall most of it.

Canfield was one for amateur dramatics. He left a poignant pause at the end of the prayer. Hollie was pleased to see that in spite of AI, smartphones and blockchain technology, kids still peeped during prayers, fluttering their eyelids at great speed to conceal their subterfuge.

'I have brought us all together today because it is at times like this that we need to draw upon the strength of our small community. I'm sorry that some of you will have been upset by the presence of police officers in our academy.'

It felt like the entire school had just turned to look at Hollie. She gave a sanguine nod, hoping to exude a little of Canfield's gravitas.

'Thank you for helping your teachers and the police today, by allowing them to check your bags and sharing the things that you may have seen. It took patience and resilience, and I know that I can always rely on you when fortitude is required.'

He'd be quoting Churchill next. Hollie wished he'd just get on with it. It had already been a long afternoon and they'd just got started.

Canfield paused as he looked at the children, seemingly fully confident in his ability to command this young crowd.

The hall was completely silent. At the worst moment possible, Hollie's mobile phone sounded; she'd forgotten to switch it to silent.

Every face turned to look at her and she fumbled to reject the call as quickly as possible. It was Léon; of course it was. He might be able to drop everything on a whim when working at home, but Hollie needed to pick her time for personal calls.

'I do apologise, Mr Canfield,' she said, relieved to have silenced the ringer at last.

He took it in his stride and continued, a disapproving look on his face.

'As you've been told by your teachers already, we sadly lost a member of our school community today. Our thoughts and prayers are with Kyle Wilson's mother, his family and his friends. We will close school tomorrow as a mark of respect, and we will be remembering Kyle in a celebration of his life at school first thing on Thursday. Now, I'd like us to sit in silence for one minute and pray for Kyle in our own way.'

Most of the children bowed their heads and Canfield searched for Hollie in the mass of bodies. He beckoned her up onto the stage. She felt suddenly nervous. There must have been over a thousand kids in there, that was a lot of bubbling hormones in one place. She felt daunted by the prospect but steeled herself.

Canfield let the silence run for more than a minute, and when Hollie had joined him, he spoke once again.

'I've asked DC Hollie Turner to say a few words to you.'

She let the rank error slide; this wasn't the time to be splitting hairs over titles. She was tempted to say *Thank you, headmaster*, but scolded herself for having petty and unprofessional thoughts.

'Thank you, Mr Canfield. I'm so sorry that this has happened in your school today. I know that many of you knew Kyle and will be very sad right now.'

She paused. If it worked for Canfield, it could work for her. She scanned the room and did a double take on one of the sixth formers. Something caught her eye. A sixth-form student with red hair had just moved his coat so that it covered his white T-shirt. It wasn't cold in the hall, there was no need for him to be doing that.

As Hollie looked in his direction, the student averted his gaze.

'I'd like to reassure you that Mr Canfield, your teachers, and my police colleagues are doing everything possible to make sure that you all stay safe in school.'

As Hollie spoke, the student shuffled in his chair, causing the sides of his coat to fall open. There was something on his white T-shirt which immediately caught her attention and the boy, clocking her watching him, moved his hand up so that the mark, or logo, or whatever it was, was covered.

He looked at Hollie with panic written across his face and then his hand moved to scratch the side of his cheek as if, instinctively, he was trying to deflect her gaze.

Was that blood on that student's T-shirt? He saw that she was staring hard at him now and pulled his coat more securely across his chest.

The sixth former looked like he was getting ready to get up off his chair. Even from a distance she could see he was sweating profusely, and his eyes darted about like he expected the other officers to have seen it, too. He reached down to grasp the handle on his bag.

'I know Mr Canfield will be sending an email out to parents this evening, but I'd like to remind you that it'll help us a lot if you don't post on, or read, social media for the next couple of days.'

The student was following her every move now, looking around him, a shifty expression on his face, the picture of guilt. The words of warning would have to wait. Hollie walked to the edge of the stage and leapt down onto the wooden tiles below.

There was an immediate gasp from the children who were directly in front of her, and a spark of shock leapt across the room.

The children had left a small gap along the middle of the

hall and Hollie ran along it now, never losing sight of the student, who'd sensed already that she was coming for him.

She was aware of the commotion all around her, but she could think of only one thing and that was to apprehend this sixth former before he could make a dash for it.

Mr Canfield and the other teachers were attempting to calm the children, and she knew her own team would be watching her like a hawk, trusting her instincts and knowing that something was up.

The student stood up like a massive voltage had been sent through his seat and he shuffled chairs with the people on either side so that he could better make his escape.

But Hollie reached him before he could make his exit and she planted her hand firmly on his shoulder.

'I'd like to see your T-shirt please,' she demanded.

The student was clearly in a state of panic but started cursing at her and trying to deflect.

'I haven't done anything wrong. Stop picking on me, this is harassment.'

'What's your name?'

'Zach.'

'Zach what?'

'Eastwood. Zach Eastwood.'

'Move your hand please, Zach!'

The room was in an uproar.

'Move it, Zach,' she repeated.

Zach moved his hand to partially reveal the white T-shirt, and she reached out to push the sides of his coat out of the way.

There it was as clear as day. The top of his T-shirt was spattered with red, fresh blood.

'Is that the way Humberside Police usually deals with children?' Mr Canfield scolded her.

'I'm sorry, but this is a police investigation, and that kid was going to make a run for it—'

'But did you have to create that level of alarm? The younger children were terrified; they didn't know what was happening.'

Hollie suspected they'd never had such a lively assembly and it was unlikely to be forgotten any time soon.

'Zach Eastwood's T-shirt has spatters of blood on it. He's just made himself prime suspect. I'm sorry, but I wasn't going to let him sneak out of the hall right under my nose.'

Canfield calmed down as a uniformed officer approached. It looked like he'd conceded that she was probably right.

'Everything's bagged and tagged, ma'am. We've got his coat, his T-shirt, his trainers, the lot. One of the teachers sorted him out with some temporary clothing from lost property. The suspect has been taken to Clough Road for processing.'

'Out the back way, I hope?'

'Yes, ma'am, of course, the press didn't see.'

The officer left them.

'How old is Zach? Is red hair allowed in school?'

'He's eighteen. I've spoken to his father about his hair, but he was less than supportive, and he's a school governor, too, so I sort of need him onside. Why did you ask about his age?'

'He's an adult. The parents don't need to be present when we question him. It makes my life easier—'

'You may wish to reconsider that, detective.'

'Why?'

Was he telling her how to do her job now?

'What about the two youngsters you spoke to earlier? Mickey and Finlay. They were allowed an adult with them.'

'We had your counsellor there for safeguarding purposes. We're always allowed to interview if there's an immediate risk of harm or loss. Besides, they weren't being questioned under caution. That won't be the case for Zach, I'm afraid.'

Canfield shook his head.

'Zach's a decent enough kid. He's a bit full of himself, perhaps, but a very exceptional sportsman. His father is a local businessman with a good relationship with the Hull Central MP, Magnus Burrows. You might wish to tread carefully with him.'

He'll get the same damn treatment as anybody else.

'Of course, Mr Canfield, thanks for the heads-up. We're going to question Zach ASAP, and he's going to need legal representation. We will inform his parents as a courtesy, of course. I'd appreciate it if you would join us in the conference room for a briefing with my team, as we need to discuss how we manage this situation going forward.'

The school was now empty of children, after them being sent home via the main entrance and with close supervision – as soon as they'd been settled down after the unexpected conclusion to the special assembly. Hollie checked with Anderson that teachers' cars were being given the once-over on their way out and that uniformed officers were monitoring all exits. Locker searches were being concluded and relevant details meticulously recorded.

Canfield had brought in his senior team. Hollie had gathered several members of the investigating team, as the assembly had created a natural point at which to take stock of the day's events.

'Thank you, DS Anderson, for pulling everything together while I've been busy elsewhere.'

Anderson seemed happy with the acknowledgement. Small things.

'I'd also like to thank Mr Canfield and all of you for your help this afternoon. It's an incredibly stressful situation, and everything you've done today to help us makes it more likely that we'll find Kyle's killer.'

They, too, seemed appreciative of the thanks.

'I want to share where we're up to and devise a management plan for tomorrow. You'll be aware that we've sent Zach Eastwood over to the custody suite at Clough Road, where we'll be questioning him ASAP in connection with Kyle's murder.'

She allowed them a few minutes to chat and ask questions; they'd earned it.

'Clearly, I can't divulge certain information about the case to academy staff, and I would appreciate your continued professionalism in not discussing the details that I can share with anybody beyond these four walls.'

She hoped she didn't have to remind a group of senior educationalists about their obligations, but she said it anyway, just in case.

'We're going to take tomorrow to continue searching every nook and cranny in this academy before the children return on Thursday. The outbuilding will remain cordoned off until further notice, and the vice-principal has arranged for some high fencing to make sure it's properly secured before the children return. Thank you for that, Mrs Dreyfuss.'

Olivia Dreyfuss gave the hint of a nod.

'And thank you, too, for making the school canteen facilities available to my team while we conduct our investigations here. As agreed with Mr Canfield, we'll be taking over this conference room until further notice. I know that we're also liaising over the provision of trauma experts in the academy for the next couple of days.'

She gave everybody a moment to absorb the information. Nobody offered further comment.

'We will keep a police presence here until it's deemed no longer necessary. I want staff and students to be able to speak to a member of my team at any time of day and night. We're determined to find Kyle's killer – or killers.'

There were nods of agreement around the conference room table. Then Olivia Dreyfuss cleared her throat.

'How do we know this won't happen again?'

'I beg your pardon?' Hollie replied.

'How do we know this isn't some local madman going around killing teenagers?'

'It's a fair question to ask,' Hollie replied. 'Although I can't share the precise details of the investigation, I can confirm that I believe this to be an isolated and targeted incident. We have already contacted other local schools in the area and have advised them to check their security measures. We will also maintain a police presence at the school gates, to give the parents and local community some peace of mind.'

That seemed to placate Olivia Dreyfuss.

'Is there any chance that broken fencing could get fixed sometime soon?' Hollie asked, addressing Canfield.

'We've been let down by one of our contractors,' he answered. 'We have to tender for jobs and then set new contractors up on our finance system. In the old days, it would have been done by the end of the day. It's been pending for six weeks now. Zach Eastwood's dad offered to send one of his workmen around to fix it, but we can't even do that. Everything has to be put through the academy budget in the proper way.'

There was a knock at the conference room door.

'Come in!' Canfield called at the same time as Hollie.

A man in blue overalls entered the room.

'Not now, Mr Lacey, we're in an important meeting—'

'I just thought you might like to know...'

Canfield had all but dismissed him, but by the look on his face, he had something that he needed to say.

'Go ahead, Mr Lacey,' Hollie encouraged. 'I take it you're the caretaker here?'

'Yes, officer,' he confirmed. 'I'm sorry to disturb you all, but I just found this stuffed behind one of the cisterns in the ground floor toilet block.'

He was holding up a brightly coloured rucksack. Attached to the zip was a gaudy, plastic name tag on which the owner's name was printed: *Kyle.*

TWENTY-THREE

I don't know what to do.

Mum broke down this evening.

We're behind with all the bills.

She's been paying the rent because she said the gas and elec-tricity and water would give it a while before they started making threats.

She hoped she might find something she could do at home before they started getting stroppy with us, but I see how worn out she is doing what she's doing.

I read today that she won't be able to swallow eventually.

I tried it and I could last just over a minute.

What must that be like?

I can't share anything with her, because she has enough worries of her own.

Yasmine helps, but she can't do anything, not really.

I'm stuck in this, and I can't get out.

I love Mum and how I feel is really shitty.

I'm her son, for fuck's sake, who else is going to care for her?

But I'm really scared of what's going to happen.

I don't know if I'm up to it.

I called in at Aldi on the way home and asked if they'd got any jobs.

Fuck knows what I'd do at Aldi, my adding up is too bad for the tills and I'm too much of a weakling to push those big crates they have.

At least Mum managed to sell the car, but that means she has to take the bus now.

She said she'd put us on the social housing list.

I saw how much that hurt her.

She always swore we'd never have to go back to Bilton Grange housing estate, but I don't know how much longer we can hang on to this house.

I guess if we can make it until summer, at least my exams will be done by then and I could catch the bus to uni from Bilton Grange.

Anyway, it's all hypothetical, as there are no houses available.

Can you believe that we have to be homeless first before we move up the list?

The way things are going, that might not be long coming.

TWENTY-FOUR

TUESDAY, 17:32

The caretaker might just as well have walked into the room with a grenade in his hand. Hollie, DS Patel and DS Anderson leapt to their feet and rushed toward him.

'Get that bagged and for God's sake make sure nobody else handles it!' Hollie instructed. Anderson ensured that the vital piece of evidence was processed and photographed within minutes.

'Where did you find it, Mr Lacey?'

'It had been stuffed in the gap between the cistern and the wall in the main corridor toilets. The kids have worked it loose, it needs fixing really...' His voice trailed away like he'd just mentioned another repair on a long list which was unlikely to be attended to any time soon.

'How did we miss this?' Hollie barked, agitated and frustrated with herself.

The members of her team looked at each other and then back to her.

'It was easily missed,' Mr Lacey suggested. 'I only found it because I thought the kids had been at it again and was checking it's still safe. There's something else I need to tell you, too.'

'Go on.'

'Whoever put it there emptied the contents into the cistern. They're drenched in there. I'll need to get a stepladder to hook them out.'

For fuck's sake!

'DCs Forsyth and Philpot, go with Mr Lacey and retrieve those items, please. Get them bagged and tagged and sent to HQ for testing. If there's anything of immediate interest, let me know straight away, please.'

The two DCs left with Mr Lacey, and Hollie sighed deeply before continuing the briefing.

'So, Mr Canfield, if you and your team would liaise with DS Patel, I'd like all sixth-form students to be available in school tomorrow, as well as those members of the lower school who indicated that they might have seen something of interest. We'll conduct one-to-one interviews with all of them tomorrow, and we'll need teachers present for safeguarding purposes.'

They worked through the finer details then Hollie wound things up with the academy's senior team. She waited for them to leave the room.

'So, let's review where we're up to. Tilly Mann's phone has been returned to her now. We've found nothing on it and we're not able to arrest her, so we've no justification to hold onto the phone. Kyle will have texted any number of people and, much as I'd like to, we need to have a good reason to confiscate their mobile devices. I'm as sure as hell she's up to her ears in this, but without firm evidence – and because of her age – I want us to tread carefully.'

'I think she's scared,' Jenni suggested, 'but I couldn't coax it out of her. I can't believe she was willingly involved in any violence, she's as quiet as a mouse.'

'I agree,' Hollie replied, 'but we're going to want to speak to her again tomorrow. Hopefully she'll have settled down a bit by then. This is a sixth-form issue, I don't believe we're looking at the lower school. I'm going to haul in all the sixth formers tomorrow.'

She noticed a slight grimace from Harry.

'Go on, DC Gordon. If there's something on your mind, please share it.'

'I can't help thinking about the chisel and the coat. The most likely scenario is if somebody exited via the gap in the fence, stuffed the coat down the drain on their way, then doubled back into the school to drop off the chisel in that bin. I supervised the searching of those bins myself – that chisel was placed there after we'd searched the premises.'

'Agreed,' Hollie confirmed. 'I saw for myself that the bin in the foyer had been processed correctly. We can't rule out one of the kids dropping it in there after the lockdown, but how?'

'Or it was one of the teachers?' Anderson added.

'Did we follow up with Canfield about which parents came into the foyer?' Hollie asked.

'We have a list of names, but by his own admission it's only partial. He was distracted by the media presence, so it's not a lot of help.'

'Okay, thanks, DS Patel. Would you follow up directly with the confirmed names of everybody we know was in the foyer at that time and see if they can add any further IDs to that list? That's parents, staff and press. Also, ask them if they saw anything which might help us.'

Hollie ran through her hastily scribbled list of items to follow up on.

'Okay, I'm going to check on the team who are scouring the CCTV after this, and I'll see if they can get me the footage so we can take a closer look at who was in that foyer.'

With the meeting concluded, Hollie was immediately on

the phone to DCI Osmond who had long since exited the building, his public-facing obligations now delivered.

'We're going to need Zach Eastwood's T-shirt and this chisel fast-tracking through forensics testing,' she urged. 'They can't get caught in the backlog. How long are we looking at?'

'I can push for you, but it's going to be two days minimum.'

Hollie resisted the temptation to demonstrate her firm grasp of expletives in front of her superior officer. With more budget cuts and increasingly limited resources, it was a wonder they were able to put anyone behind bars.

'I'd be grateful if you could do your best, sir. There's Kyle's bag and coat and his lanyard, too. Any one of those items might hold a vital clue.'

She could sense the DCI bristling on the other end of the phone.

'You know how it is, DI Turner. This is a priority case and I'll do my best for you.'

Sometimes Hollie wished it was as easy as they made it look on the TV. Items were sent to the forensics teams, and they were back within the hour. Unfortunately, real life was nothing like the dramas, where budget and staffing constraints never featured in the plots.

She ended her call with the DCI, making certain he knew how grateful she was for his efforts.

'Ben, I'd like you to brief me on your interview with Nick Yerbury. I want to compare notes.'

'Yes, boss, no problem.'

'And DS Patel, would you let the CCTV team know I'm on my way? I'll want a full debrief.'

'DC Norton is on it, ma'am, she's working with one of the teachers in a small office off the foyer where the CCTV server is stored. You'll see it's marked on the door.'

'Okay, DS Anderson, let's walk and talk. What can you tell me about Yerbury?'

As they left Canfield's office, she took a moment to collect herself.

'He's a bit sure of himself, that's for sure,' Anderson replied. 'He's not what I'd call a likable guy.'

They walked along the corridor into the heart of the academy. All the students had been sent home after the special assembly which meant Hollie and her team had free rein around the academy now.

'Did he have anything useful to share when you spoke to him?' Hollie asked hopefully.

'I'm not sure. I didn't like him, so I'm trying not to let that influence my judgement. All I'd say from my short time with him is that I'd expect a little more distress from a teacher who's just found a corpse on the school grounds.'

'Noted, Ben. I agree with you. Let's make sure he's hauled back in ASAP, though what with the blood on Zach Eastwood's coat, he has just slipped down the priority list.'

She decided to share a nagging concern with her colleague as they walked on.

'Do you think Harry Gordon missed the chisel?' she asked.

Anderson paused before giving his answer.

'They've worked systematically through the bins, I know that. But even though the school is on lockdown, teachers have had to let kids out to use the toilet block. They're like a bunch of geriatrics – it seems nobody teaches them bladder control in this place. We've had uniformed officers stationed in key locations, but we can't watch them taking a piss. I know some people moan about police powers, but that really would be a step too far.'

Hollie sighed.

'I don't think I've ever felt so stressed about my ability to protect a crime scene.'

'It's a tough one, that's for sure.'

Anderson was unusually reassuring in his reply.

'Listen, boss, at the risk of sounding like DCI Osmond on one of his mental well-being drives'—Hollie braced for what was coming next—'you look knackered and in need of a good night's sleep. I suggest you finish off here, go home to whatever it is you do in your home life, sleep on it and come back refreshed tomorrow. By that time, we'll have kicked all this information into some sort of shape. We can then start on the interviews with the kids who reckon they saw something and the sixth formers.'

He was right and she knew it. His choice of words was not as delicate as DCI Osmond's when he was in full mental health mode, but his diagnosis was spot on. She needed to walk away and let it sit overnight. But the thought of that empty flat was not appealing, with only her packed-up boxes for company. It felt better to be on the crime scene, keeping busy, shutting out thoughts of her screwed-up marriage.

'What's your hypothesis?'

She changed the subject. She'd mull it over about going home.

'Who knows?' he answered. 'It could be anything with teenagers. I think we're looking at two separate acts. There's a beating gone on; that's a warning or a punishment. Doctor Ruane will give us more details when he gets to the post-mortem examination.'

'From what I've heard, Kyle was a bit of an outlier, but he seemed completely harmless. Who'd want to hurt him?'

They were missing something, and it was probably obvious.

'Okay,' she picked up, 'somebody had a bigger grudge than the rest of them, big enough to come back and finish the job.'

'We mustn't discount the possibility that everybody involved in the beating might have seen the murder,' Anderson added.

'Agreed, but I find that less likely. It's one thing to beat someone up, and another thing entirely to kill them.'

Anderson looked at her as she held open one of the fire doors to let him pass through.

'So do you think it might be a parent or a member of staff?'

'We can't discount it. What we need to figure out is the why—'

Hollie was distracted by the sound of footsteps rushing across the foyer. It was Amber Patel, a look of urgency on her face.

'Have you got a minute, boss? DC Norton's found something on the CCTV.'

Hollie and Amber hurriedly made their way to the small room where the CCTV was being examined.

'Thanks for doing this, DC Norton,' Hollie said as she entered the small room.

'No problem, ma'am,' she replied, motioning to the teacher who was standing at her side. 'This is Mr Bridges. He handles administrative queries around the CCTV and was the teacher who last saw Kyle alive during the lunch break.'

Hollie looked at him.

'Yes, Kyle was in the homework group just before he was... killed—' Mr Bridges began, his voice breaking into a sob. 'He seemed like he had something on his mind. I asked him about it, but Mr Canfield called me, and I had to lock up the classroom. I feel so guilty.'

'Have you spoken to us formally about it yet?' Hollie checked.

'I've spoken to your officers in passing.' He sniffed. 'I've been in here all afternoon, working on the CCTV.'

'DS Patel, you know the drill.'

'Yes, boss. I'll need to conduct a formal interview with you before you leave this evening, Mr Bridges.'

He nodded. 'No problem. If I can help any more, I'd like to.'

'What does your role with the CCTV entail?' Hollie

wondered, irritated that none of her colleagues had interviewed this man in any depth yet.

'It's mostly just data protection these days, to be honest with you,' he said.

'Show me what you've got,' Hollie urged. It was a tight fit in there with the four of them.

DC Norton already seemed to have a firm grip of the software as she located the saved digital files with no problem at all. Mr Bridges looked like he'd taken a back seat.

DC Norton teed up a CCTV file and her finger was poised on the mouse.

'So, what have you got for me?' Hollie asked, sensing DC Norton's impatience.

'Someone entering the school premises at midday, just before lunch break began, ma'am.'

'A contractor?'

'No, ma'am. A teenager who definitely shouldn't have been there.'

TWENTY-FIVE
TUESDAY, 17:46

Hollie watched the footage intently as the teenage boy furtively stood outside the school gates, checked around him, and then strode confidently onto the academy grounds.

After the boy's initial checks, he seemed more assured, glancing up at the camera, but that was only conjecture on Hollie's part.

'Why wasn't he in school already?' Hollie asked. 'He looks like a sixth former, yes? He's not wearing a uniform.'

'That's Quinn Varney,' Mr Bridges began. 'He left school almost two months ago.'

'Why?' Hollie and DS Patel asked at the same time.

'He's now home-educated.'

'What does that mean?' Hollie wondered.

'He's no longer in school and his parents have taken responsibility for his education at home.'

'Is that allowed, Mr Bridges?'

'It's perfectly legal,' the teacher replied. He looked to Hollie like a man who needed some fresh air; it was stuffy in that tiny room.

'I won't bore you with the details, but it's been legal – in theory at least – since the 1944 Education Act. Lots of parents do it.'

'Well, I didn't know that,' Hollie replied. 'What can you tell me about this lad?'

'This is strictly in confidence,' Mr Bridges continued, 'but Quinn was badly beaten up, just before he was due to take mock A level exams. He's a bright kid; they've offered him a place at Oxford.'

'So he's upper sixth then?' Amber checked. 'He would have left the academy at the end of this year?'

'Yes, that's right. His parents took him out of school under a bit of a cloud.'

'Why was he beaten up?' Hollie pushed.

'Well, you know kids...'

'Actually, I don't know the kids that well, Mr Bridges,' came Hollie's sharp reply. 'That's why I'm asking you. Why was he beaten up?'

'We never got to the bottom of it,' he answered, chastened. 'There's been something going on for some time – they've been fractious, that year group. It's like a fever that needs to burn itself out.'

'I'd have thought most kids get beaten up at least once at school,' Amber remarked. 'I'm not excusing it, of course. But why didn't the parents kiss and make up?'

'They claimed the principal was unable to provide assurances about their son's safety. It was a bit tense among the staff at the time, I believe.'

'You believe?' Hollie queried.

'I wasn't – um – here at the time, I – er – was on sick leave. But I've heard it split the staff. Many of them sided with Quinn's parents; they agreed that bullying at the academy was out of control.'

'Did Quinn have any reason to be in school today?' Hollie continued.

'Yes, he didn't sever his ties with us. He'll use the school as an examination centre when he does his A levels.'

'So he doesn't do that at home if he's home-educated?'

'No, he has to sit the same formal exams. He has to pay to take exams if he's home-educated, so he may have been here to sort that out.'

Hollie wondered if it was a coincidence that Quinn's lunchtime visit coincided with Kyle's death.

'Does he have friends here still?' she resumed.

'Yes, of course, he was a popular lad at school.'

'Not so popular that someone wouldn't beat him up.'

DC Norton's face was expressionless. Hollie hadn't expected such a blunt but incisive contribution.

'She's right' – Hollie picked up the thread – 'somebody still beat him up.'

'Who knows?' Mr Bridges shrugged. 'I stopped trying to figure out the lives of these kids a long time ago. I can't imagine what it's like to be a teenager these days.'

'Who beat him up?' Hollie asked.

'This is confidential?' Mr Bridges checked.

Hollie nodded.

'It was rumoured that it was Zach Eastwood.'

Hollie and Amber exchanged a look. Maybe they had the right person locked up in the Clough Road custody suite.

Hollie thought about how different school life was even for Isabella, compared with Noah and Lily. She'd given Isabella her first phone when she started at secondary school, but it was a cheap Motorola with limited storage and functionality. She'd even read somewhere that Noah's and Lily's phones were more powerful than the guidance computer used on Apollo 11. Only she hoped NASA didn't use all that computational power to look at funny cat memes like Noah and Lily did.

'Could you please give me Quinn's address?'

Mr Bridges gave Hollie a nod.

'The office will have to give you that, but I'll get it sorted out for you.'

'Is he eighteen? Please tell me he's eighteen,' Hollie continued.

'Yes, he's eighteen,' Mr Bridges confirmed.

'Great, I want to question him ASAP, Amber. Can you get that organised? Do we know where he went after he entered the school grounds?'

'He just disappears, ma'am,' DC Norton replied, 'but there's a lot of footage still to work through, so we may yet find him.'

'Might he have exited school grounds via that gap in the fence?'

Mr Bridges nodded.

'Okay, this is good work. Quinn Varney is getting a home visit.'

'There's something more,' DC Norton interrupted.

'Go ahead.'

'DS Patel told me you wanted to see what had been captured on the foyer camera when you delivered your briefing earlier.'

'Yes, have you got me some names?'

DC Norton handed over a sheet of A4 paper, on which were written eight names.

'That's the list the principal drew up from memory,' she said, reaching over for a second piece of paper. She handed it to Hollie. 'There were four more people that we couldn't identify, though it's hard to be precise about the number of people in the foyer because they're not all caught on the camera.'

DC Norton double-clicked on a file at her workstation and CCTV footage began to play. Hollie watched as she saw her own image, alongside DCI Osmond, Mr Canfield and a stream of journalists and parents following behind. She froze the frame, and Mr Bridges pointed to the screen. He worked through the list, pointing to the parents as he did so.

The quality was better than Hollie had expected. She'd spent so much of her career studying grainy surveillance videos, it still surprised her how rapidly things had moved on. She wondered what the parents thought about their youngsters being subjected to this level of scrutiny, or if they even knew about it. She couldn't recall reading anything from the kids' schools about on-site surveillance, but then, if they had sent a letter about it, it wouldn't be the first time it had accidentally been thrown into the bin.

DC Norton advanced the footage and froze it again. This time she pointed out the reporters who'd been present. Most of them were carrying cameras or audio equipment, so they were easy to spot.

'Okay, good, so where does that leave us?' Hollie asked.

'I'm going to play you a bit more footage and I want you to watch what's happening on the right-hand side,' DC Norton explained. She clicked *Play* on the video file.

'There!'

'Sorry, I missed it. What am I supposed to be looking at?'

'I'll play it again,' DC Norton replied impatiently. Hollie was about to tick her off but held back. Norton had done some good sifting work.

Hollie watched carefully.

'There! Can you see it?'

She'd spotted it that time. It was fast and if you blinked, you'd miss it. She'd just watched somebody – male or female, it was impossible to tell – entering the foyer at the back of the group, obviously wary that it was covered by CCTV. Their head was down, and they were keeping close behind a tall reporter.

'Play it one more time please, DC Norton. Take it frame by frame, rather than playing it at full speed.'

DC Norton scrolled through the frames, the scene in the corridor playing out on her screen like a 1930s cartoon.

'There!' Hollie declared, pointing at the blurred figure in the frame by the cloakroom bin, and Norton stopped scrolling.

Hollie leaned into the screen. 'All we need to do is to zoom in on that face and we'll find out who dropped that damn chisel into the foyer bin.'

TWENTY-SIX
TUESDAY, 18:51

If Zach Eastwood's attitude had been captured by an artist on canvas it would have been titled *Bolshy Teenager Displaying Bad Attitude*.

That made sense to her now, as she'd just met his father in an adjacent interview room. If that was the warm-up act for Zach, this was going to be a prickly session.

Rupert Eastwood had swiftly established himself as the pain-in-the-arse type of parent that no detective wanted to deal with. He was, she'd learned, a successful businessman with high-up contacts throughout the city. He'd made the usual threats – that they had videos of what happened to Zach in the school hall, and they'd use them as evidence of heavy-handed policing if they needed them.

'The guy's a prick,' Anderson summarised. As profiles went it was succinct and neat, but it wouldn't be winning any literary awards. At least Rupert gave something away. Hollie now knew that Zach had had an altercation with Jake Tate, Tilly's boyfriend. That made their unpleasant encounter fruitful at least.

Where Rupert recognised that a little charm oiled the

wheels, even if you were looking at the nice detective like she was a piece of shit on your shoe, his son had no such grace.

The app was recording; DS Anderson sat at her side and Zach sat there with arms folded, bright red, dyed hair, and a snarl that threatened to stay fixed on his face if he didn't relax his top lip soon. The solicitor had spent a moment with his young client prior to the interview.

'So, Zach, I'm DI Turner—'

'Whatever.'

God, please don't let my kids turn out like this oaf.

'—and all I want to do is to figure out where this blood came from and send you home with your father.'

'No comment.'

'You don't actually need to say no comment there, Zach,' Anderson advised. His clipped words suggested to Hollie that he was struggling to maintain his patience.

The solicitor whispered something in Zach's ear.

'So, will you be going to university after A levels, Zach?'

He looked at the solicitor, who nodded.

'Yeah. I've got a place at LSE.'

'LSE?'

'London School of Economics.'

Hollie made a whistling sound. 'Nice, you've done well. What are you studying?'

'BSc Management. I want to work with the old man.'

God forbid you might achieve something for yourself.

'What grades do you need for that?'

'I need 120 UCAS points.'

Hollie nodded like she understood what that meant. She'd have to get to grips with this soon; it wouldn't be long until Lily was looking at universities. They'd have to figure out how she and Léon were going to manage the costs given their present situation. Hollie had a feeling Zach wouldn't have to worry about such inconveniences as student loans.

'What about your friends – are they all sorted out for university places?' Anderson added, doing his best to engage.

'You'll have to ask them,' he mumbled.

'Let's talk about your friends,' Hollie began.

Zach stared at her like she was some unpleasant object obstructing his path.

'Who are you most friendly with in the sixth form?'

'I dunno. Matt. Evie. Quinn. Sammy... Tilly.'

At least they were forming an idea of friendship groups, even though Zach's monosyllabic responses were beginning to wind Hollie up now.

There were a couple of names in there that she knew: Quinn and Tilly. She decided to push him a bit, to see if she could fire up his engines.

'So you stay in touch with Quinn, even though he's not at the academy anymore?'

'Yeah, Quinn's the goat, you know?'

'Goat?' Anderson asked, a bewildered look on his face.

Hollie knew this one, she'd picked it up from Izzy.

'Greatest of all time,' she announced, trying to conceal her pride at being down with the kids for once in her life. 'It means he's a great guy.'

'Oh,' Anderson acknowledged, clearly nonplussed.

'Were you disappointed when Quinn left school?'

'I suppose so.'

'Only I heard you and he had a falling out.'

Zach looked at his legal counsel.

'No comment.'

'It was a fight, wasn't it?'

Nothing.

'And Quinn left school as a result of that altercation.'

She might as well have been speaking a foreign language. Hollie stared at him. It was clear that was all she was getting on that subject.

'Tell me more about Tilly,' Hollie encouraged him.

That got the best reaction she'd had in the few minutes since she'd met him.

The solicitor gave Zach a nod; they'd obviously discussed this in their pre-interview sojourn.

'What about her?' Zach asked.

'What can you tell us about her?'

'I dunno. She's a student. She's going to Oxford Uni.'

'Nice,' DS Anderson chimed in. 'She must be a bright cookie.'

'We call them intelligent women nowadays.' He scowled.

That was DS Anderson put in his place. If Zach proved to be innocent, she'd have to pick up some management tips for handling her colleague. It sounded to her like Zach didn't need that BSc after all.

'She seemed upset about something when I spoke to her earlier today. Do you have any idea why that was?'

'Perhaps because one of her school friends just died?' Zach replied, like she'd just asked the dumbest question ever.

Hollie moved on. This was hard work.

'How do you get on with your friends? Was Kyle ever part of your gang?'

It was time they squeezed some juice out of this kid.

'What's this got to do with the blood on my T-shirt?'

'I was hoping you'd tell me—'

'No comment.'

'Come on, Zach, I'm just interested in you and your pals.'

'It's okay,' the solicitor signalled.

'There's nothing to tell. We knew Kyle, but he wasn't part of our group.'

Hollie decided to circle back to Kyle later; she didn't want to hit the dead end of constant no comment responses.

'What can you tell me about Jake? Didn't you two get into a fight earlier?'

It was Zach's father who'd told her as much, so she hoped this tack might prove more fruitful.

'No comment.'

So much for her change in strategy.

'You seem to be handy with your fists, Zach.'

He looked at the solicitor, who gave him the go-ahead.

'Jake's a pov, I don't know why she's with him anyway.'

'A pov?' Anderson queried.

'Not got much money. Poverty – a pov.'

Hollie bristled.

'Who was with him?' she continued.

'Tilly and him. They're an item. He caught us talking privately and he was jealous.'

'And was Jake angry with you?'

'Of course he was. He couldn't get his head around it. He was hostile.'

'Hostile enough for you to fight about it earlier?'

'Maybe.'

'Maybe or yes?' Anderson pressed. He was doing a less effective job of hiding his impatience.

'What were you and Tilly talking about?'

'Nothing. Stuff. You know.'

'Can you be more specific, Zach?' Anderson asked.

'School stuff. Homework. The usual shit.'

Tilly had given a similar response. These students seemed to spend a lot of time talking about homework. In her day, that was the last thing on their minds.

Hollie could feel the tension between Anderson and Zach. The two of them regarded each other like stags about to wrestle it out.

'Has anybody offered you a drink, Zach?'

'Nothing decent. Just coffee and tea, the usual Boomer shit.'

'How do you fancy a can of something?'

His eyes lit up at that.

'Coke would be great.'

Hollie slipped Anderson a pound coin from her pocket.

'We've got a machine downstairs; it'll be cooled, too. Would you mind, DS Anderson?'

She gave him a small nod as he shot her a look that said *I'm not the bloody intern.*

Hollie noted his absence for the benefit of the recording and time-stamped it for the record. She reset the conversation with something simple again.

'Who would you say are your closest friends at school?'

'I told you already. Matt, Sammy, Tilly, Evie and Jake, when he's not negging me.'

'So you'd still call Jake a close friend?'

'Yeah, sure. Once he gets over me talking to Tilly, he will be again.'

'Tell me more about Kyle Wilson, Zach. Was he ever a mate?'

'No comment.'

'I'm not going to ask you anything else, Zach. I'm just interested if he was ever a friend of yours.'

Zach turned to the solicitor again.

'Nah, not really. It wasn't that I didn't know him. He just seemed to like hanging with the girls more, you know?'

'Have you ever had an argument or falling out with Kyle?'

He was about to say *no comment* but resisted.

'Nah, he kept himself to himself. He was just there. He was a bit of a loner, to be honest. A weirdo.'

'Why was he a weirdo, Zach?'

'Well, there was that filming incident for starters. He thought he was Steven Spielberg or something. He was filming people in the Sixth Form Centre without permission. A couple of the guys had a few words with him.'

Something flashed in Hollie's mind. One of the scraps of paper in Kyle's locker had made a Spielberg reference.

'Why was he filming you, Zach?'

Zach shuffled in his chair. 'No reason, he was just practising framing shots and shit, I guess.'

'Is that why he was beaten up in the outbuilding, Zach?'

Hollie noticed the solicitor tense. He moved his hand to Zach's arm to get his attention.

'No comment.'

'It would be helpful if you told me what went on, Zach. We can get you out of here straight away if you'll just talk me through it.'

The solicitor whispered into Zach's ear once again.

'Look, Jake and I fell out at the mid-morning break today, that's all.'

'So, just before the 10.45 midday lessons, that's how the timetable is carved up, isn't it?'

'Yeah. We were just sitting about, you know?'

'Okay, go on.'

'I was talking to Tilly and all of a sudden, Jake walks by and he goes off on one. I think it was because Tilly was upset.'

'Was there any provocation?'

'Nah, just jealous, I reckon. He thought I'd upset her, so he punches me in the face.'

'Why was Tilly upset?'

'You know – girl stuff. She was fretting about some homework.'

'And she spoke to you about it, rather than Jake?'

He shrugged.

Hollie examined Zach's nose; it didn't look sore.

'How hard did he punch you?'

'Hard enough for it to bleed. Not hard enough to break or bruise.'

The solicitor nodded his head slightly. The slimy bastard – Zach was briefed to say that.

'Did you punch him back?'

Zach looked at the solicitor once again. She wondered if she could save them all some time and just get the solicitor to share whatever crap he'd concocted with Rupert and Zach so they could all be on their way.

'I was going to, but I stood down. Tilly asked me not to.'

Hollie sat and looked him directly in the eyes, sitting in silence. He averted his gaze after trying to outstare her for a couple of seconds.

'How did the blood get on your T-shirt, Zach?'

'The fat guy asked me that already.'

'I beg your pardon.'

'The guy who's gone to get my Coke. He's taking his time. Probably still struggling up the stairs.'

She paused before replying; she was more than ready to tear a strip off this kid.

'That's Detective Sergeant Anderson to you, Zach.'

'Whatever.'

Hollie took a long breath.

'Just run me through it. Jake punched you; Tilly urged you to let it pass. Then what?'

'Evie said that my nose was bleeding.'

'Was it bleeding?'

'Yes.'

'So you dabbed it on your T-shirt?'

'No, it dripped on my T-shirt. Tilly gave me a tissue and told me to pinch my nose. I did and it stopped bleeding after a few minutes. As I said, it was a lame punch. Jake is no Tyson Fury, that's for sure.'

'Why were you on the school field when the school bell rang at the end of lunch break?'

'No comment.'

This time Zach leaned over to the solicitor and whispered something in his ear. The solicitor nodded.

'We were getting some fresh air, that's all. Tilly suggested it, so we could all cool off.'

'And did you?'

'Yeah, I was chill.'

'Did Jake come?'

'Sort of. He hung back with Matt, Sammy and Tilly. I think he was embarrassed. I would be if I'd thrown a lame punch like that.'

Anderson entered the room, and Hollie acknowledged it for the recording. He handed Zach the can of Coke.

'Sweet.'

Zach picked it up and pulled back the ring pull. It made a woosh and he took a long, deliberate drink. He smacked his lips, made a sound of satisfaction, placed the can back on the table and then burped.

There wasn't much that surprised Hollie, but that shocked her. Her phone sounded and she was relieved; it excused her from finding a suitable response.

It was the forensics lab. DCI Osmond must have done some heavy leaning, as they'd turned it around in no time. Murder cases tended to get that kind of response. She listened as she absorbed the details of what had been found.

'Zach Eastwood, you're free to go. I've just received the details of the forensic report on your T-shirt and the blood is indeed yours.'

He gave a smug smile and stood up, reaching for the can of Coke. He was about to give them the finger, but he backed off before it was fully formed.

'Excellent. I'll be taking this with me then. We wouldn't want it to go to waste now, would we?'

TWENTY-SEVEN

I hate myself sometimes.

I went to the food bank today.

I haven't said to Mum, but I can see what's happened with the food shopping.

We're on own brands and budget ranges now.

It tastes like shit, but I don't say anything.

Anyway, even the food bank turned me away.

We have to be referred to them apparently, and fuck knows who does that.

Mum reckons we might be able to apply for benefits, but it takes ages to come through.

She said we might even get carer's allowance.

I'd be a carer.

It feels too young at seventeen.

Am I a horrible person because I don't want to have to do it?

I won't let Mum down, of course I won't.

But I wish I wasn't on my own.

I feel so lonely sometimes.

Zach has turned everyone against me, so I just hang out in the study sessions at lunchtimes.

Ever since they all ganged up on me about that filming, it's been really tough.

They were supposed to be my friends.

I said I was sorry.

Now, whenever I take my phone out, they give me a hard time, like they think I'm going to do it again.

Zach's the worst though, he's always the leader.

The others just follow him.

Mr Yerbury has been a lifeline, he's so cool.

He's talking about me coming over to look at his editing gear.

He even said I could use it to catch up on my homework.

I'd never end my life, but I have been thinking about it recently.

I wouldn't do it, I really wouldn't, but I do think about it a lot these days.

Sometimes I think it would be a big relief if all these problems went away.

Good job I'm too big a coward though.

TWENTY-EIGHT
TUESDAY, 20:11

Hollie's mind was still buzzing on the short drive back to her flat. She'd been so absorbed in thought, she'd navigated the roads on auto pilot. She had to divert her route home via The Avenues to pick up her tea there, what with her favourite chippy being closed. She made a point of passing Dirty Little Secrets. It was closed, of course, but she wanted to take a look around the place. That business card had to have some significance.

Hollie pulled up the car at the side of the road, leaving the engine running while she nipped out for a swift look. The windows were blacked out; it wasn't like they'd have a big display, given the items they sold. There was a metal grid padlocked across the door and a second entrance to the right-hand side of the shop which looked like it led up to the flat over the shop.

Hollie got back in the car. It was late, she was hungry, and they'd pay the shop a visit during opening hours.

As soon as she arrived back home, she slumped on the sofa and ate the fish and chip supper with her hands. She used the remote to see what was on the TV. She didn't very much care, so long as it was mindless and had nothing to do with crime.

Now satiated, Hollie placed the polystyrene tray to one side and closed her eyes. It was so quiet in the flat with nobody there. Not so long ago, back in Lancaster, she'd have come home to a warm house that was filled with activity and chatter. Now, all she had to greet her was the abandoned Pot Noodle container from lunchtime. That seemed like days ago already.

Hollie checked her WhatsApp. Noah was too young to use it, but Léon and Lily were online. She couldn't face Léon, and she didn't want to imagine him with Veronique; it was just too painful. He'd get back in touch if his earlier interruption during the whole school assembly was anything important.

She dialled Lily, who answered almost immediately.

'Hey, Mum!'

Her daughter's voice immediately nourished her as if a burst of sunshine had just appeared in her living room.

'Hello, darling, I just wanted to talk to you.'

Lily carried on whatever it was she was doing, barely bothering to look directly into the camera. Hollie positioned herself so that she could be seen fully, not that Lily seemed to require it.

'How are things at home?'

'Much better now we know Dad's not taking us to France. I think Veronique might come here to stay.'

Half of that house was hers. Hollie wasn't so sure how she felt about her husband's lover setting up home in Lancaster. She'd only just won a temporary reprieve over Léon taking them to France, and here she was feeling resentful again.

'Well, at least Noah can finish primary school and you won't have to leave your friends.'

'Yes. And you can drive up and see us, too. When you haven't got a case on.'

Hollie experienced a sharp pang in her chest. Either it was

her heart warning her after her fish and chip supper or another stab of heartache seeing her kid's face and longing to be with them in person back in Lancaster.

'Lily, can I ask you a couple of things about school? We don't talk that much about it since – well, since I've not been at – since I've been living in Hull.'

'School is fine, Mum, I told you.'

She paused, not wanting to alarm Lily.

'Do they do emergency drills at your school?'

'Yeah, we do one a term. They're quite a laugh, actually. We all have to hide under the tables. Once, when we had a really old supply teacher, we all changed desks, and she didn't even notice.'

Hollie resisted the impulse to offer a parental coaching moment.

'What are your favourite social media sites at the moment?' She tried to sound nonchalant, but knew that if she was interviewing herself, she'd have immediately clocked that she was up to something.

'Is this all about what happened at that school in Hull today?' Lily asked. She was looking directly into the camera now.

'Are you wearing make-up, Lily?' Hollie asked. Since when was this a thing?

'Just a bit. I'm experimenting. We're not allowed to wear it at school.'

'Does Dad know?'

The absence of a reply gave her the answer.

Cleverly, Lily diverted her.

'We're all on TikTok now. Sometimes I use Snapchat. Instagram is good, too. We meet up on WhatsApp.'

'Does Dad talk about this stuff with you?'

'Yes. No. Sometimes. He's more interested in Veronique these days. He reminds me of the older kids when they have boyfriends and girlfriends and they're snogging in the play-ground. They can't keep their hands off each other. It's yucky.'

Another pang. If Lily kept it up, Hollie would be rushed to hospital with a terminal anxiety attack before the night was out. She gulped and decided to broach the issue. Lily was old enough; if she was experimenting with make-up and using TikTok, the unsuitable web content wouldn't be far behind.

'What sort of things are you doing? On social media, I mean.'

'Are you checking on me to see if I've had any dick pics, Mum?'

She hadn't meant that at all, but suddenly her state of alert had rocketed into the stratosphere. Sometimes, Hollie wanted to scream. It was becoming impossible to protect her kids from this stuff. She wished there was a guidebook to help her navi-gate her way through this. Life was so much easier when a magic kiss would banish all the nasty things from her children's lives.

'Are you being serious with me, Lily?'

'Mum, everybody's had at least one dick pic!'

She sounded like she was twenty-one.

'What, even at your age?'

'Yes, Mum. Everybody gets them.'

Hollie wanted to cry. If this was Lily at thirteen, almost fourteen, what chance did she stand?

'Does it bother you?'

'A bit. But my friends get them, too, so it makes me feel a bit better about it. A boy from the next year group was sending them.'

'Did you report it to the teachers? Did you show it to Dad?'

'Mum! No, of course not. It's way too embarrassing to show any grown-ups. I just deleted it. It only happened once.'

Hollie changed the subject; this was something she'd have to discuss with Léon and with Lily's school. She switched to more general topics, but she couldn't shake her worries about the things her children were being exposed to. When she was a kid, her mum would just turn off the TV when she thought they'd watched enough.

'Go and read a book or do your homework,' her mother would say, and it was done with. They'd got the parental controls on the router in Lancaster, but Hollie knew from her work how easy it was to cheat. A quick change to an incognito browsing window, or even worse, the Tor privacy browser, download a free VPN, and the kids could look at whatever they wanted to without her knowledge.

Immediately after speaking to Lily, she dialled Léon, who was blasé about the topic, convinced that the children were fine.

'I've got a filter on the router; they can't access porn or anything unsuitable like that,' he said, after Hollie explained why she was calling.

'All the kids know about this stuff, Léon. We haven't got a clue what they're up to.'

'But they're good kids, they know how to behave—'

'Did Lily tell you she's received an obscene image from a boy?'

There was an awkward silence from Léon; now she'd got his attention.

'No, surely not, she's way too young. She's exaggerating, she's probably just read something about it happening to other kids. I was still building plastic model kits and playing football with my mates at that age. It can't be that bad.'

'It was a dick pic, Léon! To a thirteen-year-old girl. And it's so normalised at school, she didn't even think it worth a mention.'

Léon tensed and his eyes flashed.

'I'll tear the little shit's balls off—'

'Yeah, great response, Léon. Very proportionate, that. And

all my former colleagues at Lancaster police station will see when you're arrested after the assault of a minor.'

'So, what do we do? Don't the schools deal with this stuff? Should I talk to Lily?'

He sounded appropriately worried now. She'd not felt this pressure when Izzy was growing up, yet now it was snapping around their heels like a yapping terrier.

'Leave it well alone if you're going to kick off about this dick-pic kid. If Lily knows you're going to get all shouty and defensive with her every time, she'll clam up. We need to talk to the kids when I'm in Lancaster next. Together.'

'Maybe Veronique could have a word, they seem to like chatting to her—'

It was Hollie's body which tensed this time.

'Veronique is not their mum. You and I will do it. I might even speak to Izzy; I think she's going to have a crucial role to play with Lily as she grows up. It'll be easier for her to hear it from her rather than two old farts.'

Hollie looked around the flat, at the stacked-up boxes, a domestic life in limbo. She wasn't in the mood for TV now, her body was tired, but her mind was still overactive from the case.

She placed the photocopies of school registers to one side and took a sip of black coffee. She wasn't normally a late-night coffee drinker, but it was a case of needs must; somehow her eyelids had to remain open until she'd worked through the pile of paperwork that had been generated as a consequence of that day's investigative activities.

An hour later, she'd made some sense of it all. There was a register from each class, the names of the children printed out from an electronic database, as Olivia Dreyfuss had promised, with notes at the side as to whether the children had seen anything or not. The comments were brief: *nothing, saw 6F on field, saw Kyle with 6F, lunch activity.* The team had swiftly moved to using *6F* as shorthand for sixth formers, and Amber Patel had highlighted the students who would require follow-up interviews with bright, yellow highlighting pen.

Some poor police officers had spent the evening calling round parents whose children would be needed in school the following day. Much as she'd been put off initially by Canfield's self-importance, she had to hand it to him, he and Olivia Dreyfuss had been a dream team when it came to getting shit done. Though, they were as keen as her to find their killer and get the academy back to normal.

She took a short break to enjoy one of her favourite Runrig songs from the Spotify playlist she'd clicked on earlier. It was sung in Gaelic, and she hadn't got a clue how to pronounce the words, but she made a stab of it and enjoyed the short detour anyway. It brought back happy memories of a day in glorious sunshine, watching the band perform live with her parents at Balloch, on the banks of Loch Lomond.

Amber Patel had given her a copy of Kyle's timetable, with some additional notes about what they'd pieced together about his final movements. It was good to have Patel away from her desk. She ran the office superbly, but her research skills and attention to small details were just what they needed in the academy building. She'd never worked with anybody like Amber when it came to finding needles in haystacks.

The timetable took her back to her own school days. The relentless procession of subjects was not something she'd ever missed, and she'd really begun to flourish when she went to university. For someone with such a distaste for the rigidity of school life, she'd adapted to the disciplines and hierarchy of the police force with remarkable ease. She'd long since concluded that it was because she valued the work of the police, whereas school had largely bored her.

It didn't take long to get to grips with the timetable. Kyle had been in the lunchtime study session, supervised by Mr Bridges, until ten minutes before one o'clock. She'd already met Mr Bridges during their study of the CCTV footage, and he'd since been interviewed after that, though he was unable to throw any light on Kyle's state of mind, other than he'd eaten his lunch in the study room, rather than consuming in the school hall, as was the normal custom.

Was he hiding from somebody, perhaps even staying out of the way during lunch break?

He was due in a General Studies class immediately after lunch, but he'd never turned up. She cross-referenced the register for that class. That was an upper sixth class, and most of them seemed to be on the list; as far as she recalled from her own school days, that subject didn't require any particular study and gave an easy extra A level qualification if needed.

Kyle was marked as absent, and several others were recorded late. She scanned the late attendees: Zach Eastwood, Evie Keane, Jake Tate, Tilly Mann. How many people did Doctor Ruane think were involved in assaulting Kyle? As many as five or more people involved in the attack, he'd surmised from an initial look at the body. And if the home-educated student from the CCTV footage – Quinn Varney – was involved, that made five. Five students who most likely knew exactly what happened to Kyle. And very possibly one or more of them was his killer.

TWENTY-NINE
WEDNESDAY, 08:06

The coffee from the school canteen was hot and strong; Hollie had expected neither, and the caffeine was already working wonders.

'You promise me you'll let me know if you feel even the slightest bit ill?' Hollie said to Jenni, using her sternest mum's face.

'I promise, I'm just pleased to get out from behind the desk again. Besides, what can go wrong here? It's an academy, not a war zone.'

She was right about that; it was beginning to look like life at the academy had been difficult for Kyle.

'Besides, it just looks like a side shave,' Jenni continued. 'You can barely see the scar now. All the kids will think I'm a super-cool cop.'

It was great to have her back again. She'd already earned that month's salary with Tilly Mann, preventing her from deleting all of the messages on her phone. There was something about Jenni that put people at their ease. When it came to people skills, Jenni was the master. Her instinctive empathy was impressive for her young age. Also, Hollie needed the extra pair of hands and Jenni was more use to her at the school than over at HQ. They might have got more out of Zach Eastwood if she'd sat in on the interview, but she'd made the judgement call to bring in Anderson as she had sensed his thick skin might have been needed for that one.

Hollie walked through the academy and over to the classroom which the school had agreed to let them use for their morning briefing that day. It was just past eight o'clock and the room was packed. Everybody quietened as she stepped through the door.

'If you turn to the rear page of your briefing notes, I'd like you to take a look at an item that was underneath Kyle's body when it was removed from the scene. This is a business card from the Dirty Little Secrets establishment on The Avenues.'

DS Anderson picked up.

'There's a possibility the business card was there already when Kyle died, or it may have fallen out of his clothing. It might also have been left by the killer or killers. It was too badly soiled by Kyle's blood to extract anything useful, but it has been submitted for testing.'

'What do we know about this Dirty Little Secrets shop?' Hollie asked.

'Ask DC Gordon, he does his shopping there!' came a voice. There was a ripple of uncertain laughter. Hollie noticed how red Harry's face was. Poor lad, the old guard was pulling his leg.

'Let's just remember a seventeen-year-old boy died here yesterday,' she interjected, raising her voice. They settled down immediately, like kids scolded by a head teacher.

'Any sensible answers?' she tried again.

'It's what you'd call a sex shop, ma'am.'

It was DC Philpot. She reminded herself to ask him what they'd pulled out of the cistern the previous night. She assumed there was nothing of any interest in there as nobody had thought it worthy of an update.

'It's the old-fashioned variety; girlie-mags, sex toys, DVDs, that sort of thing,' Philpot continued.

'Do people still shop at those places?' Hollie wondered. 'Haven't they heard of the internet?'

She certainly had. Before things went completely awry with Léon, she'd placed an order, thinking they might try and spice things up. She'd been so caught up in work, that the batteries passed their sell-by date and leaked all over her hopeful purchase. It had been thrown out with the rubbish, to her shame, concealed in a discarded cornflakes box.

'So it's different from, say, an Ann Summers then?'

'I'm no expert, ma'am, but these shops are more specialist, I think. They do all sorts, whereas Ann Summers is lingerie and the more playful and mainstream side of the market.'

Philpot's face began to colour. It was like being back in a sex ed class at secondary school. All she needed was a room full of sniggering detectives, poking and prodding each other, and the scene would be complete.

'Okay, why does a seventeen-year-old boy have this on his person? He's too young to go inside.'

Jenni stood up.

'When I phoned the shop yesterday, I was assured they check ID if they think customers might be underage.'

Hollie could see a couple of stifled smiles. She was part-amused, part-annoyed. They were going to have to get through this if they were to make any progress.

'Perhaps he was just curious,' Amber suggested. 'Maybe there were safety controls on his internet at home so he couldn't look at stuff like that on his laptop. Not all employees are diligent about checking ID.'

'Good thinking, DS Patel, thank you, we do have some adults in the room.'

'Did he know somebody who worked there?' DC Norton

suggested. 'Perhaps one of the people who assaulted him was there?'

'This is good, keep these ideas coming. Anything else?' Hollie encouraged.

'I was a dirty little git at that age,' came DS Anderson's voice. 'We used to buy and sell porn mags all the time. I had a secret flap in my sports bag where I used to hide them. Maybe this is just regular school kid stuff, you know, buying porn mags and selling them to the younger kids.'

Although she didn't relish the insight into Anderson's teenage life, it was a fair point.

'Okay, we're paying them a visit after the briefing. I want to understand why Kyle might have been interested in that shop.'

Harry Gordon raised his hand for attention.

'Yes, DC Gordon.'

'I put a call in to Lance Fairclough in the tech labs, and he confirmed what I told you about the video files last night when we found that textbook in his locker.'

Harry had done well; he'd chased that before she'd even remembered it was on her list of things to do.

'It looks like Kyle was learning how to upload anonymous video files. The book that Nick Yerbury loaned him explained exactly how to do it. There are all sorts of reasons he might be doing that. Lance said we need to know where he was uploading them to. He also pointed out it might just be a part of what he was studying in his course.'

'Okay, good, let's get that confirmed with Nick Yerbury, please, DC Gordon.'

She cursed that her chat with Yerbury had been cut short the previous day.

'Yerbury was the teacher showing Kyle how to do all this techie stuff. I want to know why he was uploading material anonymously and which sites he might have been uploading to. I also want to know what Yerbury knows about the sharpening block inside the desk drawer where he's already told us he left his phone. Now Zach's been cleared, that just became even more important.'

Harry made a note on his pad. Hollie observed how well he responded to a bit of positive feedback.

'Did Lance find anything on Kyle's computer?' she asked.

'He asked you to call in if you get a moment,' Harry replied. 'The short answer is nothing that moves things on for us. I get the impression they're a bit snowed under over there.'

Hollie made a mental note to call in on Lance and apply the personal touch. She knew what staffing was like with the budget cuts, but still, she needed some results.

'Now, DS Patel has kindly created a timetable of who will be interviewing which children and where. For safeguarding purposes, we have placed two teachers in each interview room, which was also a preference expressed by Mr Canfield. Interviewing teams will work through sessions with all children who thought they might have seen something useful. Those children who we've asked to come into the academy today will assemble in the main hall at half past nine. If anybody learns of anything that is case critical, escalate it immediately through DS Anderson.'

Hollie reckoned they'd most likely get a patchwork of jumbled information, but they had to sift through it all, and this seemed like the most efficient way to do it. The senior teaching staff were more comfortable with the interviews being conducted in the familiar surroundings of the academy, and Hollie agreed with that.

'I also want to speak to the sixth formers as soon as we can fix it up,' she began. 'Can you set that up, DS Patel? I'd like to get them all in one room first, then we'll separate them off and speak to them individually.'

'Yes, boss,' Amber replied. She knew her colleague would have it planned out like a military operation in no time.

'Here are our other priorities for the day. DS Anderson and DS Patel will be leading on the interviews with children, so if you get anything of note, report directly to them. Top priorities are finding Kyle's phone and his laptop. I'll take the home-educated student, Quinn Varney, as soon as the briefing finishes. DC Gordon, I'd like you in on that with me.'

'Yes, ma'am.'

Hollie scanned the room. Isla Wilson's Family Liaison Officer was present.

'How's Kyle's mother holding up, DC Hayes?'

'Distraught, as you might expect, ma'am. The doctor came round to give her something strong so that she'd sleep. I'm heading over at ten. Her sister was with her overnight.'

It was unbearable to even begin to imagine what Kyle's mum was going through, and Hollie steeled herself knowing she needed to pay her another visit – she'd add that to the list.

There was a knock at the door and Mr Canfield entered, a slip of paper in his hand.

'I've just taken a call from your HQ,' he began. 'Apparently a Doctor Ruane is ready for you at the mortuary.'

THIRTY
WEDNESDAY, 09:12

As they stepped out of the academy's main doors, Hollie immediately spotted a group of about ten parents gathered beyond the gates. Some of them were carrying placards.

KEEP OUR KIDS SAFE!

FIND THE KILLER!

'Oh hell,' she muttered to Harry under her breath, 'this is all we need. I thought yesterday's little get-together in the foyer would put this to bed.'

Two constables were posted outside the gates, so at least there was no danger of it spilling over onto the academy grounds.

They climbed into the car and drove off. There was a shout behind them as they exited.

'What are you coppers doing to keep the school safe? When are you going to make an arrest?'

That's all Hollie needed. The parents were saying pretty well the same thing as the brass.

'This is going to be a challenging day for you, but I'm keen to push you a bit on this case.'

'It's fine, boss. The more experience I can get, the better.'

On the drive over, Harry confessed that he'd never been to the mortuary before, but he had seen several dead bodies in the course of his short policing career.

'I've got to get it over with some time, it may as well be now.'

'So long as you're sure. It's somehow very different when the bodies are laid out on a table. Doctor Ruane will have had to examine internal organs as well.'

As they parked up outside the mortuary, she unclipped her seatbelt and got out of the car. Quinn Varney was preying on her mind; they'd drop in on him while they were doing the rounds.

Charles Ruane was his usual calm and professional self when they joined him in the mortuary. She'd not seen him in his full medical gear before. He was in the middle of examining another body when they walked in on him.

Hollie entered first, to be greeted by the sight of a cadaver with its chest cut open and the ribs pulled apart on both sides. She'd seen it before, but it was always shocking. Harry walked into the room, took one look at the body on the table and rushed out.

'First time in the mortuary?' Doctor Ruane smiled.

'I'm afraid so.' Hollie shrugged.

Harry returned a couple of minutes later, a sheepish look on his face.

'I'm sorry, ma'am. I thought I'd be okay.'

'Never be embarrassed to express emotion around a body, DC Gordon,' Hollie attempted to reassure him. 'It shows that you're human and haven't been so tarnished by the job that you've become impervious to sights like that.'

He seemed bolstered, but still embarrassed.

Doctor Ruane had now covered up the corpse with a white

sheet. He led them over to a second body, which was also covered.

'I'm going to reveal the head only,' Doctor Ruane warned, looking directly at Harry. 'I'll tell you before I show his torso, okay? If you stay where you are, you won't be able to see where I've examined his brain.'

Harry nodded. He looked like he was ready to make a run for it.

'I'll give a bit more detail than usual so that your colleague can get a better understanding of the terminology,' he began, and reached over and pulled back the sheet to reveal the face, but left the neck concealed.

Harry took a sharp intake of breath. Hollie felt a churn in her stomach.

Kyle's face was almost completely purple. His eyelids were swollen and there were smears where the blood had been cleaned from around his nose.

'I know you won't believe me, but it looks much worse than it is,' Doctor Ruane continued. 'This is what we call blunt-force trauma, DC Gordon. In simple terms, it's a physical trauma to the body, and non-penetrating in nature. So you'd expect to see bruises like this after an assault, a road traffic collision, a sports injury, a direct blow – something like that.'

Harry exhaled loudly as if he was still uncertain if he was going to stick around. Hollie remembered being that way once upon a time. She managed to get through these sessions, but it never got any easier.

'Although Kyle was the victim of a sustained attack, he would not have died, despite the bruised state he was left in. Miraculously, there's no sign of TBI—'

'Just explain TBI if you would, doctor. For my sake, too, I'm not too good with acronyms.'

'Of course. TBI stands for traumatic brain injury. I suspect that whoever assaulted him wore soft shoes, such as trainers or plimsolls, though there is evidence somebody was wearing a heavier shoe – a boot even. It's all caused a lot of damage, as you can see, but an examination of young Kyle's brain shows that he would have walked away from that beating.'

Hollie moved to the top of the body. He'd done a neat job of the skull examination; she hoped something could be done to make the viewing less traumatic when Kyle's mum came to see her dead son.

'I'm going to move the sheet down a little now, DC Gordon. This is what we call penetrating trauma, where an object pierces the skin and creates an open wound.'

Doctor Ruane pulled back the sheet to just above Kyle's shoulders. The wound had been cleaned since she last saw it, to the extent that it almost looked like nothing at all.

'Here's where the chisel entered the neck. This is what killed Kyle. I can also confirm with a high degree of certainty that the discarded chisel found in the foyer bin was of the same type used to inflict this wound.'

'Not the same chisel?' Hollie checked.

'Well, you and I both know that, circumstantially, that's extremely likely. The forensics team will have to confirm the rest, of course.'

Harry seemed interested in the neck wound, peering over, as if testing himself to ascertain his limits.

'Thank you for sending over one of the other chisels from the school. It was extremely blunt, I noted, so I'm assuming the one that's with forensics was a lot sharper?'

It was – she'd seen it for herself when she retrieved it from the bin in the foyer. She gave Doctor Ruane a confirmation of that.

'I'm going to reveal the rest of the body now.'

Doctor Ruane pulled back the sheet so that it rested on Kyle's feet. Hollie was used to seeing grown men in situations like this; they were more often than not the victims of beatings.

She'd also seen a depressing number of women with similar injuries, as a result of domestic abuse, violent attack or sexually motivated assault. The sight of a child – there was no way that was the body of a man – took her breath away. DC Gordon screwed up his face. Dead bodies always looked so peaceful, like they'd already shrugged off what happened to them. But their bruises and wounds told another story.

Kyle's chest was stitched in a Y-shape where Doctor Ruane had opened it up to examine the internal organs.

'I estimate at least thirty separate kicks to his body, delivered by at least four assailants.'

'How can you tell that?' Harry asked.

'I can't be completely certain, but it's extrapolated from wound pattern, direction and severity. Everything here is suggestive of four, maybe five, people surrounding Kyle and kicking him while he was on the ground.'

'What about organ damage?' Hollie asked. 'Would it have killed him?'

'There's some internal bleeding and minor bowel damage via trauma to Kyle's abdomen. There's also some damage to his spleen, though, unusually, his liver was not damaged.'

'Could that have killed him?' Harry asked.

'No, not unless there was some pre-existing issue or damage. It's my belief that Kyle would have recovered from this assault. He would have been in hospital for some time, and it would have required some rehabilitation at home, but he would not have died.'

Hollie walked around the body, examining the bruising and the entry wound caused by the chisel. Something made her want to reach out and touch Kyle's hand and promise him they'd catch his killer. She didn't, but the sight of him lying there made her desperately sad for his mother, who was going to have to see her son like this. They'd dress his body in familiar clothing, and they'd make him look as good as they could for her, but it made Hollie shudder imagining what it was going to be like for the poor woman.

They were silent for several minutes, each needing a moment to take it in and wrestle with their thoughts. When Hollie's grip on her emotions was steady enough, she looked at Doctor Ruane.

He was watching her, like he was waiting for her to compose herself.

'Is there something else you wanted to tell me, Doctor Ruane? You look like something is on your mind.'

She liked and respected the doctor, but he was like a slow-release pill: he revealed his findings one step at a time.

'Yes, there is one more thing,' he continued, his face straight and his tone even. 'Kyle had swallowed something shortly before his death. I retrieved it from his digestive tract.'

He reached into the pockets of his scrubs to retrieve something that had been placed in a small plastic bag. He handed it over to Hollie. It took her a moment to work out what it was. Kyle had swallowed a small slip of paper, which was crinkled where it had been screwed up. Doctor Ruane had flattened it in the bag, and Hollie could see that something was written in pen. She held it closer so she could be sure of what it was. There were four digits scrawled on the small scrap of paper: a PIN perhaps? It read 4-7-9-2.

THIRTY-ONE
WEDNESDAY, 10:11

'We're meeting Quinn and his mum next at Chevening Park; it's off Runnymede Way apparently,' Hollie remarked, relieved to be out of the mortuary.

She'd updated the team about the PIN and made sure the forensics guys had been given the scrap of paper. What did those digits 4-7-9-2 mean, and why was Kyle so keen to conceal them?

She checked the slip of paper that Amber Patel had handed her with Quinn's home address. 'Can we park near there?'

'No problem, ma'am, it's easy enough.'

'You know, you don't have to keep calling me ma'am,' Hollie said as they crossed to the main road. 'Boss or guv is fine.'

'Yes, ma'am,' Harry replied. 'Boss.'

'We've worked a couple of cases as a team now, you can relax a bit.'

Harry didn't say anything. Hollie was concerned she might be scaring him. She'd be happier if he felt more comfortable in coming forward with his ideas. The old guard took some handling at times; she didn't want them intimidating the younger detectives like Harry Gordon.

'I'm sorry if you felt uncomfortable in the briefing earlier when someone made that silly joke about the sex shop. Sometimes the older members of the team can be a bit of a blunt tool. They forget what it's like to be young, I think.'

'It's all right, boss. It doesn't bother me. I'm used to a bit of teasing.'

'Well, let me know if it ever turns spiteful. We're a police force, not a school playground. I expect everybody to behave like adults.'

Hollie felt her hackles rising over Ben Anderson once again. She'd have liked his detective skills when she dropped in on Dirty Little Secrets, but she wasn't sure she could face the inevitable barrage of schoolboy jokes. She diverted herself from thinking about it.

'Got any plans for this evening, Harry?'

What she really wanted to know was if he had a partner, where he lived, if he had kids and how he spent his time. It didn't feel appropriate to ask those questions directly, so she kept her fingers crossed he'd be in a chatty mood.

'I live in a shared house with Ulryk and Daisy,' he started, checking his wing mirror. 'We all started around the same time.'

It made sense that he was living with DC Philpot and DC Norton, they were all a similar age.

'Wow, so you don't get much time away from work then?'

'It's okay. We're all ambitious to work our way through the ranks. Work is my life really.'

Hollie was about to give him a lecture about work-life balance when she thought of her own domestic set-up. She'd been working long hours to hide her loneliness, so she could hardly quote pages from the health and well-being manual to him. She'd be giving him recipe suggestions for Pot Noodles next.

'How about you, ma'am? Do you get to see your kids much?'

Hollie didn't dwell on her marital issues, though it was obvious to all that hers was not a normal domestic situation.

'You know what it's like with this job,' she replied. 'My husband is French, so it can create some interesting situations with geography.'

'I didn't know about him being French, ma'am.'

'Yes, I use my maiden name at work for simplicity. My kids use it at school, too. My married name is Desrosiers. Once you've had to spell a name like that out half a million times, you tend to give up on anyone in the UK ever getting it right.'

They got to Chevening Park faster than expected. It was located on a modern estate with a walled entrance. The houses appeared to be mainly detached, as far as Hollie could see from a quick scan, and they circled around a central grassed area, with smaller roads leading off at several points. She read out the details of the property they were looking for and Harry pulled up in the spare space on the Varneys' drive. It was middle-class suburban heaven.

'Nice place,' Hollie remarked. 'They'd just started building on this land when I was a student. It's grown vast.'

They got out of the car and walked up to the door together. The academy was not that far from where Quinn lived. She figured as the academy had been built to accommodate the estate, it made sense that the majority of the youngsters lived in the new houses. Harry rang the bell. There was movement inside and a woman opened the door, probably mid-to-late forties, Hollie assessed. She was casually dressed, but her bearing suggested educated and possibly professional.

Hollie held out her ID and DC Gordon followed.

'Good morning, Mrs Varney. DI Turner and DC Gordon. I believe you're expecting us.'

'Yes, come in. Quinn is here, I'll give him a shout.'

She ushered them into the living room. It was show-home tidy, with tasteful curtains, a thick carpet, colourful and worldly ornaments and modern, effervescent artwork on the walls. Holly suspected there would be no red bills in this house.

'Quinn! The police are here,' she shouted up the staircase.

She didn't sound too worried about the visit. It was the calm assurance of a middle-class woman who was confident that little could touch her.

As Mrs Varney disappeared into the kitchen to make coffee, Quinn made his way down the stairs.

His hair was stylishly unkempt in a way that teenagers managed so effortlessly. Hollie's hairstyles ranged from *a bloody mess* to *just about acceptable in public*. They'd have called Quinn cool when Hollie was at school. He wore a Nirvana T-shirt and a pair of jeans with large rips in the knees. When Hollie was small, her mum would patch her trousers when she wore them through at the knees. She needn't have bothered; if she'd just left them as they were, she'd have been ahead of her time in the fashion scene.

Hollie made the introductions and Mrs Varney brought in the drinks on a modern art decorated tray. She'd laid out a selection of mixed chocolate biscuits. Hollie spotted Breakaways; she was having one of those before they finished. She wasn't accustomed to this high standard of catering.

Harry activated the recording app on his phone and explained what he was doing.

'So, Quinn and Mrs Varney—' Hollie began.

'Call me Eloise, please.'

She was well-educated, not local, and sure of herself.

'Great, that keeps things relaxed. This is an informal interview; we're just getting a bit of background after the tragic incident at the academy yesterday.'

'Sure thing,' Quinn replied. Neither of them seemed remotely concerned about having two detectives in the house.

Eloise and Quinn seemed too cold to Hollie. She'd have expected more concern over what happened to Kyle and the pain his mother was going through, but this felt more like a chit-chat.

'So, you're eighteen now and home-educated, I believe, Quinn. Why is that?'

'I've been home-educated for a couple of months,' he began. 'School wasn't working out for me, but I just have to get through the exams.'

'Why was school not working out for you, Quinn?'

He seemed reluctant to answer.

'He was beaten up,' Eloise replied. 'The school didn't handle it very well.'

Hollie liked when information got confirmed in interviews. That was two altercations Zach had got involved in, both of them confirmed by more than one source.

'You're aware of what happened at the academy yesterday, I assume?'

'Yeah, it was terrible—'

'We were appalled,' Eloise added. 'That poor boy.'

They seemed to be working like a tag team. Hollie wondered if they'd got their story rehearsed before they'd arrived.

'Do you know why we're talking to you today, Quinn?'

'Yeah, sure. I was visiting the academy yesterday—'

'You didn't tell me that,' Eloise said, sharp and accusatory. That bit was definitely not pre-planned.

'It's fine, Mum. I popped in during the lunch break. I was just sorting out something with my exams.'

Eloise visibly relaxed.

Hollie remembered Mr Bridges suggesting something similar.

'What time did you enter the school premises, Quinn?'

'About midday. It was just before the lunch bell went off. I wanted to check the exam timetables with Miss Drake.'

'Yasmine Drake?' Harry checked.

'Yes. She's one of the young teachers and she works as the school counsellor, too. It was Yasmine who pushed the school to agree to take me as an external exam student,' Quinn explained.

Hollie clocked the use of a first name. Was this how the older kids addressed the staff these days?

'You call her Yasmine, not Miss Drake?' Harry queried.

She was pleased to see her young colleague had clocked it as well.

'Sure, she's cool with it and seeing as I don't go to school now, she's more like a friend or a colleague than a teacher.'

'She has a lot of responsibilities,' Hollie remarked as much to herself as to everybody else.

'Yasmine is chill. She's really helpful, I couldn't have gone home-educated without her,' Quinn continued.

'What time did you leave?' Hollie picked up.

'I was there for about a quarter of an hour.'

'Which entrance did you come in by, Quinn?'

'The main entrance. Everybody has to go in that way.'

'And how did you leave?'

'The front entrance, same way as I came in.'

Hollie waited for a few beats, examining Quinn's face.

'Only, my colleagues checked the CCTV footage, and they can't find a record of you leaving the academy via that entrance—'

Eloise interrupted. 'These seem to be very accusatory questions, detective. Should we be doing this at the police station with a solicitor?' She sat forward in her chair, prickly now.

'It's just background information at this stage, Mrs Varney.'

She didn't seem happy about that but allowed Hollie to continue. She looked at Quinn, waiting for his answer.

'Oh right, I remember,' he replied, not at all convincingly. 'I took the gap in the fence at the side of the school field. It's a shortcut, it takes you by the shops.'

'Why did you do that, Quinn?'

'I was hungry and bought myself something to eat.'

'If we check out the CCTV in the shops, will we see your face?' Harry asked.

Quinn's reply was uncertain. 'Yeah, sure. That's if the newsagent has CCTV.'

'Did you speak to anybody else while you were in school, Quinn?' Hollie picked up.

'Yeah, I saw a couple of the guys there.'

'Which guys?' Harry asked, pen poised.

'Evie, Matt, Tilly, Zach—'

Hollie and Harry exchanged glances.

'Zach Eastwood?' Hollie checked.

'Yeah, that's him.'

'That's the kid who beat up Quinn,' Eloise interjected.

'Really?'

'It was nothing, Mum, I told you. Just a falling out. I don't know why you and Dad made such a big deal of it.'

'Mr Canfield just swept it under the carpet at the time,' Eloise continued. 'He was beaten black and blue. It was only because Quinn begged us not to that we didn't involve the police. I don't know why he still talks to that boy—'

'Zach's all right, Mum. We made up. I was as much to blame as he was. It was just a stupid thing.'

This seemed to be an ongoing source of friction between the two. Quinn seemed exasperated with his mum.

'Can you give me their full names?' Harry asked.

'Sure. Matthew Urquhart, Evie Keane, Tilly Mann... oh, and I chatted to Sammy and Jake, too.'

'Can I have their full names?' Harry prompted again.

'Samantha Ingram and Jake Tate.'

'Great, thank you.'

'I assume these are your old school friends, Quinn?'

He nodded. He seemed reflective when he spoke about them, like he still missed that part of his life.

'Where did you chat to them?'

'In the sixth-form common room. It was just quick, you know?'

'And then you left the school completely.'

'Yes.' He paused before speaking, and his voice faltered. He reached out and took a drink.

'Was this before the lunch break ended?'

He hesitated, but only for a moment. His right hand tensed before he replied.

'Yes. I'd have heard the bell if I'd been there when lunch break ended.'

Hollie studied his face. He was good and he was sharp, but something didn't quite add up.

'I'm struggling with your timeline, Quinn. We have you on CCTV entering the school grounds just before midday. You say you spoke to—'

Hollie looked at Harry.

'Yasmine Drake.'

'You spoke to Miss Drake then what, you met with your old school pals in the sixth-form common room?'

'That's right.'

She could see him thinking it over before he answered. A bead of sweat had formed on his forehead, but the room was cool and unheated. His answers were becoming clipped and brief now. Eloise seemed tense, shuffling from side to side in her seat.

'I've got a problem, Quinn. We know you were on the school grounds when lunch break began, but my team has been unable to find a CCTV record of you after that. This suggests to me that you can't have gone to the sixth form area because we'd have caught that on one of the cameras, wouldn't we?'

'Maybe I'm mistaken then.' He frowned. His right hand was shaking now.

'Perhaps you are. It's just that it would have been possible, in theory, for you to kill Kyle, wouldn't it? Given that you've already confirmed your movements for us—'

Eloise stood up.

'I think we're finished here, detective. This was supposed to be an informal chat. I don't like your tone. If you wish to speak to Quinn again, you'll need to arrest him, and we'll want a solicitor present. Now, please leave my house.'

THIRTY-TWO

I fucking love Mr Yerbury!

I've been over to his place a couple of times since he made the offer to use that granny flat.

His editing kit is freaking amazing.

I've made so much progress on my project work, I'll be caught up soon.

He just leaves me to it.

I even play my music through his cool speakers; it sounds incredible.

I managed to give Mum some money today.

She looked at me like I'd stolen it.

I sold some old video games on eBay.

I was hoping to keep them, but I made twenty quid, so I had to do it.

I sold a pack of Yugioh cards to a kid on the lower school, too, that made another fiver.

It's not much, and I know it's not enough, but I'm doing what I can.

I'm trying to eat fewer snacks.

My stomach rumbled in class today, but it's worth it if it keeps the shopping bill down.

Something weird happened tonight though.

Usually, him or Yasmine give me a lift back home, but they said they had visitors tonight, so asked if I could catch the bus.

I was just packing up and switching off the lights when two people came into the living area.

I work in the bedroom, but there's just a Z-bed in there. I think Mr Yerbury sleeps in there when him and Yasmine have a row.

I didn't know what was going on, so I peeped round the door.

Fucking hell, Tilly and Jake were snogging on the sofa!

They were giggling, I'm sure they'd been drinking.

Nick and Yasmine must have had some of the sixth formers round to their place.

I'd heard rumours about it, but I'm not in with the in-crowd, so nobody would invite me anyway.

I don't care, I love having this place to myself.

I didn't know what to do when they came in, so I waited until they'd gone and then sneaked out.

I like Tilly and Jake, or at least I did until Zach started spreading lies about me.

They aren't nasty like the others, but they might find the balls to stick up for me every once in a while.

Anyway, I didn't see anything, I think it was just a snog. It's not like they haven't been going out with each other for long enough.

Oh, I forgot to say.

Mr Yerbury says I can have a key for the annexe.

He says he trusts me to come and go and I can't come to any harm in there.

I could have hugged him when he told me.

It's like having my own place.

I forget all about my worries when I'm in there.

It's like my little den, when I was a kid and Mum pulled a blanket over two chairs.

I know mine and Mum's problems won't go away, but it helps life feel a bit better when I'm over at Nick and Yasmine's.

THIRTY-THREE
WEDNESDAY, 11:21

'Are you okay if we drop into this sex shop before we head back to HQ?' Hollie asked.

'Of course, boss,' Harry replied. 'We may as well while we're out in the car.'

As they parked up, Hollie observed that there were residential homes nearby, and there were clearly no problems with the neighbours as it looked like it had been there for some time.

As they were walking through the door, a buzzer sounded. Hollie thought they probably should have planned it a bit better. There was only one other customer in the store, and for two to walk in at once, they might be mistaken for a couple.

She nodded at the man behind the counter, who appeared to be sorting out a pile of magazines which were about to be placed on the shelves. Harry made directly for a DVD shelf at the back of the shop, and Hollie nonchalantly stood in front of the magazines.

Hollie scanned the shop. The lighting was low, otherwise it might just as well have been a supermarket. Everything was labelled on shelves, with clear pointers to the various sexual proclivities on offer: BDSM, Bondage, Couples, Gay, Toys, it was all there. It felt surprisingly normal to Hollie, not as seedy as she'd expected, and more of a shop for adults than anything too far off the beaten track.

The man working behind the counter seemed perfectly at ease, and the other customer was taking his time examining various tonics. Hollie wondered if there was anything to help her stay awake at night that might have helped her and Léon in the bedroom. Did they sell quadruple espressos?

She decided to put Harry out of his misery and declare what they were up to. She walked up to the counter. 'Good morning, I'm DI Turner and this is DC Gordon, from Humberside Police.'

'I did wonder,' the man said. 'You people have a way of moving. I can spot you a mile off.'

The door buzzed as the shop's single customer made his exit.

'Thanks for chasing the customers away,' the man complained. 'What's this about? We're properly licensed by the local authority, you know. Are the residents moaning about us again?'

'It's nothing like that,' Hollie stopped him. 'We're investigating a murder. One of your business cards was found at the crime scene. We're just wondering if you have any idea where it might have come from.'

'You mean these?' He held up a pile of business cards which had been sitting next to the cash register.

Hollie and Harry walked over, and each took a card.

'That's the same card,' Harry confirmed.

'May I take a couple of these? We've been working from a photograph of the original so far.'

'Of course, knock yourself out. You can share some around the office if you want. I'd always be happy to see members of the local constabulary shopping here. We've even got fluffy handcuffs if that's your thing.'

Hollie noticed Harry's face colouring again.

'Who would be handed these cards?' she asked.

'Well, I place one in every bag when we make a sale, and people often take one, so they remember the website address.'

'You're online?' Harry asked.

'Yes, we wouldn't survive without online orders. I sell all over the world on the internet. This is an international business thanks to the World Wide Web. I'm Patrick Frisby by the way, I'm the owner here.'

That's who Jenni spoke to on the phone.

'There's no way of tracking these cards?' Hollie asked. 'You don't use referral codes or anything like that?'

'On the website, yes. But with business cards, no. Anybody might have taken one of these.'

'What do you publish on your website? Is it just sales?'

'Mainly, but we host couples' videos, too, you know, nothing illegal, all ethical stuff. We revenue share with our contributors. As I said, we're licensed.'

'What makes people upload videos like that?' Hollie asked. It wasn't a case-related question, she was just curious.

'Some are exhibitionists, others do it for the money, others make it a part of their relationship and some like the thrill. There are all sorts of reasons for it. I post videos there myself. It's a celebration of sexuality as far as I'm concerned. Some people get so hung up by this stuff.'

'You're not embarrassed?' she checked.

'Why would I be?'

Hollie wouldn't even use a communal changing room so there was no chance of her uploading home videos to an adult website any time soon. It made her feel old-fashioned. She'd never posted things online which used to be considered private, and she couldn't understand why people were so happy to throw caution to the wind when it came to their most intimate moments.

'Do you have CCTV?' Harry asked, looking around, keen to stick to more comfortable topics.

Patrick shook his head. 'It's a tricky one, that. I do get some shoplifting here, but it puts the punters off if we have CCTV. That's why the shop is called Dirty Little Secrets – people can come in here and be anonymous. It's up to them what they get up to, I don't judge.'

'I'd like to take a look around,' Hollie informed him. 'I want to figure out how that business card made its way to our crime scene.'

'Be my guest,' Patrick replied. 'There's not much to look at, just the kitchen area, the staff toilet and the storeroom. There's no upstairs; I rent out the top floor to students.'

'Oh yes, what kind of students?'

'Mainly from the university. I've got a younger girl up there, too, at the moment. She works in the shop sometimes.'

'What is it, like a flat arrangement?'

'Yeah, it's cheaper than regular digs because they share a bathroom. They don't have to come through the shop; there's an entrance at the side.'

That filled in a gap for Hollie, who had spotted the side door on her cursory investigation the previous evening.

Hollie and Harry wandered off, making for the beaded curtain which separated the staff area.

To the left was a small sink and water heater, with a kettle, cups, tea bags and jar of instant coffee on the tiny worktop. To the right was the staff toilet. Beyond that was the storeroom, packed with boxes, some ready to dispatch and others, it seemed, ready to unpack.

To the right, as they walked in, Hollie spotted a staff noticeboard, on which were pinned various pieces of paper. She scanned them as Harry inspected the boxes.

'He's telling the truth, ma'am, this package is being dispatched to Copenhagen.'

There was the usual information on the board: a health and safety at work notice, insurer's liability certificate and staff rota. One of the names caught Hollie's eye.

'Just check, would you? One of the names of the students in that little group – Evie something, wasn't it?'

Harry pulled his notebook out of his pocket and checked it.

She was pleased he'd got the information to hand.

'Evie Keane, boss.'

Hollie checked the name again. 'Got it! Evie Keane works here twice a week. She's our link to that business card.'

As the sixth formers filed into the drama studio, Hollie checked in with her colleagues, making sure they were primed for what was going to happen next. Two of the team – DC Langdon and DC Gordon – were not so far removed from the youngsters who were pulling up chairs all around her. These were young adults, but they were also still children.

The team had been given photo sheets of both year groups by Olivia Dreyfuss, on which were written names, birth dates and subjects being studied.

'Thanks for pulling all this together so fast,' Hollie said as Amber sidled up to her.

'So you're still going to try to flush them out?' Amber asked, lowering her voice further so she wouldn't be heard.

'Yes, I'll wait until the end, it's got to be worth a try,' she replied. Amber was the only member of the team she'd briefed about her plan, and she still wasn't completely convinced it was going to pay off. But it was worth a shot.

Hollie observed as Tilly Mann slunk into the room. She looked scared and fragile. Tilly clocked Hollie immediately and averted her gaze. Jenni walked over.

'Look who's here,' she remarked. 'Could the girl look any unhappier?'

Tilly's eyes were red, like she'd been crying. She looked drawn and exhausted.

'Did we get anything off her phone in the end?' Hollie checked.

'No, what wasn't deleted was sent via WhatsApp. It's all gone now, with no trace. But we know she and Kyle were close. And we know they'd fallen out about something.'

'Yes, but what? What's got to these kids?'

'Or who?' Jenni added. 'Who's got to these kids?'

Zach Eastwood glared at them as he slouched into the room, and she wondered what she'd do as a parent if any of her children turned out like that. She seemed to have made it through with Izzy okay, but what if Noah turned into a scowling Zach Eastwood? She hoped that was one problem she wouldn't have to confront.

'Which one's Evie Keane?' Hollie asked, leaving Jenni to catch Amber. 'She knows I want to speak to her after this?'

'Yes, she's primed and ready,' Amber replied. 'Don't expect a hearty greeting and jovial company. She's a scowler, that one.'

Hollie observed that Evie was sitting next to Zach, the two of them looking old enough to be students at a university rather than pupils in an academy.

At last, it seemed that they were all there. At a rough count, Hollie reckoned about forty, made up of both lower and upper sixth formers. She suspected they were dealing with the older kids as far as the case was concerned, and there was nothing so far that suggested what happened to Kyle had bled through to the lower sixth formers.

Hollie clapped her hands once to get their attention; she'd noticed a couple of teachers doing it around the academy while they'd been based there, and it seemed to work. Mr Canfield had just slipped in the door, and his presence also seemed to do the job; the chatter stopped, and Hollie made a start.

The majority of them were thumbing their phones but slipped them into bags as Mr Canfield moved around the group pointing at them to put them away.

DS Anderson and DC Gordon were standing together at the rear of the drama studio, while DC Langdon and DS Patel had stationed themselves by each of the two doors.

'Good morning, everybody, and thank you for coming in today. I want to be clear from the outset that this is not an interview, and you are not under suspicion because you are sitting in this room.'

Her eyes fell on Zach, and she swiftly moved them away. She tried not to catch any glances in particular, but it was difficult with them all in front of her.

'We're all shocked and saddened by the death of Kyle Wilson and I'm certain that there's not a person in this studio who doesn't want to bring Kyle's killer or killers to justice. So, I'm just asking for your help right now. We've got a number of leads from the interviews that have been conducted so far, but we need more. I'm going to ask some questions today to see if we can get a better idea of who Kyle was and why someone might want to hurt him.'

Hollie paused for a moment and scanned the faces. She wondered what it would be like to teach youngsters of this age. Their expressions were blank as if completely disengaged, and most of them looked like they wanted to go back to bed. Chasing criminals seemed like the easier career choice.

'So, who can tell me about Kyle, what kind of boy was he?'

'He hated sports!' someone called from the back. It wasn't one of the teenagers in the main group. There was a ripple of understanding laughter.

'What did Kyle like?' Hollie encouraged.

'Music – he loved his music.'

'Reading. If I think of Kyle, he usually had a book in his hand. It was often something about films or psychology or something like that.'

'He was always filming stuff.'

That made Hollie's ears prick up. She'd heard this from several people already, including Kyle's mum. Everybody seemed to equate Kyle with filming.

'Who said that?' she asked, searching the room.

'Shut the fuck up, Matt,' Zach mumbled, loud enough for Hollie to hear.

Amber pointed to the person who'd spoken up, and Hollie searched him out. He was a fresh-faced kid, with no tattoos or piercings; he might have slotted in fine with her own generation of students. Matt was next to a young woman who was sitting close enough to him to suggest they might be in a relationship; their body language certainly indicated that could be the case.

'Tell me about that, would you, Matt?'

Zach Eastwood was sitting directly behind Matt and although she didn't see it clearly, he must have poked Matt from behind, as Matt jerked in his seat and the girl turned around to give him a dirty look.

'It's nothing, I shouldn't have said anything—'

'No, please continue. It might help us.'

'Kyle just likes to record stuff. He was in Mr Yerbury's media class. We used to rib him about it. Sometimes he could be a nuisance because he'd be filming you when you didn't want him to—'

'Yeah, he was a right nerd,' Zach spoke out loud, and there was a ripple of laughter. Mr Canfield moved in a manner that suggested he might be ready to intervene, but Hollie was pleased to see DS Anderson discouraging him from getting involved.

'What do you mean by that?' Hollie pushed.

'Nothing.'

Zach folded his arms and said nothing.

'He wanted to be a filmmaker,' said Tilly Mann, who was sitting to one side, slightly apart from the main cluster of chairs. She was upset and tearful, as if thinking about Kyle was distressing her.

'Was he going to study that at university?' Hollie asked. She knew the answer already, but it was interesting to see who was speaking up as if Kyle had actually been a friend.

'Kyle was going to Manchester Metropolitan University to study film, but he had to change to Hull because of what happened to his mum,' Tilly continued. 'I guess that dream's all over now—'

She stood up and her chair scraped on the wood floor.

'I'm sorry, can I leave, please?'

She was crying now, a look of distress across her face. Mr Canfield was about to step in when Jenni rushed over to Tilly.

'It's all right, boss, I'll take care of her.'

Hollie gave a nod. Jenni had been quick to respond. Tilly probably had more that was interesting to share away from the main group. She caught Zach Eastwood flicking Matt's ear and sniggering about it behind his back with Evie at his side. It was difficult to guess what Evie was thinking; her face was fixed in a permanent look of aloof distaste.

Hollie moved her hand to her pocket and pulled out an enlarged print of the business card from Dirty Little Secrets that was found at the crime scene. She watched Evie's expression change when she saw what it was. There was some tittering from the younger students. She braced herself; this is what it must be like to have to deliver a sex education class as a teacher. She reckoned most of those kids probably knew more than her already, what with the plethora of unsuitable content that was available online.

'I'd like to know which of you has visited the Dirty Little Secrets adult shop,' she began. 'I know it's embarrassing to talk about, but we want to know how this business card found its way to the outbuilding where Kyle was killed. You can speak to any of my colleagues about this in confidence afterwards if you prefer—'

'Maybe ask the teachers about that!' came a boy's voice from the back.

'Wiggins!' Mr Canfield barked across the drama studio.

'Ask Evie Keane, she works there,' another younger student said. 'If you want a porno, Evie can get it for you.'

'Shut your face!' Evie erupted. 'He's talking bollocks, it's just a job.'

Her face was red.

'Evie, watch your language, please,' Mr Canfield cautioned.

Hollie clocked that for later. Evie was clearly touchy about this topic, but it would be better handled away from her peers.

'Come and talk to us afterwards if you can help with that. Now there's one last thing.' She pulled the piece of paper out of her pocket that Amber had handed over at the beginning of the session. 'We're still trying to locate Kyle's phone and laptop.'

Hollie pulled her mobile phone out of her other pocket and keyed in the number that she'd written down on her visit to Isla Wilson. She was dialling Kyle's mobile number.

She looked across at Amber Patel to make sure she'd clocked what she was doing.

'If you can help us locate either of those objects, it would really help—'

A phone rang. Its ringtone was *Mama Mia*. Everybody looked in the direction of the sound.

Hollie had just called Kyle's mobile phone, considering it a long shot. But the victim's phone was ringing loud and clear. And the sound was coming from the bag that Tilly Mann had abandoned at the side of her chair.

'Where is Tilly Mann?'

Hollie rushed out of the drama studio to find where Jenni had taken her. There was no sign of either of them, but Mr Lacey, the caretaker, was mopping the floor further along the corridor.

'Did you see which direction my colleague headed?' Hollie asked.

'If she was the one with that young lass, then she drove her home. Poor kid threw up in the corridor. I think it's all proving very stressful for them.'

'Thank you.'

Hollie took out her phone and called Jenni.

'Hi boss, I've got you on speaker phone and Tilly is in the car with me—'

'Is she ill?'

'Yes, boss. It's a good job she left the room. I think it might have been the end of your meeting otherwise.'

'I'm going to follow you over. What's Tilly's address? I'll be ten minutes behind.'

Jenni gave Hollie the address and they ended the call.

Hollie returned to the drama studio, where the atmosphere had become tense and nervy. DS Anderson had taken charge in her absence.

'Where are you up to?' she asked. The sixth formers were behaving like they were in an exam, such was the level of silence in the room. There were some worried faces, and a couple of students were crying.

'We need to remember these are kids,' she said before Anderson got a chance to reply, 'and some of them are under eighteen. Steady as you go.'

'We've isolated the phone and DC Gordon is getting it bagged and tagged up in the conference room now, with the help of DC Philpot.'

'Good. I'm going to see Tilly; she's been taken ill. You need to interview everybody in this room about what they saw and what they did. Make sure Evie Keane is still here when I get back, as I want to speak to her directly. It doesn't ring true to me that Tilly would leave a bag in which she knew she was hiding Kyle's phone. Talk about ramming your hand into a wasp's nest. I want to work on the hypothesis that it might also have been placed in there. If so, who by?'

'Yes, boss.'

DS Anderson had a multitude of ways of saying those two words. This was his *I don't agree with you* tone.

'You don't seem convinced, DS Anderson?'

'I think we caught her red-handed, boss. We're not dealing with hardened criminals here. As you said, they're kids.'

'You may be right; I'll find that out shortly. But work on that basis before you release this lot from the room. We don't want to have to close the stable door after the horses have bolted.'

'What gave you the idea to do that?' Anderson asked. For one moment, Hollie thought she sensed a hint of admiration in his tone.

'I wished I'd done it during that school assembly, on the day of Kyle's death. I only realised when I got home last night and was thinking about it in bed. We were so busy assuming the phone had been dumped, but it struck me afterwards that it was most likely in the school still, being hidden by somebody. We missed a trick, to be honest, but at least I got to play catch up.'

'It was a good call, boss, I'd never have thought of it.'

This man was full of contradictions. One moment he was undermining her, the next he was pinning a medal on her chest for good police work.

Hollie clapped her hands once again to get the attention of the room. She didn't need to, they were all on alert, waiting to find out what would happen next.

'Okay, everybody, I'm sorry that we're going to have to keep you here a little longer. My team will need to chat with all of you before you leave the room. We need to know why Kyle Wilson's phone was in Tilly's bag. If you can help with that, now is the time to come forward. Mr Canfield, would you be able to organise a couple of teachers to sit in on each interview?'

He gave her a nod and exited the drama studio.

'What if we need to pee?'

It was Zach Eastwood. Of course it was. He had that same cocky look on his face, and a smirk, as he played to the crowd. There was nervous laughter from a couple of the other students.

'I'm sure my colleague, DS Patel, will be happy to accompany you if you're unable to wait,' she replied, 'but I'd like to think that a lad like you would be able to exert a little bladder control.'

There was more nervous laughter and Zach let it pass, a scowl on his face. She didn't want to get into a run-in with this kid, especially with Mr Canfield now out of the room.

Hollie handed over to Ben Anderson and had a quiet word with Amber before leaving.

'Watch we don't scare the life out of the kids,' she warned. 'I'll send DC Philpot and DC Norton down to help with the interviews. I know it's not enough bodies but do the best you can. I want to know how Tilly Mann got that phone and if anybody saw anything.'

'Will do, boss. It's like being a teacher – I can't say I fancy it.'

Hollie lowered her voice.

'Me neither. Watch Zach Eastwood, will you? I get a bad feeling about that kid.'

Hollie left them to it, knowing it was a tough job for them with so few officers available, but keen to plug all potential leaks.

Hollie checked in on the conference room on her way out and found that Harry had already got Tilly's bag processed and sent over to HQ. They'd get the phone fingerprinted and then the tech guys would be all over it.

She dispatched DCs Norton and Philpot to the drama studio, then exited the building via the front entrance, relieved that they'd now succeeded in dispatching the crowd of parents. The pack of reporters was still there though, immediately alert to the case lead exiting the building.

'Anything new to report, DI Turner,' a radio reporter called to her.

'As soon as we have anything to share, we'll let you know' Hollie fobbed them off as she walked through the car park to her car.

Hollie felt sorry for the reporters and was tempted to throw them a bone by letting him know about the phone. Her inclination to sympathy was overruled by her copper's air miles and she kept quiet about it. The weather wasn't bad; there were worse days to be stuck outside in the hope of catching some breaking news.

Hollie checked the address and tapped the postcode into her sat nav. It was another property on the Kingswood estate;

she was much better off being guided in rather than going old-school and trying to figure it out as she went along.

On the drive over she reflected on what she knew about Tilly. She had been suddenly closer with Zach – apparently – but there was tension with Jake, who'd been jealous as a result. There had been some violence, too, instigated by Jake. Her instincts told her there was more to this than simple jealousy.

She pulled up outside Tilly's house. DC Langdon's vehicle was still parked outside, so it was easy to identify the correct property. It was detached, modern and well-kept; someone in Tilly's household had a decent job.

Jenni opened the door.

'Tilly's mum is here, she's a lecturer at the university,' she whispered.

Hollie shared with her what had happened after she'd left the drama studio.

'You're kidding?' Jenni said, an incredulous look on her face. 'Why would Tilly carry Kyle's phone into a room full of coppers? Surely somebody slipped it into her bag—'

'Well, we're about to find out. What did you make of her on the drive over?' Hollie checked.

'She's up in her room now, waiting for her stomach to settle. I'd say she's scared out of her wits. Something's up, but she wouldn't talk to me about it.'

'Okay, what's the mum like?'

'Fine, but worried, as you'd expect. I told her you were coming.'

Jenni led the way back into the house.

'Mrs Mann, this is my boss, Detective Inspector Turner.'

'Hello, detective, I've seen you on the TV news. Come in, take a seat.'

Hollie shook her hand. She had a confident grip. It was an academic house with textbooks strewn all over; it seemed like she had several books on the go at once. Mrs Mann had the same kind of facial expression that she might have had if Hollie were a doctor about to deliver terrible news about her daughter's health.

'Tilly is upstairs – her face was white when she came in.'

'I'm afraid we're going to have to interview Tilly under caution,' Hollie started.

There seemed to be a lot of movement upstairs. Hollie knew how noisy and creaky modern floorboards could be, but it sounded like Tilly was moving furniture up there.

The expression on Mrs Mann's face changed. She'd seen it so many times before; she was getting ready to protect her child.

'Why, what's Tilly supposed to have done?'

'After she left the drama studio, we located Kyle Wilson's mobile phone in Tilly's bag—'

'That's impossible—'

'I'm sure there's a reasonable explanation for it, but we'll need to interview Tilly at the station, and she will need legal representation—'

'For fuck's sake! Ever since she got involved with that Eastwood kid, it's been nothing but drama.'

'How so?'

Tilly's mother had just gone from zero to one hundred miles per hour on the emotional front.

There was a thump on the floor overhead.

Hollie glanced at Jenni, and they started getting out of their chairs at the same time.

'What on earth is she doing up there?' Mrs Mann said.

Hollie rushed towards the staircase and took the stairs two at a time. Jenni followed directly behind her. There was thudding, like something was striking one of the doors.

It wasn't difficult to see which was Tilly's bedroom, as it was the only door that was closed. Hollie didn't bother knocking; she burst into the bedroom, with an overwhelming sense that something wasn't right.

The moment she pushed at the door, it felt heavy, and she could see something tied up at the corner. Hollie pushed at the door and gasped as she realised what the obstruction was.

Tilly was hanging from her bedroom door, a scarf around her neck, her hands bound with a thin red belt, and her feet thumping against the wood as she struggled for life.

THIRTY-SIX

WEDNESDAY, 13:02

'Jenni, help me get her down!'

Tilly's legs were thrashing violently, her face was purple, and saliva was coming out of her mouth.

'Hold the door still.'

Hollie wrapped her arms around Tilly's waist and lifted her body. Her mother was now upstairs, screaming at them to save her.

'Tilly... no... Oh my god... Do something... please... Get her off the door, get her off... is she breathing still?'

'Grab the scarf!' Hollie said to Jenni, calm and methodical. If they lost their cool, Tilly wouldn't make it out of there. Hollie was supporting Tilly's weight, but the noose she'd made was still hooked over the corner of the door and it was pulled tight. Hollie kicked behind her to move the computer chair out of the way; that's what she must have stood on to raise herself to a suitable height. Jenni unhooked the scarf and then assisted Hollie in lowering Tilly gently to the floor. She'd stopped thrashing now, but the scarf was still tightly pulled in at her neck. Hollie slipped her fingers behind Tilly's neck and loosened the ligature; it had drawn blood. Tilly gasped for breath.

Her mother was out of her mind, in a blind panic.

'Tilly... Tilly... what have you done?'

Hollie needed her out of the way and occupied.

'Mrs Mann, I need you to listen to me carefully. Call an ambulance right now,' Hollie said calmly but authoritatively, her hand gently pressed against the devastated woman's arm.

Mrs Mann managed to pull herself up and out to the landing and used her mobile phone to make the call.

'Tilly, you're okay, we've got you,' Hollie spoke softly. Tilly's face was a terrible colour, and her breathing sounded contorted.

'I'm going to gently place her in the recovery position,' Hollie announced. Jenni moved to the side but held Tilly's hand while Hollie carefully manoeuvred her into a better position. The ambulance was no time coming, it was all a blur, but Hollie reckoned she heard its siren before Mrs Mann had even finished the call.

As the colour returned to Tilly's face, she began to sob, her voice raw from the ordeal she'd just endured.

'I blame you for this!' Mrs Mann shouted. She was screaming at Jenni. 'What did you say to her on the drive over? You must have scared the life out of her. You made her do this!'

Hollie turned her head and could see her colleague was out of her depth.

'Mrs Mann, I'd like a glass of water for your daughter. Can you go and get that for me?'

She'd learned some useful skills as a beat bobby, often first on the scene in a crisis situation. She'd found giving loved ones a job a useful distraction; it allowed those with calmer heads to get on with saving lives.

For a second, Hollie saw Lily's face as she looked down at Tilly's fragile body. What was so bad that it had made suicide an option for a girl like Tilly?

The paramedics were downstairs already; she heard them

thundering up the stairs and she stood back to let them take over.

'Talk me through how you found her and what you did.'

Hollie spoke while the medics worked. When the questions had stopped, she left Tilly's bedroom, leaving them to it. Mrs Mann was standing on the landing, her face white, her hand trembling, as she held onto the glass of water which she'd gone to fetch.

'Let's go downstairs,' Jenni said, taking the glass with one hand and guiding her with the other. Mrs Mann's panic had now turned to shock. The sounds coming from Tilly's bedroom were not pleasant to hear, so Hollie led the way downstairs.

'Get a hot drink on,' she whispered to Jenni as she sat Mrs Mann on the sofa. Hollie sat next to her and took her hand, giving it a gentle squeeze; it was ice cold.

'Was she breathing?' Mrs Mann asked, her voice dazed and robotic.

'She's alive. We got to her in time. You did well; the paramedics will look after her.'

Mrs Mann started to sob, but it was choked, and her tears wouldn't come.

'Why would she do that? We were downstairs, she could have talked to us.'

Hollie thought of Lily and Noah. She wondered where Izzy was and if she was safe. She wished she could have hugged them at that moment and made sure they were all okay. A world in which a child felt suicide was the best option was a desolate one.

'I think Tilly may be caught up in something which is beyond her control,' Hollie said softly. 'I think that was probably a cry for help. I know it's a terrible time to ask you this, but it will help us if we can work out what's going on here. Has Tilly been behaving differently?'

Jenni brought in a mug of tea for Mrs Mann, and she took it gratefully. Jenni sat in the opposite armchair.

'Something's not been right, but I just put it down to exam pressure,' she began. 'She's been withdrawn recently, but sometimes it's so difficult to reach teenagers. She may have been scratching her arms, too. I challenged her about it the other day, but she fobbed me off, saying the washing powder we're using is irritating her skin.'

One of the paramedics appeared on the staircase.

'Any allergies or adverse reactions we need to know about?' she asked.

'No, nothing,' Mrs Mann replied. 'Is Tilly okay?'

'She'll be fine, but we'll need to take her to hospital so she can have a psychological assessment, too.'

The paramedic returned upstairs.

'What does that mean?'

It wasn't the time to speak to her about sectioning; hopefully it wouldn't come to that. Either way, Tilly would be placed on a suicide watch. She wondered how long it would be until they could talk to her.

'She's in good hands,' Hollie answered. It seemed best not to overwhelm her; she'd get embroiled in all of that detail soon enough.

'She's got a place at Oxford, you know.'

That seemed to come out of the blue. Hollie exchanged a look with Jenni.

'That's good,' Jenni replied. 'She must have worked hard to achieve that.'

'She did. She is working hard, too, to get her grades. That's why I was so upset when she started talking with that Eastwood boy. I don't like him. I wondered if she and Jake might get married once upon a time – they made such a sweet couple.'

'Is Tilly's father around?' Hollie ventured. She couldn't see any photographs, but she thought he'd probably want to know what was going on.

'He's dead. He died four years ago. It was a brain tumour.'

'I'm so sorry.'

Hollie and Jenni both spoke at once.

'It was horrible. We were actually still in love. It destroyed our world at first. But I thought Tilly and I were good – I thought things were okay now. Tilly was looking forward to going to Oxford. I don't know why she'd do something like that.'

Hollie felt wretched. She'd got to thinking about Léon like the villain of their relationship, but up until his affair, she'd been happy in the marriage. And he was still the father of two of her kids – no, he was a brilliant father to Izzy, too – he was a parent to all of her kids. The children would be bereft if he died; she had to remember that while they were tussling about their future. It all felt so silly and pointless when she heard stories like the Manns'.

'What did you know about Zach and Tilly's relationship?' Hollie pushed gently. 'Were they just friends?'

She could hear the paramedics getting ready to take Tilly out to the ambulance. They had a short window in which to gather as much information as possible.

'I'm not sure you can even call it that. She just seemed suddenly to be talking to Zach all the time. He came round to the house once, and I didn't like him. He has his own car; his dad is some local business hotshot. He wasn't good for Tilly—'

'That's us, do you want to ride in the ambulance with her?' The paramedic looked down on them from the staircase.

'Yes, of course, can I?'

Mrs Mann stood up and walked over towards the staircase.

Hollie and Jenni followed behind.

'Oh, Tilly will want her phone in hospital, would you get it for me, detective?'

She made it sound like Tilly was popping in to have her tonsils removed.

'Of course,' Hollie replied. She knew already that they'd returned it to Tilly after they'd failed to retrieve anything useful from her text messages.

'Do you want to accompany Mrs Mann to the ambulance, DC Langdon?'

Jenni took her arm, and they stood to the side as Tilly was moved down the stairs on a stretcher. There was a red-raw wound around her neck where the ligature had pulled tight. It was a damn good job they'd rushed up there to help her.

As Tilly was taken out of the house, Mrs Mann handed Hollie the door key, then followed her daughter out to the ambulance.

Hollie made her way back to Tilly's room and scanned for her phone. It was discarded on the bed, so she picked it up and, by habit, looked at the screen. It hadn't reverted to phone lock yet. The last thing Tilly had read was still active on the screen. It looked like a text message, but no name had been assigned to the number.

> They found Kyle's phone in your bag. That copper's heading over to your place now. I told you to keep your fucking mouth shut.

THIRTY-SEVEN

I did something really stupid tonight.

I'm still shaking, I still can't believe I did it.

Mum told me we're going to lose the house if we can't make a full payment by the end of next week.

They send bailiffs round if things get too bad.

They can take your TV and computers and stuff.

I don't know why I'm making these recordings, they're just stupid.

I'm stupid.

There are CCTV cameras in the annexe.

I was messing about with the unit this evening and it switched on.

It's never been on before, I don't think Yasmine and Mr Yerbury use it.

Nick, I mean, Mr Yerbury, told me to start calling him Nick when he gave me my own key.

What a fucking legend that man is.

Evie and Quinn-bloody-Varney were making out in the living area tonight.

I think they had another one of their get-togethers on.

Canfield would shit his pants if he knew.

Anyway, I was just messing about with the CCTV, and they came in when I was recording.

It needed an SD disc, so I slipped one of mine in to test it.

They were all over each other. I thought Evie hated men.

I could see everything.

It's got microphone pick-ups, too, so I could hear what they were saying.

I was going to turn it off, I really was—

I didn't look at what they were doing. I turned the monitor screen off, but it kept recording.

I didn't want to listen either, so I turned the volume down.

It was private shit, it was embarrassing, too.

I was going to step out and let them know I was there, but Evie had her bra off and I didn't want to... well, I didn't want to embarrass them.

Evie's mum and dad are really posh; they give her an allowance to live on.

Quinn's the same, he's well off, and sometimes it feels like we're the only family without any money.

Jake's the only one who's broke like us.

Anyway, I'm not proud of myself, but I took the SD card out and I edited the video file so you can see them getting down to business.

I didn't watch it, it makes me feel sick, but I've had an idea—

I'm sure I won't do it, but I've thought of a way I could make that money for the rent.

I'd be a right bastard if I did it—

No, I won't do it.

They'd never forgive me.

Hollie was still shaking from the shock of what Tilly had done when she got back to the academy. She'd instructed Jenni to do some desk work in the canteen and stay out of harm's way. Hollie was annoyed with herself for exposing the young officer to such a traumatic event when she was supposed to be recovering.

Hollie had rung ahead to make sure Evie Keane was still on school premises. She was waiting in a private room with Amber Patel, ready for a follow-up interview.

'You do understand why we've asked you to speak to us, don't you?' Hollie began.

She counted the piercings in Evie's left ear; she reckoned there were five, though she might have missed one. She had small tattoos on her neck and arms. Hollie thought them tasteful and artistic and wondered for a moment if she ought to consider getting one where it wouldn't be seen at work. There was a time, as a young girl, when it was mostly men who sported traditional markings, usually on their arms, with messages like *Mum* and pictures of skulls and anchors. Since then, the entire industry had undergone an overhaul and there was some wonderful artwork on peoples' bodies. She knew Léon wasn't particularly keen – but then he'd written himself out of the script now, hadn't he?

'Not really,' Evie replied to her question in a monotone voice. 'You know what my mum does, right? If you're not following the correct procedure, she'll be on your case.'

Hollie knew all right. Anderson told her they'd run it by DCI Osmond before they hauled Evie into the small room. She was definitely eighteen years of age – an adult in the eyes of the law – and Mr Canfield and Mrs Dreyfuss were sitting in for safeguarding purposes, even though it wasn't strictly required. Hollie had asked DS Patel to sit in with her, too, fearing that Anderson might be a little too blunt and land them in trouble. The school had tried to reach Evie's mother, but she was in court. She was a barrister, ironically. At least Hollie's arse was covered.

'This is not a formal interview, Evie, you're not under suspicion and you're not under arrest. I'd just like to ask you a couple of background questions about Dirty Little Secrets—'

'It's just a shop, you know. We sell stuff, people buy it. Everybody gets all silly about it 'cause it's sex stuff. Well, get over it, I say, it's completely normal.' Evie seemed older than her years.

'When I was eighteen, I pulled pints in a pub,' Amber remarked like she was chatting to a friend. 'What made you choose an adult shop, Evie?'

Mr Canfield shuffled in his chair.

'Probably the same reason as you worked in a pub. They advertised a job, and the hours fitted in with school, I applied, and I got it. I like the customers, too, they're cooler than most places. They're more open-minded.'

'What did your parents say?' Hollie wondered. 'Your dad runs a firm of solicitors in the city centre, I believe? I'll bet they have an opinion on that, don't they?'

'My mum and dad have an opinion on everything. They don't like it, but they can get stuffed. I'm eighteen now and I can do what I want.'

'I notice from a previous interview with one of my team that you don't live at home, Evie?' Hollie said, checking the notes that Amber had provided.

'No, I live in a flat above the shop—'

'The adult shop?'

Evie nodded.

'How long have you lived there?' Hollie wondered.

'Three months, maybe.'

'Why don't you live at home?' Amber followed up. Mr Canfield and Mrs Dreyfuss didn't appear to know that information, certainly not from the look they had just exchanged.

'Me and my parents don't get on.'

'How do you pay the rent?' Hollie pushed, mindful that they had to maintain a light touch for now.

'I get an allowance. Dad pays it.'

'Even though you don't get on?' Amber continued.

'Yeah, sure, I'm still his little girl, aren't I? We agreed to do it while things were so tense at home. We weren't getting on, like I just told you.'

'Why not?' Hollie said.

'You know, stuff. They're not comfortable with my life choices. They still think you get married to the first person you sleep with and then marry for life—'

Hollie and Amber let that hang for a moment, hoping she'd carry on without prompting. It looked like the two most senior members of the academy's leadership team were also getting an education about modern relationship goals, too.

Evie filled the silence as they'd hoped.

'They didn't like Zach for starters.'

Amber got in there faster than Hollie.

'You were dating Zach?'

'Not dating, it was casual. I've slept with a couple of the boys in our year group, so what? Zach's hot, even if he is a bit of a dick sometimes.'

Mr Canfield's face was beetroot red. He looked like a vicar who'd just stumbled upon a copy of the Kama Sutra.

'Quinn, too, it's just a laugh though, you know? It's just messing about.'

'Were you sleeping with Quinn before or after he left the school?' Hollie asked.

'Before and after. He stayed in touch when he left. He still drinks with us in town.'

Hollie thought about Lily, who was almost fourteen. A time bomb had just started ticking in the part of her mind where anxiety lurked.

'Where do you all drink?' said Amber.

'Melvins. That's where you'll usually find us.'

She saw from Hollie's face that further explanation was required.

'It's a bar in the Old Town. It's nice and lively there, they have bands sometimes. We all like it.'

'So, just for clarification, Evie,' Hollie checked, 'you had close relationships with Zach and Quinn. Not Kyle?'

'Not relationships, just casual stuff, you know. Kyle wasn't interested in relationships, at least I don't think he was. I did try my luck with Sammy once, but she and Matt are joined at the hip.'

'Sammy?'

'Samantha Ingram, she and Matthew Urquhart are a couple,' Olivia Dreyfuss explained. Hollie recalled that Matt had spoken about Kyle in the earlier session with the sixth formers, and she'd noted that he and the girl he was sitting next to seemed to be close.

Mr Canfield was clearly struggling at the thought of all the heterosexual combinations, and the suggestion of bisexuality made him look like a Neanderthal shopping in an electrical store.

This was a revelation to Hollie, and it threw new light on the case. Was this all about messy relationships, spurned lovers and wounded egos? Yet Evie just told her that Kyle wasn't interested in relationships, so perhaps it didn't involve him.

'Did any of your friends ever come into Dirty Little Secrets?' Amber changed the topic. It was a good question, and Hollie wished she'd asked it. It might explain how the business card made its way to the outbuilding.

'Yes, on Saturdays when I was working there on my own. They'd just come in for a chat.'

'Who came in?' Hollie encouraged her.

'Zach, Quinn...' Evie seemed to be considering something. 'And Kyle,' she added. 'Never Matt and Sammy, they're too loved up and besides, you've got to be over eighteen for me to let you in. Oh, and it wasn't Tilly's thing either, she's far too puritanical for that. Jake didn't come because Tilly wouldn't like it.'

'Why did Kyle come in?' Hollie wondered. 'What would he be doing there? He was only seventeen, wasn't he?'

'He only came in once,' Evie answered, hesitating a little. 'Perhaps he was looking for a job.'

'So any one of those boys might have picked up that business card?' Amber confirmed.

'Yes, sure. As well as anybody who came into the shop when I wasn't working there and their parents and any of the teachers or support staff who work at the academy. It's a shop. Anybody over the age of eighteen is perfectly entitled to be in there.'

Hollie had hoped speaking to Evie might help to clarify a few points, but every time she answered a question it seemed to throw up more possibilities. She changed the subject.

'How do you think Kyle's phone found its way to Tilly Mann's bag?'

Evie's expression suggested she hadn't been ready for that question. She recovered quickly.

'I guess you're the detectives, you'll figure it out.'

'Did one of the students place it there?' Amber pushed her.

'Once again, I'm sure you'll figure it out.'

Hollie wondered if this was how things would be with Noah and Lily when they got older. She'd been mercifully spared this ordeal with Izzy, but that was only because her older daughter had taken on so many adult responsibilities, looking after the younger kids while she was late at work.

Hollie was about to snap, but she checked herself. She considered for one moment revealing what Tilly had done, but that was confidential information and not hers to share with a student.

'Tilly seemed so upset. Doesn't that bother you? She's a friend, isn't she?'

Evie shrugged. 'Yeah, I suppose so. I mean, she hangs around our group. She's a bit of a mouse for my tastes, but she's okay.' Evie appeared to have thought of something. 'Hey, maybe she was looking after Kyle's phone for him. They used to be good pals, Tilly and Kyle. Maybe that's why she had it.'

Yes, and pigs might fly, Evie.

Hollie was struggling with her patience. These kids were holding something back, but without a compelling clue or incriminating evidence, her hands were tied. She couldn't go arresting young students at random; it could screw up their future careers if they messed this up.

'Is there anything else you can tell us which might help us to track down the people who hurt Kyle?' she asked at last.

Evie looked her directly in the eye and didn't hesitate before answering.

'You're looking in the wrong place. Try Nick Yerbury and Yasmine Drake. They'll be able to tell you what Kyle was up to.'

THIRTY-NINE
WEDNESDAY, 15:06

Hollie made directly for the canteen once they were finished with Evie Keane. The catering staff were long gone, but they'd left an array of crockery, beverage options and several catering flasks which had been filled with hot water. She found Jenni Langdon there working alone on her police issue laptop.

'Hi, how's it going?' Hollie asked. 'I'd like you to check in for some trauma counselling when you can find a suitable time. That was horrible what happened earlier.'

Jenni had a printout of the interior of Kyle's locker sitting on the table. She'd added several scribbles to it. That seemed odd, but Hollie assumed it was there for a good reason.

'That poor girl.' Jenni grimaced. 'How soon until we can talk to her?'

'Not soon enough,' Hollie replied. 'There's something bothering that girl and we need to know what it is.'

They were silent for a couple of moments, before Jenni turned back to her laptop.

'I checked in with DC Hayes. Isla Wilson doesn't know what that PIN refers to. She said the numbers four, seven, nine, two don't hold any significance as far as she knows, so I'm guessing they're just random. Perhaps his bank card?'

'Yes, I thought of that. Kyle's bank card was retrieved from his bedroom; one of the team is checking it out.'

Hollie sighed. There were so many crumbs but none of them seemed to lead anywhere.

'I need to get over to see Lance Fairclough about Kyle's tech. Have you heard anything more yet?'

Jenni shook her head. Hollie knew anything crucial would be flagged immediately but still, it was like pulling teeth.

'The students' social media profiles have drawn a blank so far.' Jenni changed the subject. 'These kids are far too well trained – they have their social accounts locked down.'

'They seem to be so tech-savvy these days,' Hollie remarked. 'It would make life a whole lot easier if they weren't so adept with their devices.'

'I can see that most of the students are on Tinder. I can't believe that at their age. I'm still in my twenties and even my generation was still doing things the good old-fashioned way—'

'What, courting with a chaperone and asking fathers for permission to get married?' Hollie smiled.

'Not quite.' Jenni grinned. 'But we weren't all on hook-up sites... not at eighteen, at least.'

'You look like something's on your mind,' Hollie observed. 'Come on, you can confess it to me.'

'I want to be doing something useful, boss. I want to be interviewing the students and doing something more active.'

'Checking the social profiles is crucial to the investigation,' Hollie began. 'And I already feel guilty enough about what you saw with Tilly Mann.'

Jenni screwed up her face.

'You know what I mean, boss. There's loads that I could be doing here, and I'm stuck with light duties again. I promise you

I'll tell you the moment I have any health worries, if you'll just let me get my hands dirty.'

Hollie studied her young colleague. She'd certainly missed having Jenni about; she enjoyed their banter.

'Okay, here's the deal. You have to promise me not to get involved in anything that even raises your pulse level. And you're certainly forbidden from going off and doing any investigating on your own. If you promise me that, I'll assign you to something more interesting. Promise?'

'Of course, boss. I've written up everything I found online and sent it to you as a report. The TL:DR version is that several of the sixth formers are using Tinder, their accounts are locked down, and I can't find any trace of Kyle, but he may have all his accounts locked down, too. I've trawled far and wide. Now, can I give you two bits of information that I think you'll find useful?'

Hollie pulled up a chair next to Jenni. Once again, it was the uncomfortable, plastic variety that even Hollie recalled from her secondary school days. Some things never changed.

'Okay, go ahead. I'm all ears.'

'Well, it's been interesting just being here and lurking, watching the comings and goings. I've seen things that the rest of the team might not have observed.'

'Like what?'

'That Nick Yerbury fellow, the teacher. Did you know that he and the counsellor are romantically involved?'

'No. That's interesting. How do you know?'

'I've been sitting here working for a couple of hours. They came in between interviews; I caught a hand touch while they were waiting for their drinks to be served.'

'Does it have a bearing on the case?'

'It might do. I've seen a number of sixth formers speaking to the counsellor. She's very chatty and relaxed with them—'

'That's to be expected, bearing in mind what's happened—'

'Yes, but the pattern seems off somehow.'

'What do you mean?'

'Just lots of one-on-one, earnest and hushed chats.'

'They're all coming up to exams. And one of their group just died.'

'I know, I know. But later, when I was visiting the ladies' loos, I saw Nick and the counsellor arguing about something in the car park.'

'A lover's tiff?'

'It seemed more earnest than that.'

'How old do you think Yasmine Drake is?' she deflected.

'My kind of age? Twenty-three or twenty-four maybe? Why, boss?'

'She's almost the same age as the sixth formers here. I mean, there's not much in it, is there? What about Nick?'

'Older, I'd say. Thirties?'

'Where are Yasmine and Nick now?'

'They'll be helping with the interviews. Amber has been meticulous with the safeguarding stuff.'

Hollie was just getting up from her chair, which was already making her backside sore, when Jenni put out her hand to encourage her to sit down again.

'There's one more thing, boss.'

'Blimey, you can't keep a good woman down. You've been busy while you've been sitting here.'

'Yes, boss, I've been trawling through all the evidence that we've gathered so far. And I've got a ridiculous hunch that I'd like you to indulge me with.'

'This is getting better by the minute. I'm going to get you an armchair and a pair of slippers and a pipe. I reckon you'll have the case cracked by the end of the day.'

'I want to get another look inside Kyle's locker if I can.'

'Really? Why?'

'I think I spotted something in the photos that were taken

when it was first located, and I want to be sure. I want to take a second look, rather than having to study a photo.'

'Can you give me a clue?'

'Sure. I think Kyle has a second locker.'

'How the hell did you reach that conclusion?'

'That picture of Olly Alexander – did you notice he'd got a number written on his T-shirt?' She picked up the image of Kyle's locker. Sitting underneath it was a list of locker allocations provided by the academy for reference.

'I did and I didn't. I saw it, but it's just a number.'

'I think it might be more than that. Have we searched all the lockers yet?'

'Not all of them, there's a lot to work through. The sixth-formers' lockers are clear. Why?'

'Well, the lockers are numbered in year group order, so Year Seven has locker numbers 001 to 199, Year Eight have locker numbers 200 to 399 and so on. There are no more than two hundred students in each year group, with the exception of the sixth form where the numbers go down a bit as students have other options when they're sixteen. Some go to college, or they take on apprenticeships or traineeships.'

'You're beginning to sound like a careers adviser. How does this link to Kyle?'

'Well, the sixth formers get bigger lockers. They're much nicer, too. And the locker numbers start from 0 again and go as far as 100, as there aren't many left in school by that age. The number on Olly's T-shirt was 913. Did you notice it was drawn on with a sharpie? It's not part of the original photograph.'

'You sound like Inspector Clouseau warming up for his final denouement. How does this all piece together though?'

'Just before you joined me, I checked that number on the list of lockers and their owners that Olivia Dreyfuss provided for us. Number 913 is the number of Quinn Varney's locker.'

Hollie was trying to put it all together and leap ahead of what Jenni was trying to tell her.

'But Quinn's a sixth former. Besides, he's not at the school anymore.'

'Yes, but according to Mrs Dreyfuss, Quinn asked to keep the same locker he'd had in his GCSE year. They weren't short of lockers, so they agreed. Which means he was using the 800-999 lockers.'

'So how come his locker is still there now he's left?'

'The key is marked as lost. The school didn't need it, so they haven't bothered getting a replacement cut yet.'

'What are you saying then?'

Hollie couldn't grasp where this was leading.

'I think Kyle might have something stored in that locker. I think he might have had the key to it. Why else would he have written down the number like that? It's a bit of a coincidence that it matches the locker of the home-educated kid, don't you think?'

The penny finally dropped.

'Jenni, this is brilliant—'

'It might be a complete dead end, of course—'

'I'll bet it isn't. I don't believe in coincidences. Mrs Dreyfuss!'

Hollie called out to the vice-principal who she'd noticed chatting to one of the teachers at the far side of the hall.

Olivia Dreyfuss located the passkey for the relevant set of lockers and walked with Hollie and Jenni to save them from having to hunt the school to find where they were located.

'So, you don't replace keys when students lose them?' Hollie checked with her.

'No, we'd be doing it all the time if we did that. We wait until we've got ten or more to get cut, then do it as a job lot. If we're not short on locker space, it's not a problem.'

'Why did Quinn get to retain his old locker?' Hollie asked.

'We try not to be too inflexible about these things, especially with sixth formers. They're young adults, and Quinn made a perfectly reasonable case for keeping his old locker, so we let him hang onto it.'

They'd reached locker 913. Mrs Dreyfuss pushed the key into the lock and held it there.

'Quinn will have cleared this out before he left, so it'll just be empty, I think.'

'Let's see, shall we?' Hollie urged.

Mrs Dreyfuss turned the key and opened up the door.

'Bloody hell, Jenni!' Hollie exclaimed.

'Language, officer, please!' Mrs Dreyfuss scolded. 'There are still children coming and going to their interviews.'

It was worth the telling off. They were looking at a laptop. And Hollie didn't need to check to know that it belonged to Kyle.

'So did Kyle steal Quinn's key?' Hollie asked.

'Who knows, boss? Why would Kyle need a spare locker?'

Jenni was peering inside the locker from over Hollie's shoulder. Mrs Dreyfuss had a look on her face which suggested she wasn't quite done with her policing career just yet. She offered a theory of her own.

'Because there was something on his laptop he didn't want people to see? Or because he wanted his laptop hidden?'

'Have you got gloves on you, DC Langdon?'

Jenni handed over a pair from a packet in her pocket. She gloved up, too. Olivia Dreyfuss stood at a respectful distance, but looked like she was ready to roll up her sleeves and throw herself into the investigation.

Hollie turned the laptop, so she could lift its lid without having to remove it from the locker. It had numerous stickers on it; a smiley sun face wearing sunglasses, plus a selection of phrases, like *Good Vibes, Bonjour Baby, Smile, you're on camera!* and *Future Spielberg*. The last message gave Hollie pause; Kyle would no longer get the chance to realise his ambitions.

As Hollie pressed the *On* button, the laptop's screen activated for long enough for her to see that it was protected by a login prompt, before it flashed once and died.

'Damn, it's got a run-down battery and no charging lead.'

'Lance Fairclough will have one,' Jenni suggested. 'If you ever forget the charger for your phone, you can always rely on Lance's big box of cables. He'll be able to fire it back into life.'

'I wonder if that PIN Doctor Ruane found will let us in. Would you run up to the conference room and bring an evidence bag down, as well as a box to transport this thing. We'll need to get it over to digital forensics ASAP. Who knows what Kyle's got hidden on here?'

Jenni walked off along the corridor, and Olivia Dreyfuss moved into the space she'd been occupying.

'How easy would it have been for Kyle to steal Quinn's locker key and keep it concealed?' Hollie asked.

'It's easy enough,' Mrs Dreyfuss replied. 'I won't claim that we're on top of the lockers one hundred per cent. It's not the most pressing job at the academy. It's one of those things that's usually saved until the beginning of a school year, when we're forced to sort things out. I must admit, I am surprised that Quinn's locker key hasn't been replaced, but then, if we didn't need the locker space, it wouldn't have mattered.'

'You knew Kyle – would he have stolen a key?'

She shook her head.

'You think you know the kids you see every day, but I would never have thought any of them capable of what's happened at the school this week.'

'If I pushed you though, what would you say?'

'I'd say no. Kyle was one of those students who slipped below the radar. It was only in the past couple of weeks that there seemed to be something hanging in the air.'

'What do you mean by that?'

'Well, you know when you've fallen out with someone

about something, and they won't leave it alone. It's like a scab they won't stop picking.'

Jenni returned carrying a box and a paper cup container into which three steaming drinks were squeezed.

'I've been multi-tasking, boss. I thought we all deserved a coffee after that.'

She placed the coffees on top of the lockers and took a large evidence bag out of the box. Hollie prioritised the laptop over her drink, working with Jenni to get it safely secured in the evidence bag, then placed it in the box.

With the laptop safely secured and placed on top of the lockers, she reached up to take the cardboard coffee holder. As she did so, a splash of coffee landed on her shoe and created a small puddle on the floor.

'Oh heck, I do apologise, Mrs Dreyfuss, your poor caretaker won't thank me for making a sticky mess on his floors.'

'Don't worry, I'll grab a couple of paper towels to mop it up...' Olivia Dreyfuss was away before she'd finished the sentence and reappeared moments later, clutching a handful of towels.

Hollie bent down to mop up the coffee, and as Olivia knelt down to help her, she noticed something small lodged directly below Kyle's locker, in the gap between the floor and the metal structure. She forced her fingers into the small space, doing her best to flick whatever it was out into clear view.

'Here, use my pen,' Olivia Dreyfuss offered.

Hollie pushed it underneath the lockers, and it caught the object immediately. It bounced off the sole of her shoe.

'Damn,' she said, examining the item. 'An SD card. What's the betting this belongs in that hollowed out book I found in Kyle's bedroom?'

FORTY-ONE
WEDNESDAY, 17:04

It was packed in the academy's conference room despite the late time of day. Good use had been made of the canteen facilities and there were cardboard cups filled with steaming drinks perched all around. DCI Osmond had shown up, too.

'Thanks for your efforts today,' Hollie began, surveying the room. 'The team has managed to work through thirty-seven follow-up interviews with lower school students over the course of today. So that means everybody who flagged up something of relevance in yesterday's initial chats has now been spoken to in detail. That's quite an undertaking, bearing in mind we've had to have a staff member in for safeguarding for the majority of them. We've also interviewed all sixth formers today. DS Patel has been collating the information and can give us an overview now.'

DS Patel took a sip of her drink and stood up so everybody could see her.

'So, we've now heard from every child who indicated they might have seen something when we went around the classrooms yesterday. We've discounted six of those children's statements because they hadn't seen anything at all; they were just trying to be helpful. Of the thirty-one remaining interviews, they confirmed everything we knew. So we have a timeline of key moments.'

That was a lot of panning for very little gold.

'Evie Keane was evasive when we spoke to her,' Hollie added. 'She's got the job in the sex shop on Chanterlands Avenue, which connects her with the business card found near to Kyle's body.'

DC Philpot raised his hand. 'I interviewed Matthew Urquhart earlier. It all feels like a well-rehearsed script to me. It seems that Matthew and Sammy returned to the school building before the others anyway.'

'Do the eyewitness statements back that up, DS Patel?'

'Yes, boss,' Amber replied, consulting her notes. 'So, if we take what Doctor Ruane said to be correct, that suggests our list of suspects are Zach Eastwood, Tilly Mann, Evie Keane, Jake Tate and Quinn Varney.'

'But what's their motive?' Hollie asked. 'These are regular kids – everything suggests they're friends. If you'd asked me to guess, I'd say Tilly Mann has never hurt a fly. The girl just tried to kill herself, so none of this adds up. And we still have DC Gordon's theory that the killer may have escaped through that hole in the fence. Was it a parent? It might potentially be Quinn Varney. But surely he'd have been noticed in the group of parents who came into the foyer?'

The room was silent. It was interrupted by a knock at the door. Mrs Robinson, the school receptionist, apologised for interrupting.

'I've got one of the parents at the school gate asking if they can have a word with a member of the investigations team.'

'Go and check that out, will you, Jenni?' Hollie asked.

Jenni stood up and left the room.

She stared at the faces around the room. It was a couple of

hours past the twenty-four-hour mark since Kyle's body had been found.

'I want to speak to Nick Yerbury again ASAP, and I am going to speak to Yasmine Drake directly, to follow up on Evie's cryptic remark. Are the teachers still on site?'

'They've pretty much cleared off for the day,' Anderson answered. 'I thought maybe we could introduce the same working hours into the police force.'

There were some wry laughs and knowing smiles among the gathered officers. Chance would be a fine thing.

'We're also waiting for our forensics teams to report back on Kyle's coat, his lanyard and his rucksack. Please alert me as soon as we receive any updates. Chase that for me, will you, DS Anderson?'

Jenni Langdon had just come back into the conference room, and she clearly had something on her mind. She was holding an object in her hand. Hollie wound up the briefing and beckoned her over.

'What is it, Jenni, you look like you've got something to tell me?'

They moved over to a far corner of the school room where they could talk in private.

'That lady at the school gates gave me this,' Jenni began. 'She asked me to hand it to you personally.'

It was a school leaflet, describing after-school activities available to youngsters.

Hollie turned it around, then unfolded it to see what she'd just been handed.

Scrawled on the inside was a handwritten note.

I need to talk to you. I don't want to do it at school. Beverley Road Baths 7.15 tomorrow morning. Just you, and it must be in confidence.

FORTY-TWO

Tilly reached out to me at school today.

We've known each other since primary school.

We used to read books together in the playground.

There was some shrubbery at the side of the school, and we used to sit in a hollowed area inside it and read our books in peace.

I don't know what happened when we got to the academy.

People change when they become teenagers.

Me and Tilly did.

You do separate lessons for a start, that doesn't help.

And the boys and girls get separated for sport.

Somehow, bit by bit, we grew apart.

It wasn't that we weren't friends, it's just that we drifted our different ways.

She started seeing Jake in sixth form.

I never liked Tilly like that, we were just good friends.

We liked hanging together, that's all there was to it.

I miss those simpler days, it all seemed so easy back then.

I wish we could just retreat into that shrubbery and read our books and shut out the world.

She shoved a note at me in registration this morning.

I don't deserve it, I've been a complete bastard to her.

She was reaching out to me.

She made sure none of the others saw her do it, not even Jake.

We're well past that now, there's no going back.

What I did to them, threatening to expose them like that, when they thought they were alone... private.

I'm not sure I can forgive myself... I've betrayed them all, Tilly especially.

They could never recover from that if I carried out my threat.

FORTY-THREE

WEDNESDAY, 17:32

'So, we can have our academy back now?' Mr Canfield said as Hollie stepped out of the conference room and found him chatting to Olivia Dreyfuss in the foyer. Olivia tactfully walked away as the two senior team members sought each other out for a catch-up.

'Yes, it's all yours,' Hollie began. 'How will you pick up after this? I don't envy your job.'

'It's a bit of a challenge, but I'm sure we'll work through it. I'm going to see Kyle's mother this evening, just to check in on her.'

Hollie recalled Evie's earlier remark about Nick Yerbury and Yasmine Drake.

'Is Yasmine Drake still in school?' Hollie changed the subject. The young teacher had been bothering her. It was funny how some names seemed to work their way to the top of the list in any case. 'I met her yesterday when I was interviewing Mickey and Finlay, but I haven't seen her around today.'

'She's part-time, I'm afraid, she does a partial day on Wednesday and is off on Thursdays.'

That was not the answer Hollie wanted. She'd have to pay Yasmine a home visit tomorrow. She'd pull Jenni in for that one.

'What can you tell me about her?' Hollie continued.

'She's one of the academy's rising stars,' Canfield replied, without hesitation. 'Due to the way our budgets work, we find ourselves top-heavy with younger teachers. Yasmine shone from the moment she walked through the door and she's not that long out of university. She makes an excellent counsellor; the students seem to really relate to her.'

'Is she in a relationship with Mr Yerbury?'

Jenni had spotted them already and Evie had alluded to the same thing. Nick Yerbury hadn't thought to mention it, but then, why would he?

Mr Canfield looked around and lowered his voice.

'Now, you know I can't discuss confidential staff matters, Detective—'

'Consider this a policing matter. I'm just interested to understand the relationship between the two teachers. We know they're romantically involved.'

Mr Canfield sighed.

'I don't pretend to understand the relationships these younger people have nowadays, they seem to be very fluid and flexible. I think you'd describe it as an on-off relationship. It's the only time I've had to have a quiet word with Miss Drake, after a lover's spat spilled out into the refectory one day.'

'Really? What happened?'

'It was something about nothing. Miss Drake inherited her parents' house at the age of twenty.'

'Both parents are dead?'

'Yes, it was a tragedy. They died in a pile-up on the M62 coming back from a holiday via Leeds Airport. Yasmine was in the car at the time and was the only survivor. You'll notice a scar just below her right ear.'

Hollie hadn't noticed it but she sure as hell would be looking for it next time they spoke.

'It's a wonder that's the only injury she sustained. Mr Yerbury is in and out of her house, I think. I'd describe it as tempestuous, but since my warning, they keep it out of school.'

'And how would you describe them as teachers? This is strictly related to the case, by the way.'

'As I said, Yasmine is a rising star...' He paused as if choosing his words carefully. 'As for Nick Yerbury, he's what you might call a bit of a maverick. These young teachers, they have much more relaxed relationships with the students than my generation did.'

'In what way?'

'Well, they socialise out of school for starters. We would never have done that in my day, yet I see what an excellent rapport they have with the teenagers and, sometimes, I wonder if it's all for the better.'

'You said they socialise out of school – in what way?'

'If they meet in town they might join each other for drinks. If the students are of legal age, there's not much anybody can do to stop it, but it just feels...'

'Inappropriate?' Hollie tried to fill in the blank.

'I'm not sure I'd even go as far as that,' Canfield replied. 'Ill-advised, perhaps? Anyway, I've had a quiet word with Nick about it and he assures me all is well.'

'And you're happy with that?'

'I have to take his word for it unless I see something for myself, or somebody makes a complaint. I did receive one such complaint from a parent, but I was reassured by Miss Drake and Mr Yerbury that everything was above board.'

'May I know the name of the parent?'

'It was Sammy Ingram's mother, she's one of our parent governors at the academy.'

Yasmine Drake and Nick Yerbury had just worked their

way to the top of her to-do list for the next day. She made a mental note to listen to the audio from the interviews that had been carried out by other members of her team.

'That's all very interesting, thank you,' Hollie said. 'I'm going to move the bulk of my team back to HQ now, but we'll retain the uniformed officers on the school gates, and I'll keep a small team of detectives based in the conference room until we make an arrest. We may need to pull pupils and teachers out of lessons occasionally, just to fill in any gaps, but we'll try to disrupt school life as little as possible.'

Hollie concluded her handover with Mr Canfield, then sought out DS Anderson.

'I'll need you to lead on the morning briefing tomorrow. I may be delayed.'

She filled him in about the meeting she'd got at Beverley Baths the next day.

'We really need something solid from forensics – some incriminating DNA, a crucial file on that SD card... anything. It's all just eluding us at the moment.'

Hollie was ready to go home. She signed off with the numerous officers who were closing down investigative tasks around the school, then headed out to the car park. The parents were all gone now and the journalists had called it a day; an arrest would take the heat out of things, but that still seemed a long way off.

Hollie was about to head directly home but she was eager to speak to Quinn Varney again about that second locker. It couldn't wait until morning; she needed to know what was going on there. She diverted to his house on the way back. Things hadn't ended well with his mother when they'd called earlier, and she hoped they might have cooled down a little.

It was Quinn who answered the door; his mother was out

with friends, he explained to her. Quinn looked drained, and she assumed he was caught up in exam revision.

'Hi, Quinn, may I come in for a quick chat?'

'My mum's not here. You heard what she told you earlier.'

'That's okay, you're eighteen now, but I'm happy to come back if you'd rather your mum was with you. It's just an informal chat. I reckon you might be able to help me with a bit of detail. You don't need a solicitor; I just think you can help me clear something up at school. Besides, you might want to tell me things while your mum isn't around.'

Quinn was unsure, and she hoped he wouldn't block her.

'It will help us to find out what happened to Kyle.'

'Okay then,' Quinn agreed begrudgingly.

Hollie took the same seat she'd been sitting in earlier. The plate of biscuits hadn't been moved, yet some of them had been eaten in the meantime. She was ready for food and hoped Quinn might extend some hospitality. He didn't.

'So, what's this about?' Quinn asked.

'It's about your school locker,' Hollie began. 'Tell me what happened to the key.'

'I think you'd better leave,' Quinn replied, guarded and tense.

'It's just a simple question,' Hollie pushed on. 'The school have told me already; I just want to confirm it with you.'

He screwed up his face, then reached over and took one of the biscuits. Hollie watched enviously as he unwrapped it and bit it in half. Her stomach growled. Still, Quinn didn't take the hint.

'Look, I lost it just before I left school, all right?'

'Was it lost or was it stolen?'

'I lost it. That's it. Simple as.'

'Did you report it to the school?'

'There was no point, I was leaving.'

'Do you pay a deposit on the keys?'

'Yes, a fiver.'

'Didn't you want your money back?'

'It's not my money, Mum paid it.'

'Didn't your mum want it back?'

Quinn shrugged.

'Did you clear your stuff out before you lost your key?'

Quinn's face changed. He was doing his best to look calm and in control, but she could see his mind whirring.

'It's just that we opened that locker today and we found Kyle's laptop inside.'

'And? I haven't been a student there for ages.'

'Well, it was your old locker. And we know you've been in and out of the academy since you left.'

'So?'

'Well, here's a wild suggestion. If you hadn't lost your key and you lied about it, that would be a great place to hide Kyle's laptop where nobody would ever think to look for it.'

'You need to leave. My mum's right, this is more than just friendly questioning. You're accusing me—'

'Quinn, I'm not making accusations. They're simply observations. If you put me right on the facts, there won't be a problem, will there?'

'Look, I lost the key. Maybe someone found it or stole it. That's the person you need to find. I've been gone from that place for two months.'

'Only, you haven't really, have you, Quinn? You still see your friends socially. And you're in and out of school seeing Miss Drake.'

'Yes, none of that means anything. I'd like you to go now. I'll call my mum if you don't.'

Hollie stood up, taking a final glance at the plate of biscuits. They were gone forever now, there was no way Quinn was going to offer her one after that exchange.

'I'll just tell you, off the record, that we can bring you in for formal questioning without a parent present now that you're eighteen years of age. It will help both me and you if you cooperate, Quinn. I don't want to have to drive you into the police station, as I know how that looks for a lad your age.'

Quinn glared at her; it was fight or flight time, Hollie could see from the look on his face. He let out a deep sigh.

'Would you like a biscuit?' he said, reaching for another. Hollie could have done a happy dance, right there, right then, in Quinn's living room.

'That would be lovely, thank you,' she replied, taking the largest biscuit available and sitting down again. The chocolate was like an elixir at that time of day. She was more than ready to eat.

Quinn took a while, but he eventually settled and started to speak.

'I am telling you the truth,' he started, slow and deliberate. 'They used to steal my key and then plaster my locker with rude pictures to embarrass me. They'd slip the key back when I wasn't looking.'

'Where did they get the pictures?'

'Just stuff they'd print off the internet. It was stupid stuff. They were just winding me up. It was always the same, until the last time my key went missing.'

'Okay, so what was different when you lost your key the last time?'

'I just assumed they were fooling around again. I'd already cleared my stuff out. So, when the key disappeared and didn't return, I thought fuck it and didn't bother chasing it. The school could keep their fiver and get another one cut.'

'I know you're reluctant to talk about this, Quinn, but why did Zach beat you up at school? What happened there? You've told me he was your friend, but friends don't hurt each other like that.'

Quinn wiped his eyes, and she could see he was working hard not to tear up.

'He turned on me, that's what happened,' Quinn began. 'He was supposed to be my friend. Friends don't do that. But he did.'

'Why, though, Quinn? What made two friends fight like that?'

He looked up at Hollie, his eyes now red.

'Zach and I disagreed about something. I wanted to tell the teachers about something that was going on outside school, but Zach told me not to. I guess it was something he felt strongly about.'

Hollie drove over to HQ after speaking to Quinn, anxious to chase up the forensics teams and make sure the case log was fully up to date. Quinn had clammed up after his tearful revelation. He refused to give any more details, urging her to ask Zach if she wanted to know the truth about what had happened.

DCI Osmond reassured her that he was applying as much pressure as he could to resolve the forensics issues. Hollie knew how it worked, there had been another unexplained death in the city just before Kyle's murder, so she understood that she had to wait her turn. At least they'd managed to fast track Zach Eastwood's bloody T-shirt, otherwise they might have wasted too much time barking up the wrong tree. But she still didn't like that kid.

'Did you get anything off the SD card that I found under Quinn's old locker?' she asked Lance Fairclough, the digital forensics lead. He had the family PC from Isla Wilson's house on his work bench, and it was partially stripped down, like it had been given a thorough going over.

'I'll be honest with you, we're a bit bogged down here. It's encrypted, I'm afraid, so it'll take some time to figure it out. If you asked me to guess, I'd say it fell out of his laptop. The laptop has a small SD card slot, but it seems a little worn to me, so the spring retainer was loose inside.'

'Did you try the PIN that Doctor Ruane found on that scrap of paper? Was it any use?'

'Yes, I've tried it on the laptop and the SD card. No joy, I'm afraid.'

That was frustrating. Hollie had hoped that PIN would lead them somewhere useful. So far, it had just been another dead end.

'So, what have you managed to pull off the PC so far?' Hollie asked.

'Well, you saved me a lot of time figuring out his password, so thank you for that,' Lance began. 'I'm not having the same luck with his laptop, but that's only just made its way back to me after they ran the print and forensic checks on it.'

Lance pointed to the laptop across the room. Hollie recognised it from Quinn's locker.

'So, talk me through it,' she prompted him.

Lance took the mouse at the side of the PC and began to navigate the screen.

'His mum said he used it for gaming, I think?'

'Yes, he lived on his laptop, but used this computer. Has he logged into anything interesting?'

'Well, if he does use it for his socials, it's not very often. I looked at his search history and it's as bland as anything. The problem is these kids know how to use the internet these days. They all know how to clear their cookies and delete their browsing history. So, if he was up to anything and he had any sense, he'd cover his tracks.'

'Okay, so what tracks has he left?'

'There's only one day's worth of browsing history in there. He's been on Instagram, Discord, TikTok and Snapchat. He's logged out of all four and he doesn't store his passwords in the browser, as that would be easy for me—'

'Sorry, just explain for the hard of understanding, please.'

'Several browsers offer to save your passwords. It's not a clever thing to do if you're concerned about security, but lots of people do it. Kyle uses a password manager, look, you can see how he accesses it here.'

Lance clicked on an icon at the top of the browser.

'He knows his stuff, this kid. He uses an authentication app for access, and that's impossible to crack unless I can find his one-time access codes.'

'Okay, so did he access any non-social websites on this PC?'

'Yes, take a look at this browsing history. These are the last sites he looked at on the night before his death.'

Hollie moved in closer so she could see properly. The history showed the websites that Kyle had been looking at and the times he'd searched them.

'That's the MND Association website and the Brain and Spine Foundation website,' Hollie observed. She could have cried when she saw how Kyle had been burrowing down deep into the worst symptoms of MND: *progressive muscular atrophy* and *amyotrophic lateral sclerosis*.

'No kid should have to deal with this stuff on their own,' Lance remarked.

He continued to work down the list of websites. Kyle had been looking at Humberside Police web pages headed *Report a crime* and *What happens after you report a crime?*

'Do you think he was a victim of crime?' Hollie said aloud.

'Or maybe he wanted to hand himself in?' Lance countered, clicking on the final page in Kyle's web history: *What Laws Are There on Surveillance in the UK?*

'This could be homework,' Hollie suggested.

'Yes, it might also be something else,' Lance replied. 'Hadn't this young lad been in trouble at school for filming people without their permission?'

Lance walked over to Kyle's laptop, and Hollie followed him. It was like being in Q's lab in a James Bond film.

'I've accessed the hard drives on Kyle's laptop, but he used a secure Tor browser on this device and that hides all his browsing tracks.'

'Any files that we can look at?'

'He was a clever kid. He used a piece of software called a Shredder. So, there's evidence of him using this laptop, but he doesn't delete his files, he shreds them. That means we can't retrieve them, not without some FBI-level tech tools.'

Hollie sighed. These teenagers were running circles round them with their technical know-how. Since when did normal kids learn the tricks that had once been the preserve of fictional spies?

'Don't worry, I'm not going to let you leave empty-handed.' Lance smiled. 'I've saved the best until last. Come take a look at Kyle's phone.'

Lance clicked on his mouse and a mobile phone screen appeared on the flat screen TV that had been set on the workstation.

'This is Kyle's mobile phone. It's only been in my hands for a short time, but I made some fast progress. We can gain access simply enough using a bit of software, and this is usually where we'd find out everything about somebody. However, Kyle used biometric security on all his main apps—'

'Just explain that, please, Lance,' Hollie interjected.

'It means I can't access Kyle's messaging app without his fingerprint or a retinal scan. And before any tech experts suggest it, you need to be alive to use fingerprint activation; we can't do something grim like using a dead body to activate a phone.'

Hollie was pleased he'd pre-empted that one, as she'd been wondering about the possibility herself.

'However, we did request access to Kyle's unread message history from the social media companies and, in a rare example of them moving their arses, we hit gold.'

Lance had her full attention now.

'For the uninitiated, we can access unread messages on encrypted apps, but not read messages. Snapchat deletes them permanently once read, WhatsApp encrypts them, and even Mark Zuckerberg can't crack that open.'

As he spoke, Lance whizzed around Kyle's phone, and Hollie followed it all on the larger screen. He pulled up a text file on which were written three messages; they were too small to read on the screen.

'These are the three unread messages, retrieved from Kyle's phone in the hour of his death. Now, this isn't strictly my remit, but I'd assume if Kyle didn't read them, his phone had already been taken from him at the time they were sent, or he was on his way over to the outbuilding where he met his death and didn't get a chance to read them.'

Hollie considered that for a moment. What Lance was implying was that whoever messaged Kyle at that time was not involved in the attack on him. Or perhaps they knew about it but did not take part in it. Or maybe they just wanted to warn him.

Lance read out the first message.

'"Go home, Kyle. They're going to be waiting for you. Tell the police, it's your best bet. 12:06"'

'That message was sent while we believe he was making his way through the school for lunch break. He would have just left lessons at this time. The message was sent by somebody identifying themselves only as T.'

'Tilly Mann, I'll bet,' Hollie said.

'You're right, we cross-referenced her mobile number with

the send address. It was sent from her phone, though from what DC Langdon told me, she's deleted it from her own device.'

Lance Fairclough read the second message.

'"Don't you dare upload it. I'll pay you like you asked. BTC okay as usual? 11.59."'

'Okay, so this one is more of a mystery—'

'What's BTC?' Hollie asked.

'It's Bitcoin,' Lance replied. 'Think of it as a method of payment. These kids will all know about this stuff. From Kyle's point of view, it's a way of taking payment which avoids the usual banking records. We can trace it, but it takes time. He could use Bitcoin to pay for computer games, drugs, or even convert it to regular cash.'

'Who sent the message?'

'Someone identifying themselves as QBoy2006. Not much use, I'm afraid, unless we can find it on other social profiles.'

'That would make the sender eighteen years old if that's their birth year,' Hollie commented. 'Quinn Varney, perhaps? It doesn't help much, but it does suggest Kyle's been uploading something that he shouldn't. But what?'

Lance Fairclough continued speaking.

'What I infer from this exchange is that Kyle was doing some sort of uploading service for which he was being paid. This supports what I've found on his laptop, which indicates the use of video editing software and private and secure web browsers.'

'What if he was making pornographic films?' Hollie began, speaking as much to herself as the room. 'He'd use private browsers, wouldn't he? He might also attempt to cover his tracks by taking payments in Bitcoin. And we have this connection to Dirty Little Secrets, too.'

'I'm strictly a tech geek.' Lance smiled at her. 'But I'd say none of those theories is wide of the mark from Kyle's online behaviour.'

'I've been thinking about what would make a young girl like Tilly try to hang herself, and it's been bothering me all day. It would have to be something extreme, something terrible. Might Kyle have been leaking private information? Is this about the distribution of nudes or private content?'

'Again, you're best sharing that idea with your team. But none of this is pie in the sky – all these scenarios are possible.'

Lance turned back to Kyle's mobile phone.

'Okay, this last message was found unread on Snapchat. I think this is probably the most useful.'

He read it out.

'"Your final chance, Kyle. You know what you have to do."'

'This message was sent at 11.58, which is when the pre-lunch lesson will have been ending. Kyle never read it, but it seems that someone was offering him a way out of whatever it was he got himself into.'

'What does it tell us, though?' Hollie asked. 'Is there a name?'

'No,' Lance replied, 'just an anonymous username. It's *Tigers06.*'

'Could be a Hull City fan,' Hollie suggested. 'Their nick-name is the Tigers—'

'And again, 2006 might be the birth year,' Lance added.

'So, one of our sixth formers?' Hollie summarised.

'You need to see this though,' Lance Fairclough continued, navigating to a new screen. 'Snapchat uses cartoon avatars and I've managed to locate the avatar for *Tigers06.*'

He clicked his mouse and the avatar appeared on the screen. The face could have been anybody, but it was the red hair that gave it away.

'Zach Eastwood,' Hollie confirmed.

FORTY-FIVE
THURSDAY, 06:53

Before heading over for her early meeting, Hollie checked in on her work emails. She'd woken up still agitated from a late-night call with Léon the previous night, so she needed the distraction. He'd used the 'D' word – divorce – and it had shaken her. That would make things so final.

Her emails did the job. Forensics had finally come back with their test results which were, almost predictably, inconclusive. DS Anderson had followed up the results with a TL:DR summary for her sent by email after she'd got home:

Kyle's blood only
All sorts of mixed DNA from Kyle's movements around the
academy
Coat soiled badly in drain
Phone, lanyard and laptop showed evidence of being cleared of
prints with antiseptic wipes

Anderson's email summary said it all.

Someone knows what they're doing and we're f***ed for evidence.

Hollie couldn't have put it more succinctly herself.

Beverley Road Baths was a substantial, red-brick Victorian building with a domed tower rising above the main entrance. It was walking distance from her flat, too, so Hollie left the car and figured the exercise would do her good.

She wondered why the contact had chosen the baths as a place to meet, as it was off the beaten track for the academy and not the sort of place you'd go to hang out. She'd passed it many times, even in the nineties as a student in the city, but never stepped beyond the doors. As she might have anticipated, it was a marvel of Victorian architecture with its beautifully tiled walls, high, ornate ceilings and stunning stained-glass windows.

This visit was a bit of an annoyance to Hollie. If it just turned out to be a carping parent, she'd give them short shrift. Her mind was on Yasmine and Yerbury, that's who she really wanted to be speaking to.

Hollie wasn't sure where she was heading, so looked around for a suitable place to sit. She was a little early, but there appeared to be an early swimmers' session about to start, so she took a seat and examined the contents of the snack machine. Moments later, a woman stepped out of the changing rooms, her hair still wet from where she'd been for a swim. Hollie caught the distinctive smell of chlorinated water, and it reminded her that she hadn't been swimming for years, other than to accompany the children to their lessons when they were younger.

'Hello, Detective Turner, thanks for coming.'

Hollie didn't recognise the woman from the gathering of parents and press in the academy's foyer earlier that week, but she stood up and shook her hand and waited for her to take the lead.

'I'm sorry to be so cloak and dagger about it, but you've seen how emotions are running wild at the moment. I'd like this to be off the record if that's all right?'

Hollie took a close look at the woman. They were probably about the same age, but she knew from past mistakes not to jump to conclusions on that count. She was well-dressed and Hollie reckoned there'd be some exclusive labels in this woman's clothing rack.

'My name is Julie Ingram, I'm Samantha Ingram's mother.'

The surname rang a bell. Canfield had told her she was a parent governor at the academy. She'd also complained about Nick Yerbury and Yasmine Drake. This was a conversation she was very happy to be having.

Julie Ingram was confident and businesslike. It looked like she had something on her mind.

'Sammy is head girl at the school,' she continued. 'I'm a parent governor there and have been for the past two years or so.'

'So you're very invested in the well-being of the school, I see,' Hollie remarked, in an attempt to establish some kind of dialogue.

'You might say that. Sammy has a place at Cambridge. We're very proud of her, she works hard.'

'I should think so! That's a prestigious place to study, congratulations.'

'Did you know she's in a relationship with Matthew Urquhart? We call him Matty, he's a lovely kid. He suffers from anxiety, as so many youngsters do these days. I don't know why it is. Maybe we put too much pressure on them, I don't know.'

Hollie waited without interruption. Sometimes it was right to push; at others, it was a case of teasing out what a person wanted to say. Julie Ingram would get there eventually; she was just framing whatever it was she needed to get off her chest.

'Matthew and Sammy are both seventeen – they're the younger members of that little sixth-form group.'

'But they're in upper sixth, yes?'

'Yes, you know how the school years work – it's odd, isn't it? Which means Sammy was allowed to go to the parties a little later than the others.'

'Parties?' Hollie wondered.

'Well, you know what it's like with teenagers. The moment they all turn eighteen, they're out in the pubs. Because Sammy and Matty have been a couple since they were in their GCSE year, they got left behind a bit with that. They can't drink legally and – thank God – Sammy is pretty particular about things like that. She understands that a pub landlord could lose their livelihood if she was served alcohol underage.'

Hollie was struggling to see where she was heading with this. So far it felt like a lame attempt to distance her daughter from the other kids. It was beginning to smell a lot like arse covering.

'I'm sorry, but why are you telling me this?'

'Matty and Sammy were excluded from some activities, because of their age. But they didn't want to be. Sometimes I'd hear them discussing it when I was in the kitchen.'

'What were they discussing?'

Hollie was beginning to wish she'd not sacrificed the morning meeting for this.

'The older members of that group go out drinking in town. They like Melvins, it's the live music and the DJ that makes it a good place to go, or so I've gleaned from their conversations.'

'So, how does this fit in with what happened at the academy? I'm struggling to see the link here.'

'From what I've heard, they meet up with a couple of teachers in the pub. They're big drinkers and partygoers, apparently, and the kids have a laugh with them.'

Hollie's face clearly gave the game away.

'I know what you're thinking, detective, the same as me probably. In our day the teachers were aloof from the kids, and we wouldn't be seen dead in their company. But it's all changed these days, they all seem very familiar with each other. I raised it with Mr Canfield as a concerned parent and a governor, and he told me there's nothing we can do about it. So long as there's nothing inappropriate going on, the sixth formers are all legal drinkers and they have as much right to be in that pub as the teachers do.'

Hollie nodded. She was right, they were all adults. But still, it was a tricky one.

'But Matt and Sammy were excluded from all this?'

'Well, they'd start off with soft drinks at Melvins, things would get more boisterous, and because they were sober, they'd leave earlier than everybody else. Which means they often missed out and only got to find out what went on afterwards from all the gossip the next Monday morning.'

Hollie was getting interested now.

'And what did go on?'

'A lot of the time, they'd end up going back for a house party with the teachers—'

'Which teachers?'

'Miss Drake. She and Mr Yerbury are the main offenders, from what I hear. Yasmine Drake has quite a house, I believe. I'm not sure how she manages it on a teacher's salary.'

Mr Canfield had given her the answer to that question, but that was not Hollie's information to share.

'What kind of parties are these?'

'This is only what Sammy and Matty were discussing, and please don't ever tell them I was listening in. I was snooping because I wanted to find out if they're sleeping together yet. I've had the birds and the bees conversation with Sammy, but I don't want her messing up her future by getting pregnant. Matty's a nice kid, but she can do better.'

'Was there anything inappropriate going on at these parties, to your knowledge?'

Hollie was trying to figure out if this might land the two teachers in deep water. At the very least, it would result in a disciplinary, surely?

'They were certainly drinking there. There may have been joints consumed, Matty and Sammy weren't sure. But I think some of them were using the place for sex, too—'

'What? You mean at Yasmine Drake's house?'

'This is overheard only; I might have the wrong end of the stick entirely.'

'Did you raise this with Mr Canfield?'

'What am I going to say to him? That I've been listening in to my daughter's private conversations to find out if she's sexually active yet? How would that look, detective?'

'Well, you're telling me now,' Hollie pointed out.

'That's because of what happened in school on Tuesday. I've been wrestling with my conscience, but I have to tell you this.'

'Go on.'

As far as Hollie was concerned, this had just tipped the case on its head.

'You see, the reason Matty and Sammy were discussing it was because they felt snubbed. They weren't invited to the parties because they're too young to drink. I, for one, am not sad about that, but they were annoyed because Sammy heard them discussing someone who was underage but who was also going to Miss Drake's house.'

'And who was that?'

Hollie suspected already but wanted to hear it with her own ears.

'Kyle Wilson. Kyle Wilson was a regular there.'

FORTY-SIX

I can't believe it.

Evie paid up.

So did Quinn.

They've got too much money floating around if you ask me.

Mum made the rent and we're okay for another month.

I told Evie I'd post the video on that Dirty Little Secrets website if she didn't give me the money.

It was her who gave me the idea, because she works there.

Everybody in Hull will see it if I upload it.

I'd never do it, of course, but she and Quinn don't know that.

It turns out the eighteen-year-olds go round to the main house sometimes.

That's why I haven't been invited, I'm still too young apparently.

Anyway, they wouldn't want me there.

Evie hates me now, but that's her fault – she should have stuck up for me when Zach was mouthing off about me being a gay boy.

I hate that bastard.

I've been shaking ever since I got the money from Quinn and Evie.

I'm making them pay me in Bitcoin; the olds won't have a clue what I'm up to.

I told Mum I've been selling my old video games on eBay.

It was kind of true, and she fell for it.

I don't feel proud of what I'm doing, but it means we can stay in the house.

It's not causing any real harm.

There's no way I'd leak those private videos onto that website, but I'm not telling them that.

That's what you get for being a bunch of traitorous bastards.

Oh, and Jake and Tilly came in again tonight.

I've been hanging around more, just in case I get lucky again.

I like Tilly and Jake, and Tilly's parents are okay for cash.

Jake's strapped like us, I reckon, not much point pushing him.

If Mum needs the money again, I'll shake them down.

Not for as much as Evie and Quinn, but they should be good for a few bob.

I reckon it might have been Tilly's first time, they were all fingers and thumbs.

It was quite sweet, really, I think they're in love those two.

I didn't watch the CCTV video. I just made sure it was recording okay.

I'll sleep on it and think about whether I'll threaten them with it.

I feel like a right shit, but a part of me likes having some power over them at last.

They've been pretty disgusting to me.

Sometimes, I think they deserve it.

FORTY-SEVEN
THURSDAY, 10:27

'Excuse my language, DC Langdon, but it's bloody huge. I had not expected this.'

Hollie had just drawn up outside Yasmine Drake's house on Pickering Road. As soon as she'd got back to HQ from her Beverley Baths meeting, she'd offered to give Jenni another break from desk work. A bit of fresh air would do her the world of good and besides, she enjoyed the chatter in the car. Jenni almost bit her hand off.

It was a non-working day for Yasmine, so they were having to meet her at home. That suited Hollie as she wanted to see where the sixth formers were – allegedly – meeting up for drink and drugs.

'I should have gone into teaching, boss. It's like a mansion.'

Hollie admired the detached, red-brick property from the roadside. It had massive bay windows at the front, a balcony to one of the upstairs bedrooms and an arched front door.

'How much do you reckon it's worth?' Jenni wondered.

Hollie whistled and looked it over again.

'In London, a billion pounds and your first-born child. In

Hull, £400k maybe? What an inheritance. I wouldn't have known what to do with it at her age.'

'I'd like to have the chance to give it a try,' Jenni retorted. 'And you say it has a granny flat, too?'

'Yep!' Hollie exclaimed. 'I suppose she has to work to maintain the place. It's all right inheriting a property, but you still need to eat, heat it, run a car and go on holiday. I guess her teaching pays for all that.'

'How the other half live. We'd better get some carpet treading done. I can't wait to see inside.'

An idea occurred to Hollie as she was unfastening her seatbelt. It was an opportunity to kill two birds with one stone.

'Oh, by the way, do you fancy a quick drink after work tonight? It can double up as your PTSD session after that episode with Tilly Mann. I'm buying.'

'Yeah, sure. Though remember what happened last time we popped out for a quick drink. Best not repeat that, eh?'

Hollie recollected the karaoke duet that they'd performed together and winced at the memory.

'No, I promise, a quick drink and a debrief only. Strictly no karaoke.'

Hollie and Jenni got out of the car, walked up the drive and knocked at the door. Yasmine didn't take long to answer; it always helped to call ahead.

'Come in,' she invited them as if it was not out of the ordinary to own a house that size.

They stepped into a massive entrance hall with wood wall panelling and a polished wooden floor.

'Let's sit in the conservatory as it's a nice day.' Yasmine smiled.

She led them through a massive lounge, furnished with expensive-looking leather sofas and boasting an oak fire surround and a chandelier hanging from an ornate ceiling rose.

The conservatory was some size, with French doors opening out onto the garden.

'It's amazing,' Jenni mouthed to Hollie as they walked through.

'This is a lovely property,' Hollie remarked, trying to remove any tinges of jealousy or resentment which might be detectable in her voice. She had her small, rented flat on Pearson Park, after all.

'Well, I'm sure you know by now how I inherited it. I'm thinking of selling it, to be honest with you, it's way too big for me. It costs a bomb to heat it in winter and I can't see myself ever using the space. It's even got an annexe around the back.'

'Really?' Hollie replied, like she didn't know already.

'So, how can I help you? I've got a couple of chores to do as it's my only full day off, so I'd appreciate it if we could do this swiftly.'

Hollie and Jenni took a seat on the sofa which looked out into the garden. It didn't look like Yasmine was much of a gardener. The grass was uncut and what looked like a once beautiful garden was now filled with overgrown shrubs and unpruned roses.

Yasmine caught Hollie's gaze.

'Apologies about the garden,' Yasmine began, looking beyond the conservatory window. 'Mum and Dad loved it, but it's a damn nuisance as far as I'm concerned. I have no interest in gardening, and I can't afford a gardener on a teacher's salary so that's the result. As I said, it might sound nice to inherit a property, but it's a big liability.'

Hollie reckoned she could cope. It made her feel embarrassed and inadequate living in her flat. The sooner she moved into her new place, the better.

'So,' she began, 'just to be clear, this is informal questioning, you're not under arrest, we're just going to get some background information from you today.'

Yasmine nodded. It looked like DS Patel had briefed her well. Jenni opened up the app on her phone and began recording.

Hollie looked out into the garden, distracted by a sound that she could hear through the windows.

'What's that?' she asked.

Yasmine listened.

'Just my wind chimes,' she replied at last. 'I was going to take them down, but they drive Nick mad and – well, you know – I left them up just to annoy him. These little things can keep a woman sane in a relationship.'

Hollie kept her face expressionless, but she understood that impulse all right. She thought back to how she'd deliberately not helped Léon come up with a costume idea for Noah. She wanted to laugh at the thought of him searching the house high and low for a last-minute costume, so she refocused on the job in hand.

'How would you say the sixth formers are coping, in your position as the school counsellor?'

As Yasmine started to answer, Hollie noticed the scar just below her right ear which Mr Canfield had mentioned. To escape from a fatal car crash with just that must have filled Yasmine with a sense of guilt. Or, perhaps, the impetuousness to throw herself fully into life by having reckless fun.

'It's been a huge shock to all of us. I think it will take some time for it to sink in. What a terrible thing to happen on school grounds.'

'Did you ever speak to Kyle?' Jenni asked.

'Yes, of course.'

'Was he working through any issues at the time of his death?'

'He'd been getting in a lot of trouble, I do know that. It was unlike Kyle.'

'What sort of trouble?' Hollie wondered.

'Well, you know, fallouts and disagreements. Things seemed fractious with the other students.'

That wasn't the first time she'd heard that word *fractious*. It was an unusual word to use, yet Yasmine wasn't alone in her decision to deploy it.

'Any idea why?'

'No, not really. Just teenager stuff. It always gets a bit tense around exam time. There's a lot depending on their results, and relationships get fraught because students don't know if they're going to have to go to separate ends of the country after summer. I think tempers were getting a bit frayed.'

'Quinn Varney is an interesting character—' Jenni picked up.

'How so?' Yasmine replied.

The wind chimes were beginning to irritate Hollie. She looked out and could see them hanging on a tree close to the annexe. They must have annoyed the hell out of Nick Yerbury on the nights when he was banished to his rented accommodation.

'Well, he was in school on the day of Kyle's death.'

'He had an appointment to see me. He'd made it the day before.'

'So it was a last-minute thing?' Hollie suggested.

'Yes, I suppose it was. I'd have preferred him to come over first thing in the morning before lessons began, but he made some joke about not dragging himself out of bed until after ten o'clock. Anyway, we were done in five minutes, it was just a paperwork query. He could have emailed.'

'He was at the academy all lunch break?' Jenni asked.

'One of your colleagues has already asked me this when you interviewed me on Tuesday. I don't know, I left him in the foyer. Anyway, you're barking up the wrong tree with Quinn, he's a good kid, he still has friends at school. It was a knee-jerk reaction, his mum pulling him out of school; she overreacted.

Whatever it was Zach and Quinn fell out about, it's long behind them.'

'I had wondered in passing if Kyle might have been exploring his sexuality,' Hollie remarked, choosing her words carefully. She was fascinated by Yasmine's nose ring which made much more of a statement than the blander one she wore in school with three pointed studs hovering above her top lip.

'I'd had a couple of general conversations with Kyle where it came up in passing. He was just one of those nice kids. He wasn't the tough guy type, the girls liked him because of it, and he didn't seem interested in romantic relationships.'

'So you don't think it's a factor in his death?' Jenni checked. 'It's just, we're struggling to find a motive for who would want to harm him.'

'I've thought about this long and hard because I sat in on several of the interviews this week and I heard the line of questioning your colleagues were taking. I do not believe this was about Kyle's sexuality. Middle-aged blokes in pubs might get hot under the collar about it still, but most of these youngsters – particularly the more cerebral type – they don't give a damn.'

'How old are you, if you don't mind me asking?' Hollie changed the subject.

'Twenty-five. I got a degree in psychology, then it took another year to get qualified teacher status. I've been teaching for three years, and this will be my fourth year when we get past summer. I wanted the job because it had counselling responsibilities, so it used both of my qualifications.'

Hollie exchanged a glance with Jenni; they'd discussed this in the car. Start with the general information and use a pincer movement to home in on the detail.

'We've heard some suggestions that you sometimes host parties here with your students. Is that true?'

Hollie had just changed the subject by doing a 180-degree handbrake turn.

Yasmine sat up straight on the sofa.

'This again,' she said.

'What do you mean?'

'This is Sammy Ingram's mum, isn't it?'

Hollie didn't reply.

'She's convinced we're having some kind of orgy here. Even Mr Canfield had a go at us about it. Look, some of the older kids come around here and we chat and have a laugh. They're all over eighteen, it's completely legal, and I'm not responsible for any of their grades. They just let off some steam in a safe environment, that's all it is. Think of it like a youth club. It helps when things get tough in school if I have a good relationship with them. As I said to Mr Canfield, I'm not stupid, I'm not going to jeopardise my career over it.'

'It's not entirely appropriate though, is it?'

Yasmine seemed put out by that suggestion.

'I don't know why you think it's inappropriate,' she protested. 'Nothing that goes on here is illegal. It's just a safe place for the kids to destress, away from home and school.'

Hollie looked out into the garden and observed the annexe which was tucked behind the garage.

'That's a lovely granny flat you've got. How do you use it?'

'I don't go over there much. My parents used it for my nan, but she's dead now. Nick uses it as his den mainly—'

'Nick Yerbury?' Jenni clarified for the record.

'Yes, Mr Canfield will have told you about that, I'm sure. We're a couple. At first, he rented it from me, and the extra money was useful. Now we're together, his stuff is still over here. But he uses it as a place to work sometimes. I think he likes being out of the way. It's his man-den or shed, you know the sort of thing. And sometimes, when we row, I kick him out to sleep over there. Every couple ought to have an annexe. It's very useful.'

'What does he do over there?' Hollie pushed, intrigued by the idea of having all that extra space.

'I couldn't tell you, to be honest. I just leave him to get on with it. I haven't been over in weeks. Video work, probably. It's his editing and filming studio.'

'Do the students wander over there?' Jenni wondered.

'Yes, sometimes. It's quite cosy, it has a small kitchen and a living room area. I think if things get a bit noisy in the house, some of them pop out for a cigarette or a vape and they probably chill in Nick's place.'

'Could we take a look?' Hollie asked.

'Ha, you'd have to ask Nick, I'm afraid.'

'You don't have a key?'

'Not anymore, not since Nick lost the spare. Or misplaced the key, as Nick put it.'

She made air quotes to illustrate her point.

'He carries the only key around with him all the time now. You'll have to ask him if you want a look. As I said, he still pays me rent on it to help with the bills, so I kind of consider it his space these days.'

Hollie and Jenni continued working through their questions, but nothing Yasmine said gave them anything new to work with. At last, Hollie decided to call time on it, mindful that Nick Yerbury was booked in to see her over at the academy.

'May we wander over and check out the annexe before we leave?' Hollie asked.

'Be my guest. The side gate latch is broken, so you can let yourselves out. Let me know if I can be of any more help.'

Hollie and Jenni exited via the French doors, and Yasmine watched them walking across the garden before heading off to do whatever it was she'd got on that day.

The annexe seemed like it might be a converted double garage; it was big enough to pass as a small bungalow. Hollie tried the door, but it was locked as Yasmine had suggested.

There were cigarette butts and a couple of empty lager bottles discarded to the side of the door.

'If I was the neighbours, I'd sneak over the fence and cut that bloody wind chime down.' Jenni laughed.

'Not if I got there first,' Hollie replied, peering in the side window. It seemed to be a basic layout inside, with a simple living room and kitchen area, and two doors at the far end, which she assumed led to a bedroom and a bathroom.

'I might ask to move in here if she ever throws Nick Yerbury out,' Hollie quipped.

As the two detectives turned towards the gate at the side of the house, Hollie looked up and studied something below the annexe guttering.

'What's up, boss?' Jenni asked.

'This annexe seems to have CCTV,' she replied, 'but it's not switched on unfortunately. Look, the external wires are disconnected.'

Jenni looked up, following her gaze.

'That's a shame,' Jenni remarked, turning away. 'That CCTV might have given us a better idea of what went on at the parties with the sixth formers.'

That's exactly what Hollie was thinking, too. Why would somebody want to cut the wires to what looked like a perfectly serviceable surveillance camera? Was somebody keen to conceal what was going on there – Yasmine or Nick, maybe? Or perhaps even the teenagers who went over there to use the annexe.

FORTY-EIGHT
THURSDAY, 13:03

Something about Nick Yerbury was getting under Hollie's skin. She was delighted to have him in a room on his own again. She'd asked Harry Gordon to sit in with her while Jenni and Amber teamed up with DCs Philpot and Norton to conduct further interviews with the small group of sixth formers.

Nick Yerbury was waiting for them in the conference room, which was the only place available to them at the time. He had his feet up on the table again. God, that annoyed her.

'Ah, detectives, it's good to see you—'

'I would appreciate it if you didn't place your feet on the table,' Hollie began. 'This is a police interview, after all, not a night in front of the TV.'

'Of course.' Yerbury smiled. He moved his feet, pulled in his chair and sat up straight. Hollie and Harry took seats on the left and right of Yerbury; it was interesting how he'd chosen to sit at the head of the table.

'So, just to clarify, you're not under arrest and this is just an information-gathering interview,' Hollie said.

'Sure,' he replied nonchalantly. He was looking only at Hollie; he had barely acknowledged Harry.

'Yasmine Drake told me about your work area in her annexe. What do you do over there?'

'Did Yasmine tell you I pay her rent? I don't take advantage. I use it as my studio. I edit video files over there and I mark the kids' projects. It has a nice plain wall, which I use to project images and videos onto. Yasmine doesn't need it, so it works well for both of us. It keeps the annexe lived in and aired.'

'Yet she doesn't have a key for it.'

Nick looked at Hollie as if to say *so what?*

'Yeah, I... lost one. I dropped my key into the key cutter this morning so he could make me a new spare. I'll be picking it up on my way home today.'

'So we can't get into the annexe today?' Hollie asked, frustrated.

'Well, no, not until school finishes and I can pick up the new key. It might not even be ready tonight. He said I'd be safer popping in tomorrow.'

For fuck's sake.

Hollie wondered if they had sufficient justification to break the door down, but she knew what the answer to that question would be. She'd have to wait.

'Does anyone else have access to the annexe?'

He shrugged. 'Like who?'

'Any of the students. There's a suggestion some of the kids may come around sometimes. Is that true?'

'Yeah, Yasmine invites them over to the house. She's a school counsellor, right? She has a different kind of relationship with them. They tell her private stuff, you know.'

'Does she ever share that information with you?'

'Of course not. Yasmine is a professional, and what the students tell her is confidential.'

'Do the students ever use the annexe?'

'Yes, I let them use it, so long as they stay in the living area and leave my video gear alone.'

'What kind of gear might that be?'

'You know, I'm a video guy. I make videos and edit them. I keep my stuff in the bedroom; it's my work area. Yasmine calls it my man-den.'

'What sort of gear do you have in there?' Harry asked.

'Cameras, microphones, my laptop, a mixing desk for audio work... that sort of thing.'

'Was Kyle one of the students who used the annexe?'

Nick studied both of their faces, then gave a shrug of acceptance.

'I knew you'd get to this eventually.'

'Get to what?' Harry pushed.

'Look, Kyle was going through a rough time. I gave the kid a break. I let him have the spare key for the annexe and he came and went via the side gate. Yasmine never fixes the bloody thing, so it's easier than him knocking at the door every time.'

'So Kyle had access to the annexe?' Hollie confirmed.

'Yes. I didn't tell Yasmine because – well, I thought she might be against it. But I like – I liked Kyle, he was a good kid. Most students don't give a crap about their subjects, but Kyle was talented, he really had a thing for film. This conversation is confidential, right?'

'So long as it's not brought into evidence.'

'I knew Kyle was going through a tough time. His mum's Motor Neurone Disease is a shitty thing for a kid to deal with, right? So, one day, on the spur of the moment, I told him to come over. It was the first time I'd seen a bit of spark in the boy since he gave up his place at Manchester Metropolitan Uni. So, I let him have the spare key. He couldn't come to any harm. These kids are as good as adults anyway.'

'But he did come to harm, didn't he, Mr Yerbury?'

Nick let out a long, resigned sigh.

'I know how this might look. I liked Kyle, I'd never wanted to harm him. He was my star student, he was going places. I can see what you're thinking with the chisel and all that. But you really are barking up the wrong tree. I let Kyle use the annexe. So what? Sometimes we let students go over there to relax or get some time alone. We're not doing any harm.'

'How come you didn't recognise Kyle when you went to examine his body in the outbuilding?' Harry asked without warning.

Hollie looked at him. He was right to ask, but it seemed to have come out of left field.

'Did you see the body?' Nick asked, looking between the two of them.

'I did,' Hollie replied.

'Then you saw how his face was pointing away from the door and facing into the ground. He was bruised and bloody, too. Maybe I should have recognised him, but a still body is very different from a living person. And as I told you, I was in a panic. I didn't handle it as well as I might have.'

This man annoyed Hollie, but he seemed sincere.

'Would you let us take a look at the annexe?' Hollie asked. 'As soon as you get the new key back.'

'Yes, I've got nothing to hide. I'm not a suspect, am I? I thought you might get a bee in your bonnet when you found out that Kyle had been at the annexe, but it's all completely innocent, I assure you. I was just giving the kid a space to get away from it all. He was grateful for it, you know?'

Nick Yerbury wasn't off the hook until she'd seen that annexe.

'I noticed there was a CCTV camera on one side of the annexe,' Hollie continued. 'The main house doesn't have CCTV, why is that?'

'That's Yasmine's grandmother—' Nick began.

'Is she still alive?' Harry asked.

'No, she died before Yasmine's car accident. But she used to live there until she went into a home. She had dementia –

there's a camera in the living room, too. Yasmine's parents used to keep an eye on her when she was losing her faculties, but it allowed her to have her independence for as long as possible.'

'Do you use it still?' Hollie asked.

Nick laughed.

'No. The students disconnected it, the little buggers. They never asked me beforehand. It was part of their *1984* privacy paranoia. I told them it wasn't switched on.'

'How about inside the annexe?' Harry wondered.

'I think it's all still connected. As I say, I never use it. The control unit is in the bedroom. I've got so used to it being there, I don't notice it anymore—' Nick stopped dead and looked up at the two detectives.

'What?' Hollie asked. 'What is it?'

'I've just remembered. A couple of weeks ago, I was grading some of the students' video assignments over in the annexe. I have my iMac over there, it's great for video work. I had to switch the CCTV unit off. It was never normally turned on, and I did wonder about it at the time. I just assumed that Kyle had turned it on by mistake.'

Hollie had spent far too much of her life in hospitals. It went with the job, she knew that, but with the hushed voices, the clinical environment and the constant sense of foreboding, she would have rather avoided them. And there was the parking, too, that never helped. Jenni found them a parking space, they paid for a ticket and walked over to the main door of Hull Royal.

This was definitely a job for Jenni; she'd seen several times how empathetic her colleague could be and this visit to Tilly Mann was going to require all their sensitivity. Besides, she was there when Tilly attempted to take her life, and it felt like the best way to play this.

'How did the interviews go with the sixth formers, Jenni? Any gaps in the alibis yet?'

'No, they're sticking to their story. I need to tell you something about that.'

'Good. Am I going to like it?'

'DS Anderson told us to hang fire with Zach Eastwood. His father has asked to see you as soon as you can get over to his office. It's a legal thing – he's blocking us speaking further to Zach unless we're going to make a formal arrest.'

'Did the high-ups agree to hold off?' Hollie checked.

'DS Anderson said DCI Osmond confirmed it. We're not to speak to Zach again until you've consulted with their legal counsel.'

'Why do I get the feeling that everybody's blocking us?' Hollie cursed. 'I'll get over there before we head out for our boozing session... I mean, our debrief—'

Jenni laughed.

'Remember, you promised no karaoke. Besides, I'm still on medication after my accident, so no booze for me tonight.'

They'd successfully located the correct ward and reported to the nurse's station.

'DI Hollie Turner, you're expecting us, I believe.'

The two women held out their IDs for examination.

'Oh yes, Tilly's consultant is over there, you might like to catch him for a quick word before you see Tilly.'

Hollie made herself known to the consultant who'd just been doing his rounds.

'Was there any serious damage done?' she asked.

'You're the detective who saved Tilly, I believe? Her mother is happy for me to share the medical details relating to these injuries.' He checked their IDs. 'Tilly is a very lucky girl; you must have got to her fast. She came in unconscious on Coma Scale 4.'

'Just explain that if you would?'

'It's related to motor responses, brainstem reflexes, eye responses, and respiration patterns. Tilly had a weak pulse and shallow breathing. The pressure on her neck caused ischemia, which is a lack of blood supply to the brain due to compression of the carotid arteries.'

Hollie and Jenni looked at each other; this wasn't sounding good, it felt like he was setting them up for bad news.

The consultant continued.

'In cases like these, there can be some long-term consequences: difficulty with speaking, a loss of vision, memory impairment, inability to walk, coordination problems, and other issues.'

'So how is Tilly?' Jenni asked.

'Due to your quick intervention, I think she's going to be all right. She'll need to recover, of course, and we'll have to check up on her for some months yet, but she's extremely lucky. I see too many teenagers in here who don't make it out alive, so thank you for your quick and effective response.'

This was one of those moments when the job felt worthwhile. Hollie was grateful for the praise and could see Jenni felt the same way, too.

'You're welcome to talk to Tilly, but you know the drill, detectives. Please don't overexcite her and keep it short.'

He motioned them towards the door of Tilly's single room; her mother was sitting by the side of the bed reading a book in silence.

Hollie lifted her hand by way of greeting.

'Is she awake?' she whispered.

Mrs Mann put her book down, stood up and walked over to Hollie and Jenni. She gave them both a deep, long hug.

'Thank you both so much. You saved my daughter's life. I can never thank you enough.'

'Has she said anything?' Hollie checked.

'Nothing about why she did it—' Mrs Mann began to cry. 'It's about that boy's death, isn't it?' she sobbed. 'What else would it be about?'

Hollie squeezed her arm. 'We think it must be connected. Is it all right if we ask Tilly some questions? Let's see if we can get to the bottom of this, shall we? Would you wake her up for me?'

'I'll get some chairs, boss,' Jenni volunteered, leaving the room.

Tilly was woken easily enough, and Hollie and Jenni pulled up the extra chairs at one side of the bed, leaving her mum sitting on the far side. Tilly reached for water and took a long drink. When she spoke, her voice was hoarse, and she seemed to have some discomfort when swallowing.

'Hello, Tilly,' Hollie began, her voice quiet and gentle. 'You probably remember me, I'm DI Hollie Turner and this is my colleague, DC Jenni Langdon. You're not in any trouble, Tilly, but I'm sure you'll understand that we need to ask you some important questions.'

Tilly was propped up on her pillows now. She nodded. Hollie could see where her neck had been dressed to cover the wounds from her failed attempt on her life. She wondered how well they would heal and if Tilly would have to spend the rest of her life hiding those scars.

'I want to ask you first, Tilly, why did you run out of the drama studio while we were talking to you?'

'I was feeling sick,' she replied. It sounded like it was some effort for her to speak.

'Was it something that was going on at school?'

'I felt sick about Kyle and everything that's been going on.'

'Is something worrying you, Tilly?' Jenni asked. 'You barely said a word to me when I was driving you home.'

Tilly closed her eyes and screwed up her face like she was trying to exorcise something from her mind.

Mrs Mann had tears streaming down her face, but she left Hollie and Jenni to their work.

'Are you scared of somebody?' Hollie pushed a little harder. 'If you talk to us, we can help you. We can protect you. Please tell us what's bothering you.'

Tilly shut her eyes again. It was as if she wanted something terrible to go away but didn't know where to begin. Her right hand moved over to her left arm as if she was about to scratch at her skin, but she checked herself.

'I – can't tell you, I just can't—'

'Why not, Tilly?'

'It's just so – it's horrible, I'd rather die, I'd just rather die.'

Mrs Mann looked across the bed, her eyes raw from crying.

'Please, Tilly. Please,' her mother begged.

'I can't.'

'Why was Kyle's phone in your school bag?' Hollie pushed.

That got a reaction. She saw it in Tilly's eyes.

'I don't know how it got there,' Tilly protested. 'I didn't even know it was there. It's only because you told me that I even know. Someone must have put it in there.'

'Who?' Jenni asked.

'I don't know. They're trying to make it look like I did it.'

'Did what, Tilly? Beat up Kyle? Stabbed Kyle? What do you mean?'

Hollie knew she was pushing her luck, but she was tiring of all the stonewalling. This girl knew something, and it was time she started sharing.

'Can you tell us who's involved, Tilly?' Hollie urged. 'If you know who hurt Kyle, can you give us some names?'

Tilly was shaking her head now, a haunted look in her eyes, her hands shaking.

'Why did you delete those text messages on your phone, Tilly? What are you trying to hide?'

'It was nothing,' she sobbed. 'Just messages to Kyle.'

'Was Kyle in some kind of trouble?' Jenni said gently. 'Had you got involved somehow?'

'I loved Kyle,' she sobbed, 'he was my friend. I just wanted him to be okay, that's all. I just wish he'd—' Her voice was raw, she was struggling to speak.

'What, Tilly? What should Kyle have done?'

Tilly kept shaking her head, the tears streaming down her face.

'Did you send this message from your phone, Tilly?' Hollie

asked, reading from a handwritten note she'd taken after her conversation with Lance Fairclough.

'"Go home, Kyle. They're going to be waiting for you. Tell the police, it's your best bet." It was sent at 12:06.'

She looked at Tilly. 'It sounds to me like you were trying to warn Kyle, Tilly. That's the sort of thing I'd expect a friend to do. Were you trying to warn Kyle that he was going to get a beating?'

'I only ever wanted to help Kyle. He wouldn't listen to me. I don't know what happened. We used to be friends.'

'Does this have anything to do with Zach, Tilly?' she said at last. 'I know you and Zach have been closer recently. Is that what this is all about?'

From the flash in her eyes, Hollie could see she'd hit the mark.

'What is it with Zach, Tilly? Is Zach the reason you can't speak to us? Did he do something? Has he hurt you in some way?'

All Tilly could do by way of response was to shake her head and sob uncontrollably. 'I can't tell you,' she repeated. 'I just can't tell you. I want to die; I just want to die.'

Tilly's fear was gripping her; whatever she was hiding had a complete hold over her. At last, she began to speak again, her voice barely there now, sounding like the life had been drained from her.

'I can't tell you anything, I just can't. But Kyle Wilson isn't as innocent as you all think. One day you'll find out. And then you'll really know.'

FIFTY

THURSDAY, 14:31

DS Gordon

School days didn't seem that long ago for Harry Gordon. Walking the corridors of the academy, hearing the teachers taking lessons behind classroom doors, watching the students filing between lessons like drones accepting their fate felt all too familiar to him still.

Something was bothering him. Jenni told him that Kyle had a key to the annexe, and it hadn't been found anywhere. That struck him as odd. If you'd had the key to somewhere like that, you'd have either kept it safe or had it attached to something like your lanyard. He already knew from his colleagues that nothing was attached to Kyle's lanyard, which meant Kyle must have lost the key or he must have hidden it somewhere secure.

Harry knew that DI Turner wanted to look inside that annexe, and he could see how frustrated she was to have to wait for a new key to be cut. So he took the initiative.

On the day of Kyle's death, Harry had interviewed Alison Robinson, the academy's receptionist. It was she who'd placed the 999 call after Nick Yerbury and the two younger students raised the alarm. He knew from his own time at secondary school that the receptionist was often the most well-informed person in the school. She observed all comings and goings and had a unique relationship with the youngsters, having the joy of not being responsible for teaching them.

'Hello again, Mrs Robinson,' he said, walking up to the reception desk. 'I see you didn't get a day off then?'

She gave a mock cynical laugh and smiled at him. Harry had been brought up to speak as respectfully to everybody as if they were his ninety-one-year-old grandmother. It served him well as a rule, and Alison Robinson had clearly warmed to him.

'These phones have been ringing off the hook.' She held up her hand and touched a button on the console to her side. 'Crestwell Academy, how may I help you?'

All Harry could hear was somebody bawling at her down the phone. He caught a few swear words. Tensions were running high, and the pressure was on from the local community to get a result on the case. Harry couldn't ever imagine being the case lead like DI Turner. He reckoned the amount of pressure on her must be overwhelming at times, but she seemed to take it all in her stride.

Alison Robinson was polite, firm and reassuring, and she dispatched the caller efficiently and professionally.

'Another parent who kept their child back from school today, wondering if it's safe to send them back to school tomorrow. I'm not sure how we're going to recover from this. I'll bet we'll have fewer children coming here with next year's intake.'

That was a problem for Mr Canfield as far as Harry was concerned, and another reason why he had no aspirations to move up into a management position any time soon.

'When Kyle's body was discovered, did anybody find a key over in the outbuilding? Did Mr Yerbury or either of the two students hand one to you and forget to mention it?' he chanced.

The blank look gave him his answer.

'Is there anywhere else he might have kept his key? Do the students have anywhere else that's private to store things?'

'Just their lockers and you've been through them already. I'm sorry, detective, I can't help you, I'm afraid.'

She lifted her hand again to warn him of an incoming call, and he gave her a small wave to thank her for her help. He moved away from reception to the seats just inside the foyer, thinking through where Kyle might have left it. Its very absence suggested to him that it was something Kyle was keen to hide or protect. That annexe had to hold a crucial clue.

DS Patel had briefed the team about her walk-through of the academy's corridors, and how she thought Kyle had taken an unusual route after the lunchtime study session ended. It was as if somebody was waiting for Kyle, and had guided him out of that exit. So, Harry wondered, if he knew he was in trouble, where might Kyle hide the key if it was something he was keen to protect?

Harry stood up again almost as soon as he'd sat down, walking over to the small room where DC Norton was still poring over the CCTV footage, like a gold prospector searching for a small nugget. He tapped at the door before entering, then walked in. DC Norton looked up to see who it was. As he'd expected, Mr Bridges was still in there with her, assisting with the meticulous trawl for evidence. They reminded Harry of vampires in that small, windowless room.

'Anything new?' Harry asked.

DC Norton scrunched up her face and carried on.

'It's been an eye-opener for me looking at all this footage close up,' Mr Bridges answered. 'We have a real bullying problem around school. I honestly had no idea.'

Harry changed the subject – he wasn't there for a chit-chat.

'When you were with Kyle during the lunchtime study session, can you remember where he was sitting?' he asked.

Mr Bridges gave it some thought.

'Yes, he was on the far right-hand-side desk as you look from the teacher's desk. He was sitting on his own. He always sat on his own now I think about it.'

'When you walked out into the corridor to leave the study session, was there anybody out there?'

'Mr Canfield was doing one of his lunchtime patrols along the corridors and he gave me a call. He wanted to have a word with me, so I was distracted. But now you mention it, I think Zach Eastwood might have been walking by. He had that furtive look on his face that students do, when they change what they're doing to avoid attention from a teacher. I told him to move along, and he did, I think.'

'Did you mention this in your interview?'

Mr Bridges looked suddenly sheepish.

'No, I'm sorry, it was such a small thing, I didn't think to. Is it important?'

'Possibly,' Harry replied. 'Was Kyle distracted during the session?'

'He was looking out of the classroom door, which I'd left open, but not in any way that particularly caught my attention. He was slow to leave the session, I do recall that, and I mentioned it in my interview.'

'What classroom were you in?'

'Room 4U, why?'

'I'm just going to check something. Thanks, that's been very helpful.'

DC Norton had barely broken her stride throughout their exchange. Her ability to concentrate was remarkable.

Harry left the room, thinking about Kyle's last movements. Everything suggested to him that DS Patel was right to think that somebody was waiting for Kyle, and he might have known that trouble was coming. If so, the chances were he'd have concealed the key somewhere; after all, he'd swallowed the scrap of paper which Doctor Ruane had found in his examination of the body. Harry had a hunch, but not the kind of left-of-field idea he'd ever dare share at a team briefing.

He rushed through the building, taking two stairs at a time to the upper level and triggering the movement activated lighting as he rushed through the corridor. At DI Turner's request, Mr Canfield had instructed the caretaker to leave all the key classrooms unlocked and unused so that investigating officers had the full run of the primary locations.

He ducked underneath the police tape that had been placed across the entrance, rushed into the classroom and stood behind the teacher's desk, quickly identifying the desk that Kyle had been sitting at. From there he had a clear view of the corridor. If someone was waiting for him, he'd be able to see them.

Harry pulled out the plastic chair and sat down, pulling a latex glove onto this right hand. He moved his gloved fingers around the rim of the desk. His hand hit a lump of hardened chewing gum, but rather than flinch, he explored it with his fingers. There it was, a small metal object pushed into the gum for safe-keeping. He crouched down and took a closer look, pulling the object out of its hiding place.

It was a door key, and it even had a sticker on it saying where it belonged: *Annexe.*

FIFTY-ONE

Fuck, I'm constantly scared these days.

I can't believe all this is going on under my nose.

It's like some fucking honey pot in this annexe.

I know I'm playing with fire, but what else can I do?

I think the other kids come over here from the house. I'm not even sure Yasmine and Nick know what they get up to.

Nobody knows I'm here, that's for sure.

But I have to take care of Mum... and it's not like they don't deserve it.

Evie was playing hardball with me today when I told her I wanted more cash.

I sent her a still image from the video to prove it's real.

I didn't show anything, but it was enough to convince her that I mean it.

I picked up the money at Dirty Little Secrets.

Ironically, they don't have CCTV there.

You should have seen her face when I took one of the business cards by the cash till and I showed her the address of their website.

That made her cough up the Bitcoin payment fast enough.

She was straight on her phone, and it was in my account in seconds.

They all hate me now.

Well, they know how it feels to be me, don't they?

Mum said there's progress with our benefits claim.

She reckons they might even be able to pay some of our rent.

If we get the money sorted out, I'll stop pushing them for money.

It's not a lot of cash to them, but it makes all the difference to us.

I'm not proud of myself, in fact I despise myself as much as they do.

And if I ever have enough money, I'll pay them back.

But I'd never release those videos, even though I said I would.

I know what it would do to them and I'm angry with them, I really am.

But I could never hurt them that much.

I just want them to like me, really.

FIFTY-TWO
THURSDAY, 16:47

'Any joy with the Dirty Little Secrets website?' Hollie asked Amber when she was back at HQ. After her conversation with Lance Fairclough, she wanted to know if the pornographic videos theory held any water.

'I've just been on to Patrick Frisby, the owner,' she replied. 'He's organising a login for me. I had to email a scan of my police ID; he wasn't too happy about it.'

'It's a public website though, isn't it?'

'Yes, I think he's more disappointed about not getting the subscription payment.'

Hollie laughed.

'I can assign this to someone else if you'd rather not have to sit through those videos,' she offered.

'Patrick Frisby assures me it's pretty soft-core material. He's big on the consenting couples and ethical porn angle.'

Hollie shook her head. She'd never understand what made people post intimate content online. She wouldn't even share a holiday bikini image on social media; then again, there were strict rules about using social sites as a copper, so she was probably overcautious on that score.

'You're looking for any of our group of sixth formers. It wouldn't surprise me at all if Nick Yerbury's or Yasmine Drake's face popped up on there, too.'

'Just their faces?' Amber joked.

'Don't, please, I really hope we don't find anything there. Things would take a very dark turn if that's what this is all about.'

Amber turned to one side and reached for something at the side of her PC.

'I hope you don't mind, boss, but I got Lance Fairclough to lend me that SD card. I don't want to teach my grandma to suck eggs, but they're overwhelmed with work in there and I'd like to have a crack at that file myself. I promise not to mess anything up. I've got an idea that I want to try.'

'Be my guest, just don't do anything that damages or erases anything on that SD card.'

Harry walked into the office, looking hot and bothered: a man with a mission.

'Kyle's key to the annexe, boss—'

Both Amber and Hollie stared at him, a look of admiration on their faces.

'How?' Amber wondered.

'It was stuck to his table with chewing gum. I just had a hunch.'

'Brilliant work, Harry. I was due to catch up with Nick Yerbury first thing tomorrow to snoop round the annexe. I think I'll be paying him a visit before I head home tonight, now I have a key. Has it been checked over, Harry?'

'Yes, it's clear, boss. Just Kyle's prints, that's all.'

'This is good work, Harry, and some great lateral thinking. And thank you for correct handling of the key, I appreciate your attention to detail.'

He smiled, clearly pleased at the praise.

'Okay, let me know if you spot any familiar faces on that website, DS Patel,' Hollie said.

'Or backsides!' she added.

'Don't go there.' Hollie grimaced. 'The sooner this case is concluded, the better. It seems to have brought out the worst of everybody with their smutty remarks.'

She smiled at Amber, keen to let her know that she wasn't making a snarky comment. She could be immature with the best of them, but someone had to be the adult in the room. And this case was as dark as they came, what with one dead teenager and another who'd tried to take her life.

She walked across the office to DS Anderson's desk, checking in with colleagues as she passed their work stations.

'Do you reckon there's some mileage to this theory of mine?' Hollie asked. 'I'm not strolling far from the beaten track, am I?'

She trusted Anderson's experience and judgement on this, and she wanted some reassurance that her instincts were right.

'The porno theory? Yeah, I think it might be a goer. These kids nowadays, they're sharing all sorts of unsuitable shit online.'

'So, let's look at what we've got,' Hollie began, casting her mind back to the various conversations she'd had as she caught up with the team.

'We've a group of five students who are of particular interest now. Zach – probably – and two other students – we think Tilly and Quinn – were messaging Kyle in the run-up to his death. Something happened that made Tilly so distraught, it was enough to make her try to take her life. Somebody moved that chisel from the murder scene to the bin in the foyer, after police arrived on the scene. And something was going on at Yasmine's house, which may or may not be connected. What are we missing here? I just can't place it.'

'Same, boss, I feel like we're so close. We just need one more piece of info to drop and it'll become clear.'

'Well, let's see what Rupert Eastwood wants to threaten us with now. Then I'm heading directly over to that annexe to see what Nick Yerbury is hiding in that man-den of his.'

FIFTY-THREE

THURSDAY, 17:48

The chat was easy and professional on the drive over to Rupert Eastwood's office. Hollie and Anderson ran through the details of the case, considering if they'd missed anything.

Eastwood Enterprises was located in a plush new office on Bridgehead Business Park. There was a black Tesla parked in the designated CEO bay.

'Looks like Eastwood's wife is driving the second car today,' Anderson quipped.

'Well, it's easy to see where Zach gets his entitled attitude from,' Hollie added.

Eastwood kept them waiting for ten minutes at reception, in spite of their arriving at the designated time. When they were finally taken to his office, his legal counsel was there.

'Good evening, Mr Eastwood, thank you for agreeing to speak to us today.'

He said nothing but waved them to the two chairs that had been placed in front of his sprawling desk. It looked solid and expensive, while his desk chair was ergonomically designed and seemed to be half robot, it had so many joints and levers. The walls were adorned with photographs of construction projects and architectural award certificates. There appeared to be a lot of money in the building game.

Hollie scanned his desk. There was a picture of Zach with members of the city's football team. Zach was wearing a Tigers football shirt. She thought back to her conversation with Lance Fairclough. *Tigers06*: was that Zach?

As they sat down, she noticed a box of disposable plastic shoe guards on the windowsill behind Eastwood. She assumed he used those on construction site visits to avoid bringing mud onto the carpets and floor coverings.

'Why did you ask to see us, Mr Eastwood? We wanted to ask Zach some more questions today, and it was not helpful that you delayed that.'

'This is now bordering on harassment, detectives,' he snapped. 'That's what this meeting is about. Geoff—'

He turned to the lawyer, who had a pile of papers perched to the far side of Eastwood's desk. It was three times the size of the desk Hollie used at work.

The solicitor cleared his throat and picked up a piece of paper. As he did so, Rupert stretched out his legs and his footwear protruded under his desk. He was wearing trainers; that was an unusual choice for the office. He was the boss, after all, and Hollie considered that he was probably doing a Mark Zuckerberg and dressing tech casual.

As the solicitor shuffled some papers, Hollie pulled a pen out of her pocket and made a note of the make of footwear coverings that was plastered across the box. SOCO had said that some of the footprints were obscured; she wondered if these plastic guards might create a similar effect.

Rupert Eastwood caught her eye as she was making her notes and she looked away, pretending to be examining a piece of artwork on the wall.

'Before you interview Zach again, I just wanted to clarify a legal point,' Geoff began.

Hollie looked at DS Anderson and they waited for him to continue.

'Mr Eastwood just wanted to be very clear from the outset that he takes the reputation of his son very seriously.'

Hollie could sense DS Anderson's eagerness to pass comment.

'Whenever you question Zach Eastwood, you throw his good character into question and that, in turn, reflects badly on Mr Eastwood and the fine reputation of his business.'

Hollie was tempted to say something now. She checked herself and waited for him to reach his point.

'This is a formal notification to Humberside Police that, should you further interview, arrest or charge Zach Eastwood, and he is proven to be innocent – which he will be – Eastwood Enterprises will be taking a civil action against your force and you as individuals for defamation of character.'

DS Anderson couldn't help himself. He shook his head and smiled.

'I think you'll find that there's not much precedent for that, bearing in mind Zach is part of a legitimate police investigation.'

Rupert touched the screen of his mobile phone, and a video began to play. It was filmed in the drama studio at the academy. It showed Hollie's briefing to the sixth formers, Tilly's early departure, and the mayhem that followed after she called Kyle's mobile phone and it rang in Tilly's bag.

'Who took that video?' Hollie asked, nervous now. 'That was a confidential briefing, and the sixth formers were asked to turn off their phones beforehand.'

'I'd suggest this demonstrates reckless police behaviour, wouldn't you, DI Turner?' Eastwood smirked. 'Particularly as a poor girl tried to end her life immediately after this little spectacle. Some might call it entrapment.'

Hollie looked at him, and DS Anderson was choosing to

stay quiet now. The solicitor shuffled his papers, then spoke once again.

'So, as well as making a potential civil claim for defamation of character, we'll also be making an official complaint with immediate effect to your Chief Constable and the Police and Crime Commissioner for using inappropriate investigative techniques to ensnare young people who aren't even old enough to leave school yet.'

FIFTY-FOUR

THURSDAY, 19:09

Jenni already knew the significance of where they were drinking, but as a copper it seemed the perfect choice. Hollie had almost talked herself out of going to Melvins, but when Jenni suggested meeting in the Old Town for their after-work debrief, it was too good an opportunity to miss. Besides, the sixth formers wouldn't even be there after all that had happened that week.

She needed that drink. Rupert Eastwood's threat was preying on her mind. People like him, with plenty of money behind them and the local influence to back it up, could create problems for her. She'd have to tread carefully where Zach and his father were concerned. This was getting referred up the chain of command.

'So, how's it been being released from your desk again?' Hollie asked as they sat down, with soft drinks in their hands. She'd scanned the bar, checking for any familiar faces from the academy, and was relieved to see that this would just be a social visit and a great opportunity to see where the youngsters liked to hang out. There was not much which helped her with the case, but it was good to see the place for context.

'It's been great, the days are much more interesting when I'm in the thick of it,' Jenni replied. 'You can't beat a bit of sleuthing on a crime scene. And there are no motorcycles, too, so that's a bonus.'

Hollie's mind flashed back to Jenni's lifeless body in the alleyway, the revving from the motorcycle only metres away. She thought she'd lost her friend; it was so good to be sitting with her again on a night out, even though it was just a quick visit.

They carried on chatting and drinking as the bar became busier and louder around them. Hollie had already got a sense of the place, it was bustling, noisy and boisterous, but she was having to shout to be heard now and was thinking of finding somewhere quieter.

Jenni's phone vibrated and she picked it off the table to check it.

'Oh, a friend of mine just texted me to say she's back from her holidays in Spain. She's at a pub around the corner. Do you mind if I pop round quickly and say hello? I won't abandon you, I promise.'

Hollie smiled, thinking about how lonely she'd felt since arriving in the city. It was all good while she was distracted by work, but the evenings without her family could seem long and quiet. There was no way she was going to make life difficult for Jenni.

'Okay, I'll stay here for a bit,' Hollie offered. 'Text me when you're coming back, and I'll run you home.'

Jenni agreed, held the table until Hollie had topped up with a second drink, and was on her way. She was only around the corner at the Wetherspoons on Lowgate, so there was very little chance they'd get separated.

'If you end up having fun with your friend, just text me and blow me off, it's no problem.'

As Hollie watched Jenni walk out of Melvins, she pulled

out her phone so she would look occupied and busy. She'd barely activated the screen before a middle-aged man in a flannel shirt and jeans walked up to her.

'Can I get you a proper drink, luv? Seems a shame you're all on your lonesome.'

Hollie looked up at him. His slurred words and bleary eyes suggested to her he might have made an early start on the beers. He also appeared unable to see the full glass directly in front of her.

'No, thanks very much, I'm just waiting for a friend to come back.'

The man looked her over for a few moments, swayed, and then moved on with a 'Be like that.'

Within minutes, he was bothering another group of women who were waiting to be served at the bar.

As Hollie took a sip of her drink, she caught a familiar face in the crowd: Zach Eastwood. He had two pints of lager in his hand and was talking to someone he knew, on his way back to a table. Hollie kept her gaze on Zach, to see who he was drinking with. Although it was busy, she managed to track him back to his table across the room. He was sitting with Quinn Varney.

Hollie immediately kicked into detective mode, her mind alert and her eyes fixed on the spot where Zach and Quinn were speaking. It seemed unusual that they should be out drinking as if nothing had happened so soon after Tilly's attempt on her life. Something about it didn't ring true.

A text arrived from Jenni.

I'm here! Won't be long, promise! Ten minutes max. Sorry to abandon you x

'Hello darling, mind if we join you?'

Two thirty-something men were standing by the table, both with pints in their hands. They were what officers would describe as geezer types, the sort of drinker with bonhomie to spare and more than willing to spread it around liberally.

'I'm okay on my own actually,' Hollie replied, 'but thanks for asking.'

'No need to be shy,' the man's mate said, pulling up a chair and looking like he was settling in. He placed his hand on her knee, and she brushed it aside, annoyed, and on the point of twisting his arm behind his back, like she might apprehend a suspect. The other man was hovering to her left-hand side, and it was claustrophobic and far too familiar.

She needed to close this down, and fast. She pushed the man's hand away.

'It's just that I'm waiting for my wife, she's running a bit late.'

'We don't mind, luv, it's more friendly if there's two of you—'

Hollie hated having to resort to it, but she put her hand in her pocket and searched for her ID card. She pulled it out and discreetly held it out so both men could see it.

'Off you go and enjoy your pints, chaps, I'm not in a chatty mood, I'm afraid.'

They got the message and made their hasty retreat. Hollie was annoyed at having to show her hand like that, as it would be more difficult to claim that she'd only been there socially if anything ever came of it.

She took a long drink and looked over at the students again. It was better than she could have hoped for: Evie Keane had now joined the group. Three of them were there, almost everybody on her watch list and they hadn't got a clue she was even watching them.

Jenni texted once again.

> Done now. Okay if I bring my friend over? We're in Wetherspoons and she fancies going somewhere a bit livelier!

Hollie thought it over. She was crazy thinking she could do anything with what was going on across the bar. She had no justifiable reason to arrest any of them and what she really wanted was to be a fly on the wall and listen to everything they were saying. She was playing with fire as it was; if they spotted her, they would be well within their rights to complain about harassment or inappropriate police surveillance. She took another large sip of her drink and texted her reply.

> Stay where you are, I'll walk over to you. It's a bit noisy here, let's move on somewhere where the music isn't so loud. With you in 5.

'Looks like your friend isn't coming,' came a voice from behind her. Whoever it was had just placed his hand on her shoulder. It was the first man who'd offered to buy her a drink, clearly unsuccessful with the other two women he'd been troubling. Hollie took another large swig of her drink, eager to finish it and be on her way now. She went to stand up, but the man pushed down on her shoulders, preventing her from moving. Her head was spinning more than it should be, bearing in mind she was restricted to soft drinks, and she was beginning to wonder if it was just too stuffy in there. Despite that, she was immediately on alert to what the man had just done.

'Excuse me,' she said, attempting to stand up once again. Her words were slurred.

'I think you're being a bit rude,' the man said. 'I only asked if you wanted a drink. I think you were trying to brush me off.'

'Look,' Hollie said as quietly as she could so that he could hear, 'fuck off and leave me alone. I asked you politely the first time, and now I'm telling you to sling your hook.'

This had suddenly become a problem and she needed to get out of there without causing a commotion. The man's foot was by her chair and, seeing he was about to move to confront her, she placed her foot on his. He lost his balance as he attempted to execute the manoeuvre and went flying into a large group of young men and women who'd been minding their own business and keeping themselves to themselves near the bar. The drunk man tripped, and his drink went all over one of the women, who shrieked at the shock.

'That's out of order, mate—'

'Right, you've had enough to drink now—'

Hollie stood up to make her exit, but as she did so, her legs weakened, and she felt herself swaying.

Did those bastards spike my drink?

Through the haze, she knew she had to find Jenni, leave her car in the Old Town and get a taxi home. While the commotion played out behind her, she headed for the pub's exit, mobile phone in hand, keeping her head down so as not to be spotted by the group from the academy.

She staggered out of the door into the street and looked around to get her bearings. No sooner was she outside, pleased for the fresh air and relieved to get away from the noise, than she sensed a movement behind her. There were two figures, moving confidently; it took her by surprise. They took an arm each, scooping her up and sweeping her along the street.

'Time to go for a ride,' a familiar voice said. She recognised it but couldn't place it. One of those bastards had spiked her drink. She felt the adrenaline coursing through her veins, but she was unable to speak – her body would not respond. As she felt herself drifting away, she was pushed into the back of a car waiting at the side of the road. The car door slammed, and she passed out.

FIFTY-FIVE
THURSDAY, 19:45

DS Patel

Amber Patel looked at the time on her computer clock; it was approaching eight o'clock. This was the second night in a row she'd had to stand up Duncan. No wonder DI Turner's marriage had imploded; it was impossible to run a relationship when a big case was on. But she was determined to get into that video file before it was handed back to Lance Fairclough and his tech team the next day. If it was important enough for Kyle to hide, it must be crucial to the investigation.

She had some rudimentary experience of cracking open videos which were supposed to be locked. As a student there had been a black market of the latest film releases available as video files. She knew that if you persisted long enough, you could usually find a bit of free software that would do the job.

She opened up her browser and began hunting around for download sites. As she clicked on the first website in the search results, she thought better of it. Using her police PC to access potentially virus-laden downloads was probably not the canniest career move, even if it did result in a case break-through.

She walked across the office to her locker where she'd stashed her rucksack. Packed inside was a change of top and underwear and a toothbrush and hairbrush, and her home laptop. There was a momentary pang as she thought of Duncan's sofa and snuggling up while they watched the next episode of their favourite Netflix series.

No, she'd bitten the bullet, Duncan knew she wasn't coming over; she was committed to another late night in the office now.

She pulled out her laptop, connected it to the guest Wi-Fi network and returned to the website she'd been looking at previously. It offered the top ten video file-cracking tools. She downloaded the first three, installed the software on her laptop and ran the video file through them, one by one.

It was useless. Without being able to open the folder with a password, she was wasting her time.

She checked the case log and noted down every bit of information that had enabled them to access Kyle's tech so far.

She tried everything: Kyle's birth date, his twin's birth date, and every combination of numbers and letters that she could think of. She entered the numbers: 4-7-9-2 which had been retrieved from the scrap of paper which Kyle had swallowed and entered them five times into the SD card's password prompt: nothing.

Amber reflected on how Harry Gordon's lateral thinking had revealed the whereabouts of the spare key to the annexe. She entered the names of the celebrities who featured in the posters on Kyle's bedroom wall; she studied SOCO images to see the titles of books on Kyle's shelves, until she'd completely exhausted every angle she could think of.

She stared at the photograph of the screwed-up slip of paper that had been found by Doctor Ruane in Kyle's digestive tract. If Kyle was so desperate that he'd swallow it before he was intercepted by his assailants, it had to have some significance.

DC Philpot had already checked it against Kyle's bank card and confirmed that it was not his PIN for the cash till.

She studied the numbers: 4-7-9-2 once again and entered them into the SD card password prompt, as if it might somehow make a difference.

Those numbers had to mean something. What was she missing?

Once again, she checked the photo that had been taken of the slip of paper after it had been retrieved from Kyle's corpse. Although it had barely been in his body long enough to pass through into his stomach prior to his death, there was some smudging of the numbers.

Then it struck her; that number 7 might just be the number 1, with a downward stroke at the top. She was so excited by the possibility that she mistyped the PIN the first time and had to erase her inputs and start again.

The folder opened; her hunch was right. There were five encrypted videos there, a series of audio files and three images.

She ran the encrypted video files through the software programs that she'd already downloaded, determined now to crack this without Lance Fairclough's help. Nothing.

Amber downloaded two more software packages from the website. She ran the video through the first; again, nothing. She opened up the second piece of software and ran the video through it. Expecting little now, she clicked *Unlock It!* on the screen prompt and it fired up straight away.

At first, she couldn't make out what she was looking at. Then, as the video continued to play, it became clearer. She expanded it to full size so she could make out the faces.

It was Tilly Mann and Jake Tate; she recognised them from her work at the academy. They were in a room somewhere, it wasn't at the academy, and they were being filmed without their knowledge, via a CCTV camera or something similar. There was sound, too, but it wasn't good quality; the camera was too far away, and they were speaking quietly to each other.

They sat down, held hands and began chatting. Occasionally they kissed, it was gentle and loving – the two teenagers clearly liked each other. Tilly was more relaxed than Amber had ever seen her; she and Jake looked comfortable together.

There was suddenly a loud crash off-screen, and Zach Eastwood burst into the room; she recognised him from his red hair. He'd been drinking or was high, Amber couldn't tell which.

'My fucking dad is coming over, I'm supposed to be at some shitty business networking event,' he said, anxious and in a state of panic. 'He'll go mental if he sees me like this.'

Jake stood up and rushed to Zach's side.

'Come over to the house with me, let's get you sobered up quickly with a black coffee. Nick and Yasmine will cover for you—'

He walked over to Tilly and kissed her.

'I'll just get Zach sorted, then I'll be back.'

'No worries, I'm quite tired. I'll have a doze while you're over at the house.'

Was this the annexe Hollie and Jenni had briefed them about? From the way they'd been talking about it, it sounded like that.

Amber turned up the audio as loud as it would go. It was still too low on her laptop, so she pulled the speaker lead out of her work PC and pushed the jack into the side of her laptop.

She continued watching as Zach and Jake left the annexe; Tilly could be seen stretching out on the sofa. She drew some headphones out of her pockets and put the pods in her ears.

Somebody entered the room, their body language angry and aggressive. They were wearing a sports cap, and it was difficult to make out the face.

'Where the fuck are you, you little shit—?'

Amber heard that clear enough.

It was Rupert Eastwood. He seemed furious and he was looking around frantically when he entered the annexe. He stopped when he saw Tilly lying there and stood looking at her for a few moments. She didn't appear to have seen him; it looked to Amber like she was zoned out, dozing and listening to her music.

Rupert walked up to the sofa, standing over her. She was still unaware that somebody was there. Amber saw his body language change on the screen, from one of anger and rage to a stance of sinister opportunism. He looked back towards the direction he'd come from, presumably the door. It was difficult to make out what was happening, but he was doing something with his trousers. Then it became clear, as Tilly jumped up, frightened out of her life.

Tilly tried to push him away. He shoved her down, moved her skirt up with his hands and forced himself on her.

'No, Mister Eastwood, please don't. I want to be with Jake.'

'You looked all on your own in here, like you need a bit of company—'

'Please—'

Tilly was panicking now, she understood what was happening.

'You young girls with your provocative clothing, you're going round asking for trouble.'

'No, please, I don't want to—'

'Shh. You don't want to be bothering with those young boys. What you need is a proper man—'

'Mr Eastwood, no, please, no—'

'Shut the fuck up, you know you're asking for this—'

Amber was about to slam down the lid of the laptop in disgust when she saw Zach walking in on his father.

'It's only me, Tilly, Jake said he left his phone—'

Amber watched as he stood there, a rabbit in headlights momentarily, trying to take in what he was seeing.

'Fuck, Dad, leave her alone, she's my friend—'

He ran at his father, pulling him away from Tilly. He paused a moment, then hit his dad.

'You stupid, fucking imbecile,' Rupert seethed at him. 'You fuck everything up, don't you?' He struck his son hard across the face with his open hand, leaving Zach sobbing on the ground and nursing his jaw. Tilly was sobbing, too, terrified at what might happen next.

Rupert fastened his trousers and pulled up Zach from the ground, aggressively.

'Nothing happened here tonight, is that clear?'

He stormed out of the annexe, half dragging, half pushing his son.

Amber couldn't watch any more. She slammed down the top of her laptop and threw up in the wastepaper bin at her side. The office was empty, it was just her, the office lighting dimmed, a desk lamp illuminating her workstation like a beacon. She reached for her phone and rang Hollie.

FIFTY-SIX

I'm really fucking scared.

I mean, really scared.

Shit, shit, shit!

I can't believe what happened tonight.

I was sick on Mr Yerbury's carpet.

I wanted to help Tilly, but I was terrified.

My legs wouldn't move.

I'm fucking useless. When Tilly needed me, I just bloody caved in.

I hate myself.

I could have helped her.

I like Tilly, really, I didn't mean to cause her any harm.

I could hear her begging him not to do anything.

She was crying, for fuck's sake, there was no way she wanted that.

I hate that fucking bastard.

I really fucking hate the Eastwoods.

I don't know what to do.

Do I talk to Tilly?

Do I tell the police?

I don't know what to do for the best.

This could cause big trouble for me and Mum.

But I've got the evidence.

I was recording it.

I have to think this through.

I'm trembling now, I'm so scared.

This has gone too far now.

I think they've been speaking with each other about what's going on.

I didn't think they'd do that.

It's got really hostile.

They've been posting notes in my locker and sending threatening texts to my phone.

I wish I'd never started this.

If Mum gets her benefits, we'll be able to survive.

If I'd hung on a little longer, I think we might have been okay.

Damn, damn, damn.

I've messed this up so bad.

Why did they have to fucking tell each other? It was supposed to be private.

They're going to get me at school tomorrow.

I don't know what to do.

I only wanted to help my mum.

FIFTY-SEVEN

THURSDAY, 20:05

'You've given me a big problem—'

Hollie felt terrible. She could hear wind chimes. Where the hell were those wind chimes coming from? Her head was pounding, her eyesight blurry and she thought she might throw up at any moment. Slowly, she pieced together the fragments that she could remember.

'You spiked my drink, you bastard—'

She wished she could recall who the voice belonged to.

'Well, if you will go spying on my kid, what do you expect a father to do?'

She'd got it now: Rupert Eastwood.

'I saw your face in my office earlier. You think you've got something. What did you see there?'

She looked at his shoes; he was wearing a pair of the disposable shoe coverings that she'd spotted on the windowsill in his office.

The penny dropped. The scenes of crime team had said there was something unusual about the footprints, this was it. Rupert was sensible enough to place the shoe coverings on his feet to conceal his prints. A sting of panic gripped her – was he the killer? She'd suspected it was Zach. Was it Rupert hiding behind the outbuilding?

Hollie scrunched up her eyes in the hope it would help her to focus better. It wasn't much use, so she tried to figure out where she was. The room was barely lit, and she was tied to an office chair using plastic cable ties. They were tight, there was no room for her to move, even for comfort. Her ankles were tied, too; as she moved her feet, she heard the sound of plastic sheeting underneath. For the first time since coming around, she felt a streak of panic rush through her body.

'What is this about?' she asked, her voice faltering. 'You've already warned me off with your legal counsel.'

'I'm not completely certain myself, yet. I need to decide what to do next.'

'What's the plastic sheeting for?'

'I'm surprised you haven't worked that one out, being a hotshot copper.'

Jesus, he's serious. Is he going to kill me?

Hollie's hands were shaking; she had to control her sense of alarm. If only her mind would sharpen, she could figure out what to do.

'What's this about? How did we get here?'

'You might well ask,' Rupert replied. 'Young Kyle has caused several people a lot of problems. But I think I know what needs to be done now.'

He's wearing latex gloves. He's suited up. How does he know this stuff? What the fuck is he planning?

'Talk to me, please. There must be a way to resolve this?'

'We may have gone too far for that—'

A projection appeared from behind her on the wall directly ahead. It was a film of some sort. It seemed amateur, but she felt immediately sick as she worked out what she was watching.

'Why are you showing me this?'

'This is young Kyle's handiwork. Take a look, then you'll see why emotions are running so high.'

The video showed Jake and Tilly kissing. It was awkward, teenage stuff; they seemed shy, inexperienced, but it was consensual and affectionate. It seemed to Hollie like it might be their first time.

'Do you see anybody you recognise?'

Clothes were being partially removed and it was obvious what this was filming.

'Turn it off, I don't want to watch this, it's horrible. Who filmed this?'

Hollie looked around the room. It had been recorded in this place. Jake and Tilly had been kissing on the sofa at the far end of the room.

Rupert stopped the video. Hollie glanced around the room. There was a CCTV camera up there, but it didn't appear to be on.

'You've seen it, I see. I made sure it was turned off. We don't want this little conversation on record now, do we?'

Rupert opened up another file which projected a similar scene onto the wall. This time it was Quinn and Evie, caught in a deeply intimate moment, but unaware of being filmed.

'I don't want to watch this stuff, it's sick. These kids have a right to their privacy. Why don't you just tell me who did this and we'll get them banged up before they can draw their next breath? This is horrible—'

'I'm not finished yet. You have to understand what's going on here. I need you to know why this is so important to me.'

Another video appeared on the wall. This time it was Quinn and Zach; Hollie hadn't even realised there was anything between them. Is that what their fallout had been over? She gasped as the video continued and pleaded with Rupert to turn it off. There were officers who dealt with material like this all the time, and she couldn't understand how it didn't send them insane.

'Look, I get it, right? I don't need to see any more—'

'One more, and then we're done.'

Rupert continued to move his hands across the laptop keyboard until a new video appeared on the projector. This time it was Evie and Zach. There was nothing going on between them, they were chatting and seemed at ease with each other. The conversation was already in full flow when the video started recording.

'—I could tell something wasn't right, Zach. Your head didn't seem to be in it. I promise I won't say anything.'

'I can't let my dad find out, he'll go spare. He's got plans for me to take over the business and it won't fit in with his macho builder image if he finds out I'm bisexual. If I can just say you're my girlfriend, it'll keep him off the scent.'

'Have you had a physical relationship yet?' Evie asked him. She spoke with the calm wisdom of an experienced counsellor.

'No, not properly... me and Quinn kissed a bit—'

'He did say he was experimenting,' Evie replied, as casually as if they'd been discussing their shopping lists.

'Look, Evie, you have to swear you won't tell—'

'I promise, Zach. How long have we been friends?'

There was a gentleness in this interaction which Hollie hadn't seen in Zach before.

'I made a pass at Kyle a couple of weeks ago—'

'How did he react?'

'He just looked shocked, then ran off—'

'Has he said anything?'

'No, but I'm scared he will. That's why I've been such a bastard to him recently. I can't risk him telling everybody.'

Rupert closed the video before it had finished. He waited in silence, like he was struggling with his own thoughts and feelings. At last, he spoke.

'So, you can see where that leaves me,' he said.

'Yes, you have a bisexual son who you need to be supporting.'

'It's not quite as easy as that, DI Turner. What you see in those videos is a group of young people who have their entire lives ahead of them. Imagine if those films fell into the wrong hands. How many young lives would be ruined forever?'

'But we can stop that, right now. Just hand that content over to the police and we'll sort it all out—'

'I'm certainly going to get Zach's videos deleted. They'll never see the light of day. Did you know Kyle Wilson was trying to blackmail everybody you've just seen in those films? Rent problems at home, apparently. That's how he was helping out his mum.'

'Jesus, so he was blackmailing them?'

'Yes, and he was threatening to upload the videos to the Dirty Little Secrets website.'

'Kyle recorded it all on that?' she said, looking at the CCTV camera. 'The camera's not even on, you can see because the LED isn't flashing.'

'Of course it's not on now. And it wasn't on when Kyle started using this place to edit his videos. But somewhere along the line, he spotted an opportunity. And hey presto, here we are!'

For fuck's sake!

'Except when he filmed my Zach, he went too far. And when he tried to blackmail him, I couldn't let that slide. He'd have been milking me for money for the rest of his life.'

'So you killed him?'

'Let's just say I set in motion a course of events which would shut Kyle up for good. And now, I've got to make sure I've blocked all the exits.'

FIFTY-EIGHT
THURSDAY, 20:18

Rupert Eastwood was looking increasingly agitated.

Hollie's head was pounding, and her mouth was dry. Her hands were shaking, and her wrists were becoming sore from the restraints. She could see his performance was reaching its conclusion now, whatever that might be. The plastic sheet and the protective clothing were causing her apprehension to surge, but she knew the only way out of this was with a level head and some sharp thinking.

She swallowed hard; she wasn't certain how steady she could make her voice when she spoke to him.

'You know that if you hurt me, my colleagues will just take my place? And when it comes to dead coppers, they don't stop?'

It was worth a try; Rupert Eastwood had a lot to lose here. She wished she could have said the words with a little more conviction.

'Is that a threat, detective?'

'It's a statement of fact. You're a successful businessman, I know you're intelligent, so you must see that.'

Her phone started to ring. She jumped, not realising quite

how on edge she was. Instinctively, she tried to reach for it, but spotted it was elsewhere in the room.

Rupert walked over to the coffee table where he'd left it. She assumed he'd taken it off her when he brought her in.

'You'd better answer this,' he said, holding it up. She could see there were missed calls. Who had been trying to reach her while she'd been out cold? Jenni, probably.

'Give the game away and you'll get this.'

Rupert held up a crowbar; it was splashed with blood. Hollie took a sharp breath – whose blood was that?

A bead of sweat dripped from her forehead onto her lap. A wooziness from the drugs threatened to overwhelm her, but she struggled to keep her mind sharp and focused on Eastwood.

'I'm putting it on speaker,' Rupert said. 'Say anything and you'll feel this against your head before you finish the sentence.'

He held her phone in front of her face and accepted the call, clicking the speaker button.

It made her skin crawl as his hand brushed her check. Was he trying to intimidate her even more? She was in danger of throwing up, so great was the grip that fear had taken on her.

'Boss? It's Amber—'

Hollie paused and took a breath to help steady her voice.

'Hi, Amber. Surely you're not still at the office?'

DS Patel was sharp, she'd sense something wasn't right.

'Yes, I'm here on my own. I've got something for you. It won't wait, I'm afraid.'

Hollie felt her stomach tightening.

'Can we leave it until tomorrow?' she asked. 'I'm out with Jenni right now.'

She couldn't let Rupert hear this, not if it was part of the case. Amber paused at the end of the line. She would know that nothing would normally stop Hollie from biting her hand off for more information about the case.

'What's that noise I can hear? You sound like you're in some hippy commune.'

Amber had heard the wind chimes outside. Rupert waved the crowbar at her, snarling.

'Oh, it's just somebody's crappy ringtone,' she blustered.

'It's about Rupert Eastwood, boss. It can't wait.'

Hollie watched as Rupert's eyes widened and with his spare hand he moved the tip of the crowbar close to her face. She felt its cold edge on her skin.

'Go ahead, Amber.'

She cringed as she spoke the words. Her hands were shaking uncontrollably; Eastwood had clocked it, too.

'I managed to break into that SD card. It's all there, boss. Rupert Eastwood sexually assaulted Tilly Mann.'

'What?'

'It was captured on video, it's all there. I've got it right in front of me—'

Rupert placed the crowbar on the floor and muted the microphone on Hollie's phone. There was a wild look in his eyes now. He was a man who'd seen the endgame coming.

'Get her to bring it to you,' he said. 'Make up some excuse. Make sure you get that SD card. And tell her not to make any copies!'

Hollie's mind was racing now. How the hell was she going to get Amber over there with the evidence? There was no way she was placing her colleague in danger, even if Amber was gullible enough to fall for it.

A second bead of sweat worked its way down her forehead, even though her entire body felt cold now. The shaking was beginning to move beyond just her hands, threatening to overwhelm her.

'Boss? Are you still there?'

Rupert must have sensed her panic, because he shouted instructions at her once again.

'Put her off for now, tell her you'll call back in five minutes. Do it!'

Hollie cowered at his voice, such was the contempt and anger that dripped from his commands. She'd seen a hint of this in their previous interactions, but Rupert seemed like a man who was losing his grip.

He pressed the speaker button on the phone.

'I'm a bit distracted at the moment, Amber, can I call you back in five? Stay where you are, I'll get back to you.'

Surely Amber could hear the trembling in her voice.

She ended the call. Amber would smell trouble a mile off. She'd know something was up.

Rupert was beginning to look unhinged now. He'd begun to pace, desperately trying to figure a way back from this.

'It's time to let it go, Rupert. It's gone too far now—'

'No, I'm not losing everything I've built because of this. One silly mistake, and she was asking for it anyway. It's not like she's a kid, she's a woman now—'

Hollie became instantly gripped by anger and outrage. In spite of her fear, she screamed at him.

'Do not attempt to blame this in any way on that poor girl. What the hell did you do to her? She was going to end her life because of you—'

'Don't miss out the video that Kyle made. He's the bad guy here. What the fuck was he doing filming people like that in the first place? I've another surprise for you—'

What the hell has he done now?

Rupert walked over to a cupboard door and opened it. A body had been slumped against the side and it slid out onto the floor. She recognised him immediately.

'What have you done to him?'

Nick Yerbury had been bludgeoned about the head. These were no warning shots; they were intended to cause harm.

'Mr Yerbury needed some encouragement to help me find

Kyle's video files. The daft bugger didn't even know they were sitting in the bedroom on his iMac. I never rated him as a teacher anyway. He even had two keys for this granny flat in his pocket when my guy followed him home from the academy. It was useful, that, he'd just got a spare one cut.'

If he'd done this to Yerbury, he wouldn't hesitate to do the same to her.

'Have you hurt Yasmine?' Hollie asked urgently.

'No, Yerbury said she's out at some folk music evening in Beverley. Frankly, she'd have more fun if she was here.'

Hollie was forcing her mind to focus, even though her head was thumping, and her eyes were heavy from the drugs. Her movements were sluggish, too, it was like wading through quicksand. She had to remain sharp.

'Is he dead?'

'Not quite, I need him alive a bit longer.'

'And what about me?'

She hardly dared ask the question. This didn't look good. Whatever ties he'd used to secure her, there was no wriggling out of them. Her mind was alert with the possible options; there weren't any as far as she could tell, other than to buy time and hope that Jenni might sound the alarm when she didn't turn up at the pub to meet her.

Come on, Amber, Jenni. You must be wondering where I am.

Hollie despised this man. But she could not afford to make him any more agitated; he had her life in his hands. She could feel her whole body shaking, but she had to stay calm; if she panicked or shouted, he'd turn on her. She wanted to see this monster banged up in jail.

Hollie knew from experience that most men like Rupert Eastwood enjoyed an ego stroke. He seemed talkative, so she'd keep him going as long as possible. If she got out of this, at least he would fill in some gaps in the investigation.

'How did you spike my drink? It had to be those two guys, right?'

'Yeah, Zach spotted you and your friend as soon as they walked into the pub. Even better when your mate ditched you, and bingo, we've got you on your own. I'll bet you thought all those guys were after your body. Well, don't flatter yourself. While my pal was touching your leg, the other chap squirted some Rohypnol into your drink. They tell me it was that diet cola shit you were drinking, so you won't have been able to taste the difference.'

He was laughing at his own comments now, his confidence clearly growing. He was a clever sociopath, that was for certain.

'So, what about me? You've really painted yourself into a corner now.'

'Yes, DI Turner, what about you? And what about your colleague—' He stopped mid-sentence. Hollie could see by the expression on his face that he'd figured it out.

'I want you to call your friend back,' he started, seemingly certain now of what he was going to do.

'What am I going to say to her?'

'You're going to tell her you're in danger. If she doesn't hand over that SD card, you're going to be hurt badly. She'll come. I could hear it in your voice, she's the type who wants to impress you.'

He looked at Hollie's phone and checked the last called number.

'It came through a switchboard,' Rupert said. 'Dial her directly on her own phone. Tell her to bring it to the Lord Line building. We'll meet her there.'

'I'm not sending her to the Lord Line building. There's no way I'm dispatching a lone female officer out there, it's isolated enough at the best of times.'

Hollie had seen the derelict building many times while driving along the A63. Once an integral part of the city's fishing industry, overlooking the deep-sea trawlers which docked there, it had long since been abandoned and was derelict.

'What's her number?' Rupert shouted.

Hollie gave it to him, her mind frantically working through the options. Amber would smell a rat. There's no way she would go to that place. Unless... unless Rupert raised the stakes.

The phone connected.

'Boss? Hollie? Are you okay?'

Amber sounded alert and concerned; she'd sensed something was up all right.

Rupert had the crowbar back in his hand now. He was holding it uncomfortably close to her face once again.

Hollie forced herself to stay calm. There were two of them in danger now and there was no way she was putting Amber at risk.

'I need you to meet me at the Lord Line building—'

'What? Are you sure everything is okay, boss?'

Rupert shook the crowbar again.

'I want you to bring the SD card with you so you can hand it over—'

She was thinking on her feet now, desperately trying to see a way through this.

Without warning, Rupert swung away from her and used Hollie's phone to take a photo of Nick Yerbury, bloodied and unconscious on the floor. He sent the image to Amber and muted the microphone.

'Tell her that's what will happen to you if she doesn't come.'

He unmuted the microphone.

'Jesus, Hollie, what have you just sent me?'

'We're in a spot of trouble, Amber. I need you to keep a cool head—'

'Are you in danger? I'll get a team there straight away.'

She watched as Rupert flinched. He muted the microphone again.

'Tell her to be there in twenty minutes. If she's not there, you'll be joining Nick Yerbury. If she brings anybody with her, you'll be joining Nick Yerbury. I'll have somebody meet her there.'

He touched the screen on the phone again and thrust it under her chin.

'You need to go there now, Amber. I'm being threatened—'

'Who by?'

'I can't tell you that. There'll be someone to meet you at the Lord Line building in twenty minutes. Go alone. They just want the SD card, Amber. Don't make any copies and don't get smart with them—'

Without warning, Rupert raised the crowbar above his head and brought it crashing down on Hollie's arm. She screamed as it struck her, a pain like she'd never known before. Rupert dropped the phone on the floor, smashing it with his foot. Amber's desperate voice was cut off mid-sentence.

'Jesus, boss, are you okay? Hollie? Hollie? I'm coming – don't hurt her! I'm coming, boss—'

FIFTY-NINE
THURSDAY, 20:26

Hollie was desperate to hold her arm, but tethered as she was to the chair, that was not possible. She cried with the searing pain.

'What the fuck did you do that for?' Hollie screamed at him.

'Keep your voice down or you'll get another one,' he warned her.

It hurt so much she was struggling to fight back her tears. She did not want this man to see her weak.

'You know that DS Patel is too sensible to go there alone—'

'She'll do as she's told. She won't risk the life of her boss. Not after what she just heard. Besides, nobody has a clue where you are. It'll all be over soon.'

Rupert's phone was to the side of the room. He put the crowbar onto the floor and walked over to it, dialling a number which was on speed dial.

'Yes, it's me. I've got two jobs for you. Send Phil and Tony over to the Lord Line building – yes, now. A copper will be there. Let her walk through the subway, then sort her out. She has an SD card on her. Make sure she has that first, then make it look like someone got her in the building. Leave the body there. If she doesn't come alone, call me immediately. Remove her mobile phone and destroy it. We'll have two disposals, too. I'll text you the address. Put them in the superstore foundations, make sure they're wrapped in plastic and covered in ballast.'

He rang off, but Hollie had caught enough of his whispers.

'So, you kill me, you kill my colleague and then what?'

'You forgot Yerbury.'

'What's he done?'

'Nothing besides being a shit teacher. That and letting Kyle use this place for his pervy video work.'

'And how does that get my colleagues off your back?'

Hollie was trying to figure it out. Rupert was making it up as he went along now. How was he going to make this work for him?

'Here's how I see it. Nobody knows about my little encounter with that girl and besides, what's the betting she'll try to take her life again? Past form suggests she's not the coping type—'

'And you're all right with that? She's the same age as your son, for God's sake.'

'Well, an anonymous source will remind her that the video with her fucking her boyfriend is still out there. I reckon she'll keep her mouth shut, don't you? Kyle was onto a good thing when it came to extortion. He just shouldn't have involved me and my kid.'

'You're a monster, you must see that?'

'I made a bad decision in the heat of the moment, that's all. Now I'm tidying up my mess.'

'You still haven't said what happens to me. Surely if you'd just left me in the pub, I'd have gone home and got on with my job?'

'Yes, and eventually you'd have ended up at my door to arrest me. That can never happen, detective, you must understand that. Your colleagues will find the videos in this room, just as if Nick Yerbury was viewing them at the time of his disappearance. Nick will vanish without a trace. It'll become a cold case, the police will assume someone got their revenge on Kyle and Nick.'

'Fuck – what? You're out of your mind.'

She'd seen the same deranged look in eyes on several occasions in her policing career. This was a man detaching himself from everyday life and preparing for something extreme and violent.

'You and your colleague, Patel, whatever her name is, will be casualties of the case. Patel will look like she was in the wrong place at the wrong time. You will just disappear into thin air.'

Hollie raced through his plan. She had to spot the gap, that was the only hope she had of stopping this; she had to make him see the flaw.

'So it was you who killed Kyle then? It wasn't Zach—'

'No, Zach's a young fool. I told him to send Kyle a warning and to find the videos. The idiot even messed that up. I have to do everything myself.'

Rupert stooped down to pick something up; it was a kitchen knife taken from the kitchenette. Sensing what was about to happen, she struggled to release herself from the ties once again. She gasped with the pain as she wriggled her wounded arm.

The only hope she'd got was if he made a slip. An error with DNA, fibres, CCTV, any of those things could screw up his plan. But that didn't sort out her immediate problem. It would be no consolation to Hollie if they figured it all out after he'd finished her.

'So where were you hiding?'

'Behind the outbuilding. You coppers are idiots. Zach brought the chisel. I ducked through the gap in the fence after that Quinn kid had pissed off, and then I dropped it in the foyer when you were briefing the press and parents—'

'You were in that briefing?'

Hollie thought back to it. It was just a sea of faces to her, and she hadn't met him then. He was a psycho if he was prepared to take a risk as great as that.

'I'm a governor there. I'm in and out of that academy all the time.'

Hollie struggled again. All the time he'd been talking she thought there might be a way out, or the cavalry would arrive in the nick of time. That hadn't happened. Jenni was probably still drinking with her new friend, wondering where the hell she'd got to.

Rupert's eyes were blank now like he'd disconnected from his soul. He walked over to Hollie, the knife in his hand ready to strike. He raised it high and as he plunged downward, she contorted her body as much as she could, so he avoided her chest. He missed her torso, but the blade slipped into the top of her leg.

'Arrghh, Jesus Christ!' she screamed, struggling and twisting in the chair. The blood was flowing freely now, dripping onto the plastic decorating sheet where it would leave no trace on the fibres of the carpet.

Rupert came at her again, and she used what little movement she'd got in her feet to push against his shins. As the knife came down with deadly force, the chair tilted backwards, the blade just missing her neck as she fell.

'You stupid fucking bitch,' Rupert cursed as he rapidly recovered himself and started to move to the side so that he could make a clear strike. He slid on the blood that had dripped from Hollie's leg, fuelling his fury.

Hollie was in excruciating pain now, and she was concerned that he'd hit an artery, as there seemed to be too much blood for a leg wound.

Rupert struggled to steady himself at her side, smearing her blood across the plastic sheeting. He raised the knife and pointed it directly at her throat. His other gloved hand was clutching her hair, so she was unable to move her head. She was completely caught now, there was no play left to make. She closed her eyes, wishing it would just be over.

There was a violent crash to the right of Hollie. She caught the movement of Rupert's arm as the knife's blade flashed in front of her face, but the blow never came. Instead, the chair to which she was tied fell backwards and her head struck the floor, disorienting her as the room filled with urgent shouting.

'Drop the knife, Eastwood,' came a male voice, urgent and on edge.

'It's over, Rupert,' came a female voice. Jenni?

Fuck, what's she doing here?

Hollie's neck was jarred, but it felt like a nest of ants was swarming into the room, and there were panicked voices all around her.

'Put it down, Eastwood,' came the voice again. She heard the distinctive crack of a Taser being readied.

'Put it down and get on the ground!'

'Taser!' came the male voice.

The Taser popped and Rupert cried out, the electrical clicking telling her all she needed to know.

'Fuck you,' Rupert screamed.

'Taser deployed,' the officer called.

'Stay down!' Jenni called. She'd never heard such ferocity in her colleague's voice.

The knife landed to the side of her face. A gloved hand retrieved it almost as soon as it hit the ground. She heard Rupert Eastwood cursing as the voltage discharged through his body and the officers ran in to deal with him.

'Stay down!'

'Put your arms out where I can see them!'

She couldn't see anything of the mayhem around her, but it was over, they'd got the bastard.

Hollie felt the blood seeping through her trousers now, her head was spinning, and she felt herself fading.

'The boss is badly hurt,' she heard Jenni shout out. 'We need a medic in here. Get a medic.'

Friday, 10:12

'Oh shit, that hurts—'

'No wonder, it was deep enough to hit bone. Try to keep it still.'

Hollie was pleased Jenni's was the first face she saw. At least she'd managed to look after herself after the hazards of the previous night.

'So, just put me right on this, because it all happened a bit fast. One minute I was bracing myself for the end, the next minute a Taser's been discharged, and all hell's let loose in Yasmine's annexe. How did you pull that off?'

She could see her other colleagues standing outside at the nurse's station; at least they cared enough to make the visit. They'd clubbed together to send flowers over; they were in a vase next to Léon's, in the corner of the room.

'When you didn't come over to the pub, I knew something was up straight away. I tried phoning you, but it went to voice-mail. So I ran back round to Melvins, and I caught a posh SUV driving away from outside the entrance. And guess who stepped outside the door to make a phone call two minutes after?'

Hollie didn't know.

'Zach Eastwood, that's who. I reckoned you must have been stalking them in there—'

'You mean investigating their movements, don't you?' Hollie smiled through her pain.

'Yeah, that's right, boss: stalking. Anyway, I rang the office to get some help and Amber was working late. She was right onto it. She said she'd spoken to you on the phone. When she mentioned those bloody wind chimes, I knew exactly where you were. They sent a team around straight away. Good job you took me to Yasmine's house, eh? Else I wouldn't have known that's where you were.'

Hollie smiled.

'You can't keep a good copper down. Good work, Jenni.'

'I'm pleased I could return the favour. I mean, I do owe you one, after all.'

The door opened and Amber and Harry joined them.

'No DS Anderson?'

'He told us to tell you he's sorting out the quote – fucking mess – you've left us to clear up,' Amber began. 'But he sends his best wishes and congratulations for clearing up the case. He'll get over here for a social call as soon as he can.'

Harry perched at the end of the bed; Amber pulled up a spare chair.

'Thank God you're safe,' Hollie said to Amber, reaching out her good arm to her colleague. Amber gave it a squeeze.

'Jenni saved the day.' She smiled. 'I didn't know what to do when I heard him hurting you over the phone. Jenni called just as I was about to leave the office. She couldn't have timed it better. I had to know you were safe, boss.'

'So, where are we up to?' Hollie asked. She felt like crap but was desperate to know. The Rohypnol was still working its way through her body, so she'd been warned by the doctor that she might feel shaky for a while.

'Well, it was a shit show, wasn't it?' Amber answered. 'Rupert Eastwood has been charged with murder, and Zach with conspiracy to murder.'

'That's some entry for Zach's university CV,' Jenni remarked.

'So it was Rupert who finished off Kyle? Zach just delivered him to the right place at the designated time. Nice work, Harry, you said that hiding behind the outbuilding was a possibility early on in the case. Well done.'

Harry's face beamed.

'Crestwell Academy's PR department is in meltdown, and we apprehended Rupert's two henchmen at the Lord Line building,' Amber continued. 'We've got all the evidence we need with those videos from the annexe and the assault shown on the SD card. They make ghastly viewing. I've never seen anything so horrible.'

'I should take more days off,' Hollie observed. 'Things seem to move just as fast when I'm not around.'

'Yes, boss, but there's not half as much drama.' Amber laughed.

'How is Nick Yerbury? Did he make it?'

'He's not far from here, just along the corridor,' Jenni explained. 'He's fine, badly hurt of course, but conscious and no lasting damage. I got his statement before I came to see you. He's feeling pretty damn stupid about what Kyle was up to. I think he and Yasmine are going to have to reflect on their pastoral style.'

Hollie had just remembered Kyle's mother. They'd all thought Kyle innocent in all this, yet it was his actions which had created this mess.

Amber pulled out a folder stuffed with papers.

'There were some audio files on that SD card, too,' she

continued. 'Kyle recorded a series of audio diaries explaining why he did what he did. It's enough to make you cry. The PIN unlocked them, too; those digits were four-one-nine-two – it was a one, not a seven.'

'This is excellent work, Amber.'

She'd not yet worked with these detectives for half a year, but they were already proving themselves to be some of the best.

'Bedtime reading.' Amber smiled, handing over the papers. 'I know you'll want to read those transcripts from the audio diaries. It says a lot about what Kyle was thinking.'

Hollie was tempted to dive straight in, but there were still unanswered questions.

'He used Nick's video editing laptop to process the videos and kept everything in a hidden folder that was tucked away on the hard drive. The SD card was for backups.'

'And Rupert found it how?'

'Zach extracted the information while they were beating up Kyle.'

'Jesus, Rupert came so close to being caught red-handed,' Hollie gasped.

'I wonder if he'd have hurt those two boys if they'd found him lurking behind the outbuilding,' Jenni suggested.

The thought of it made Hollie shudder. Who knew what Rupert was capable of? She was in two minds about Zach though. It seemed to her that he was a vulnerable boy who'd been caught in the snare of his father's expectations. Which child hadn't agonised over maintaining their parents' approval?

'Is Tilly speaking to us now?' Hollie asked. She still felt so angry about Tilly. She'd been cast aside like she was worth nothing.

'Now she knows that video isn't getting released, yes. She's told us everything, who was involved in the assault on Kyle and how Zach had got it all worked out, avoiding CCTV cameras and everything.'

'But really, it was all Rupert's work and planning?'

'It looks that way, but we'll find that out when we formally question him and Zach later. We think he got Zach to encourage the other kids to beat up Kyle, and that way they'd all be implicated in the murder. That gave Rupert cover to get the job done. Zach got sloppy though because his prints were on Kyle's phone when we took it out of Tilly's bag. Her prints weren't on it, and she reckoned Zach had placed it there when they were filing into the drama studio.'

Amber waited while Hollie took that all in.

'Where are the Eastwoods?'

'They've been charged and held at Clough Road. Ben got to them last night with Harry.'

'And?'

Harry turned to Hollie.

'DS Anderson said the two of them are falling over themselves to blame each other for what happened. Rupert has got his legal big guns involved, but the recording that DS Patel found is all the evidence we need. Oh, and guess what was found in Zach's wallet?'

Hollie's blank face must have given it away that she hadn't a clue. She was still struggling after being drugged, and she couldn't wait for her sharpness to return.

'Quinn Varney's locker key,' Harry beamed. 'He must have dumped Kyle's laptop there after the assault.'

Hollie took a moment to think through all the angles.

'Who assaulted Kyle then?' she asked at last.

'All the kids in the videos, boss,' Amber replied. 'Tilly gave us the names. So it was Zach, Tilly, Evie, Jake and Quinn. Quinn exited the school grounds via the hole in the fence. He was telling the truth about that; he just lied about the timing.'

'How did they agree to beat up Kyle? Most of them seem too gentle to do anything like that.'

'By that stage, Rupert knew about the videos – though he didn't know where they were stored. Zach threatened to leak the videos on the academy's Facebook page if they didn't help him to send a warning to Kyle. According to Tilly, Zach said it was just to scare him off. Tilly was terrified of Rupert after what he did to her. She was too scared to tell anyone, but also out of her mind that he might do it again. I'd guess the Eastwoods figured it would obfuscate our investigation to have more people involved. Tilly said Zach was brutal with Kyle; the rest of them tried not to hurt him. Their hearts weren't in it, despite what Kyle had done to them.'

'I'm never sending my kids to school ever again,' Hollie said, 'and I'm going to issue them with the oldest Nokia phones I can find, something that can't cope with images or videos. I experienced my entire childhood before I went anywhere near a video camera, but the damn things are everywhere these days.'

'I take it Yasmine and Nick will be out of jobs?'

Amber screwed up her face.

'What do you reckon?'

Hollie sighed. There were so many lives screwed up, it was difficult to count them all. The assault charges would stay on the kids' records for years, their only chance of ameliorating that problem would be if they could prove Zach's blows were the ones that caused the most physical harm to Kyle. Or, if Kyle's mother didn't press for assault charges because of the harm Kyle had caused.

Amber stood up, and the two DCs followed her lead.

'We'll leave you now, boss, we just knew you'd want an update from your hospital bed.'

'I appreciate it. I'll be back at my desk as soon as I can.'

They all laughed at that. They clearly knew her well enough already to know that she would.

'So, what now?'

Hollie grimaced and picked up the pile of transcripts that Amber had brought with her.

'Well, none of you buggers brought me any celebrity magazines or bunches of grapes, so it looks like I'm entertaining myself with these for the rest of the day.'

EPILOGUE

As Hollie watched her three children hanging together, she couldn't stop thinking about Kyle. Izzy, back from her travels at last, was sitting with Noah and Lily on the sofa, all three with electronic devices in their hands, still sociable and chatty in their high-tech bubbles. Two of those devices – a mobile phone and a laptop – had given Kyle the tools which ultimately ended his life. The technology was both brilliant and a terrible source of threat.

The sight of them sitting together, Noah's head on Izzy's lap and Lily burrowed into her other side, made Hollie want to melt. She'd desperately missed this; her three beautiful children, all together, all safe and having a lovely time. Only, they were no longer in Lancaster, and this was her rented flat in Hull. She'd had to drive them down along the M6 and M62, an almost four-hour journey just to see her youngest kids.

'Any thoughts about what you'll do next?' she asked Izzy. She didn't want to push her, but she was going out of her mind with worry that she might move on again. After so long moving from hostel to hostel and travelling between countries, she hoped her daughter wouldn't be struck by restlessness. Things had been tense when she left home, the two of them needing space, but since she'd returned, Izzy had matured and they seemed to be bonded as equals now, rather than as mother and daughter. A lot of the baggage had gone.

Izzy turned and smiled.

'I'll miss these two,' she began as she suddenly turned and dug her fingers in at Noah's side, tickling him so he yelped out loud. Noah stopped his playful squirming and returned to his tablet. Lily took it in her stride, like she was beyond such childish behaviour now. She was growing up, and fast.

The tragic situation at the academy had badly shaken Hollie. Noah was still young and naive, but she wasn't stupid, she'd heard about the surveys on the radio, and she understood that he was only one click away from a predator or an inappropriate image. Worse still, might he become tainted by the worst behaviour among his peers, and become one of the youths responsible for making lives a misery as a result of this technology?

Léon had agreed to sit down properly and discuss a plan of action when she returned the kids to Lancaster. At least he was taking it more seriously now. Hollie couldn't calm her concern that this was the sort of problem that might easily fall between the cracks while they were co-parenting.

It was Lily who was her most pressing concern. Now in the deep, anxious heart of puberty, this was when life at secondary school became a grenade with its pin removed. A cesspool of bubbling hormones, it was ripe for bullying, sexualised behaviour and shaming, with an overwhelming pressure to conform and fit in.

She remembered it from her days as a teenager, before mobile phones were everywhere, and you could make your mistakes away from the unerring gaze of the internet. She'd had boyfriends, wore terrible clothes, made bad mistakes and got embarrassing hairdos, but it was all hidden in a few grainy photographs, none of which were particularly incriminating. Her generation had it easy; Kyle's fraught relationships at the academy had shown her just how dangerous things could get.

'How would you feel about me hanging around in Hull for a bit?' Izzy replied, after some time. Hollie sensed she was nervous about asking; she needn't have been. She never had to apologise for wanting to be around her mum.

'I'd like that,' Hollie replied. 'Stay as long as you want. I'd love to have you here.'

'Can we stay here?' Lily said, looking up from her laptop. 'Permanently, I mean?'

Hollie would like nothing more than that, but even she saw now that it wasn't practical. Léon was a good dad and he'd been pivotal in her being able to maintain her crazy workload. She had to remind herself of all the good he'd brought into their lives, when her immediate instinct was to feel anger and frustration with him. Between them, they were putting the youngest two kids in an impossible position.

'We'll need to chat to your dad,' Hollie replied. 'It's not quite as easy as that. Think about your school and your friends. It won't be that long until you're doing exams. It would be a big wrench to move to Hull.'

It was only half a year since she and Léon had been building up the move, trying to put a positive spin on it. Then Léon had dropped his bombshell, and everything had been rolled back at a pace.

Lily returned to her screen, shrugging it off. Kids were resilient, she knew that. They'd work it out between them somehow.

'Anyway, we've got WhatsApp, we can call you whenever we want,' Noah proclaimed, with the sudden wisdom of an old man.

He'd got it in one, summing up the entire dilemma of the technological age in one sage sentence. All that tech was a thing of great potential, both good and bad. On the one hand it could lead to the horrific set of circumstances which had resulted in Kyle's tragic loss of life. On the other, it could bring her family together across a distance of more than two hundred miles, so it felt like her children were right by her side, even when they were staying with Léon.

She'd take the positives for now; she needed it after being so emotionally wrung out in the aftermath of the investigation. The sight of her children, all together, was exactly what she needed at that moment. It was what made catching the bad guys worthwhile. It was what made it feel like she was making the world a safer place for her own children to grow up in.

A LETTER FROM THE AUTHOR

Thank you very much for reading *The Killing Circle*. If you want to join other readers in hearing all about my new releases, you can sign up for my newsletter at:

www.stormpublishing.co/paul-j-teague

Or sign up to my personal email newsletter on the link here:

www.paulteague.net/storm

I'd be grateful if you would leave a review if you enjoyed this book as this helps other readers to discover my stories.

This book sees DI Hollie Turner and her team investigate a completely different kind of murder from the first trilogy, this time looking for the killer of seventeen-year-old Kyle Wilson.

Due to the dark nature of the story, I've set it in a fictional school but still kept the story firmly rooted in the city of Hull.

The Kingswood estate was just being built when I lived in the city. I can remember driving off at the Dunswell Roundabout to take a look at the new properties there. We were living in Hull at the time and eventually made the move to Beverley, but it was quite clear even in 1999 that this new-build area was going to become quite sizable. It's wonderful to see how established it is now; it looks like it was always there.

Crestwell Academy doesn't exist, and it is not based on any

of the city's existing schools. After all, I'd hate to frighten anybody! Instead, I just placed it where I figured there would be a need for a large, modern academy. The staff, pupils, teachers and parents are a complete figment of my imagination.

However, the book itself picks up on numerous themes which I have observed in the press, as a consequence of my own children's experiences at school, and the parts of my seventies and eighties school life which still remain relevant in the twenty-first century.

I trained as a teacher and worked in primary schools between 1987 and 1991. The world has changed considerably since those days. For instance, although I'd seen my first mobile phone in 1990, nobody really had one in those days. My teaching life was absent of surveillance and mobile devices. I really don't envy teachers these days. Not only must it be almost impossible to prevent the kids from using their phones, but there are also teacher-rating websites online and everything can be filmed and shared in an instant.

I'm so pleased my teenage life went largely unrecorded. It wasn't that you'd have spotted much that was interesting; it's more a case of cherishing the anonymity we enjoyed and being able to get away from school, shut the door and leave it all behind at the end of the day.

I think the pressure from social media and the twenty-four seven presence of phones must create huge stress for youngsters, yet as parents, it's so difficult to know what's really going on online.

Now my own children are adults, they tell me how they used to cheat the locking software that I'd placed on the family PC, and even though it was in an open and shared area, they still got up to mischief when we weren't watching. Fortunately, it never got worse than an email from a moderator on Club Penguin that the kids had been inserting rude words into the mouths of their cartoon creatures. I suppose I should be thankful.

I wanted to include a home-educated character in this story, as all of my children spent some of their schooling years learning from home. Many parents who had to teach their children at school during COVID think that's what home ed is all about, but it isn't, that's just exchanging one type of school for another.

Home ed is a lot more relaxed and free form – two of my kids went on to get degrees and the third is just about to embark on that journey. It's definitely not for everybody, but if you ever find yourself caught up with children who aren't managing in the school environment for whatever reason, check out Education Otherwise and it might provide some solutions.

This story deals with the dark world of the Web and shows what happens when a group of young adults gets caught up in something sinister and dangerous. There are so many perils lurking online, and you only have to blink to be caught out by a phishing email; they're often so clever and well-disguised.

I've managed to sneak in the usual array of Hull settings, in spite of the fictional school.

Beverley Road swimming baths are a wonderful location in the Stepney area of the city, and I was keen to include a scene there. It's a Grade II listed building and it's great that it's still a focal point for families who live nearby. I'm ashamed to say we lived just up the road from the baths and never used them; when our oldest child was a toddler in the city, we opted for the wave machine at Ennerdale Leisure Centre.

We also take a couple of trips along The Avenues, with a mix of fictional and real-life shops. Hull has many great, traditional streets just like The Avenues, there's such a huge variety there, and it's wonderful to see that the superstores haven't put them out of business. I love walking down these streets, there's such a selection of shops, and you can find virtually anything there.

Before you go, please connect with me on social media.

Thanks once again for reading *The Killing Circle* and I hope to see you over on one of my social channels very soon.

Paul Teague

facebook.com/paulteagueauthor
x.com/PaulTeagueUK

Printed in Dunstable, United Kingdom